THE
GREAT HUNGER

by

JOHAN BOJER

Translated from the Norwegian by
W. J. ALEXANDER WORSTER
and
C. ARCHER

Second Printing . . . . January, 1919
Third Printing . . . . February, 1919
Fourth printing . . . . March, 1919
Fifth printing . . . . May, 1919
Sixth printing . . . . August 11, 1919
Seventh printing . . . . November, 1919
Eighth printing . . . . March, 1920
Ninth printing . . . . July, 1920
Tenth printing . . . . April, 1921
Eleventh printing . . . . January, 1923
Twelfth printing . . . . November, 1925

Printed in U. S. A.

BOOK I

Chapter I

FOR sheer havoc, there is no gale like a good
northwester, when it roars in, through the long
winter evenings, driving the spindrift before it
between the rocky walls of the fjord. It churns
the water to a froth of rushing wave crests, while
the boats along the beach are flung in somersaults
up to the doors of the grey fisher huts, and solid
old barn gangways are lifted and sent flying like
unwieldy birds over the fields. "Mercy on us!"
cry the maids, for it is milking-time, and they have
to fight their way on hands and knees across the
yard to the cowshed, dragging a lantern that *will*
go out and a milk-pail that *won't* be held. And
"Lord preserve us!" mutter the old wives seated
round the stove within doors—and their thoughts
are far away in the north with the Lofoten fishermen, out at sea, maybe, this very night.

But on a calm spring day, the fjord just steals
in smooth and shining by ness and bay. And at
low water there is a whole wonderland of strange
little islands, sand-banks, and weed-fringed rocks
left high and dry, with clear pools between, where
bare-legged urchins splash about, and tiny flat-
fish as big as a halfpenny dart away to every side.
The air is filled with a smell of salt sea-water and

warm, wet beach-waste, and the sea-pie, see-saw-
ing about on a big stone in the water, lifts his red
beak cheerily sunwards and pipes: "Kluip, kluip!
the spring has come!"

On just such a day, two boys of fourteen or
thereabouts came hurrying out from one of the
fishermen's huts down towards the beach. Boys
are never so busy as when they are up to some
piece of mischief, and evidently the pair had business of this sort in hand. Peer Tröen, fair-haired
and sallow-faced, was pushing a wheelbarrow; his
companion, Martin Bruvold, a dark youth with
freckles, carried a tub. And both talked mysteri-
ously in whispers, casting anxious glances out
over the water.

Peer Tröen was, of course, the ringleader. That
he always was: the forest fire of last year was
laid at his door. And now he had made it clear to
some of his friends that boys had just as much
right to lay out deep-sea lines as men. All through
the winter they had been kept at grown-up work,
cutting peat and carrying wood; why should they
be left now to fool about with the inshore fishing,
and bring home nothing better than flounders and
coal-fish and silly codlings? The big deep-sea line
they were forbidden to touch—that was so—but
the Lofoten fishery was at its height, and none of
the men would be back till it was over. So the
boys had baited up the line on the sly down at the
boathouse the day before, and laid it out across
the deepest part of the fjord.

Now the thing about a deep-sea line is that it may bring to the surface fish so big and so fearsome that the like has never been seen before. Yesterday, however, there had been trouble of a different sort. To their dismay, the boys had found that they had not sinkers enough to weight the shore end of the line; and it looked as if they might have to give up the whole thing. But Peer, ever ready, had hit on the novel idea of making one end fast to the trunk of a small fir growing at the outermost point of the ness, and carrying the line from there out over the open fjord. Then a stone at the farther end, and with the magic words, "Fie, fish!" it was paid out overboard, vanishing into the green depths. The deed was done. True, there were a couple of hooks dangling in mid-air at the shore end, between the tree and the water, and, while they might serve to catch an eider duck, or a guillemot, if any one should chance to come rowing past in the dark and get hung up—why, the boys might find they had made a human catch. No wonder, then, that they whispered eagerly and hurried down to the boat.

"Here comes Peter Rönningen," cried Martin suddenly.

This was the third member of the crew, a lanky youth with whitish eyebrows and a foolish face. He stammered, and made a queer noise when he laughed: "Chee-hee-hee." Twice he had been turned down in the confirmation classes; after all, what was the use of learning lessons out of a book when nobody ever had patience to wait while he said them?

Together they ran the boat down to the water's edge, got it afloat, and scrambled in, with much waving of patched trouser legs. "Hi!" cried a voice up on the beach, "let me come too!"

"There's Klaus," said Martin. "Shall we take him along?"

"No," said Peter Rönningen.

"Oh yes, let's," said Peer.

Klaus Brock, the son of the district doctor, was a blue-eyed youngster in knickerbockers and a sailor blouse. He was playing truant, no doubt— Klaus had his lessons at home with a private tutor—and would certainly get a thrashing from his father when he got home.

"Hurry up," called Peer, getting out an oar. Klaus clambered in, and the white-straked four-oar surged across the bay, rocking a little as the boys pulled out of stroke. Martin was rowing at the bow, his eyes fixed on Peer, who sat in the stern in command with his eyes dancing, full of great things to be done. Martin, poor fellow, was half afraid already; he never could understand why Peer, who was to be a parson when he grew up, was always hitting upon things to do that were evidently sinful in the sight of the Lord.

Peer was a town boy, who had been put out to board with a fisherman in the village. His mother had been no better than she should be, so people said, but she was dead now, and the father at any rate must be a rich gentleman, for he sent the boy a present of ten whole crowns every Christmas, so that Peer always had money in his pocket. Naturally, then, he was looked up to by the other boys, and took the lead in all things as a chieftain by right.

The boat moved on past the grey rocks, the beach and the huts above it growing blue and faint in the distance. Up among the distant hills a red wooden farm-house on its white foundation wall stood out clear.

Here was the ness at last, and there stood the fir. Peer climbed up and loosed the end of the line, while the others leaned over the side, watching the cord where it vanished in the depths. What would it bring to light when it came up?

"Row!" ordered Peer, and began hauling in.

The boat was headed straight out across the fjord, and the long line with its trailing hooks hauled in and coiled up neatly in the bottom of a shallow tub. Peer's heart was beating. There came a tug—the first—and the faint shimmer of a fish deep down in the water. Pooh! only a big cod. Peer heaved it in with a careless swing over the gunwale. Next came a ling—a deep water fish at any rate this time. Then a tusk, and another, and another; these would please the women, being good eating, and perhaps make them hold their tongues when the men came home. Now the line jerks heavily; what is coming? A grey shadow comes in sight. "Here with the gaff!" cries Peer,

and Peter throws it across to him. "What is it,
what is it?" shriek the other three. "Steady!
don't upset the boat; a catfish." A stroke of the
gaff over the side, and a clumsy grey body is
heaved into the boat, where it rolls about, hissing
and biting at the bottom-boards and baler, the
splinters crackling under its teeth. "Mind,
mind!" cries Klaus—he was always nervous in
a boat.

But Peer was hauling in again. They were
nearly half-way across the fjord by now, and the
line came up from mysterious depths, which no
fisherman had ever sounded. The strain on Peer
began to show in his looks; the others sat watching his face. "Is the line heavy?" asked Klaus.
"Keep still, can't you?" put in Martin, glancing
along the slanting line to where it vanished far
below. Peer was still hauling. A sense of something uncanny seemed to be thrilling up into his
hands from the deep sea. The feel of the line was
strange. There was no great weight, not even the
clean tug-tug of an ordinary fish; it was as if a
giant hand were pulling gently, very gently, to
draw him overboard and down into the depths.
Then suddenly a violent jerk almost dragged him
over the side.

"Look out! What is it?" cried the three together.

"Sit down in the boat," shouted Peer. And
with the true fisherman's sense of discipline they
obeyed.

Peer was gripping the line firmly with one hand, the other clutching one of the thwarts. "Have we another gaff?" he jerked out breathlessly.

"Here's one." Peter Rönningen pulled out a second iron-hooked cudgel.

"You take it, Martin, and stand by."

"But what—what is it?"

"Don't know what it is. But it's something big."

"Cut the line, and row for your lives!" wailed the doctor's son. Strange he should be such a coward at sea, a fellow who'd tackle a man twice his size on dry land.

Once more Peer was jerked almost overboard. He thought of the forest fire the year before—it would never do to have another such mishap on his shoulders. Suppose the great monster did come up and capsize them—they were ever so far from land. What a to do there would be if they were all drowned, and it came out that it was his fault. Involuntarily he felt for his knife to cut the line—then thrust it back again, and went on hauling.

Here it comes—a great shadow heaving up through the water. The huge beast flings itself round, sending a flurry of bubbles to the surface. And there!—a gleam of white; a row of great white teeth on the underside. Aha! now he knows what it is! The Greenland shark is the fiercest monster of the northern seas, quite able to make short work of a few boys or so.

"Steady now, Martin—ready with the gaff."

The brute was wallowing on the surface now, the water boiling around him. His tail lashed the sea to foam, a big, pointed head showed up, squirming under the hook. "Now!" cried Peer, and two gaffs struck at the same moment, the boat heeled over, letting in a rush of water, and Klaus, dropping his oars, sprang into the bow, with a cry of "Jesus, save us!"

Next second a heavy body, big as a grown man, was heaved in over the gunwale, and two boys were all but shot out the other way. And now the fun began. The boys loosed their hold of the gaffs, and sprang apart to give the creature room. There it lay raging, the great black beast of prey, with its sharp threatening snout and wicked red eyes ablaze. The strong tail lashed out, hurling oars and balers overboard, the long teeth snapped at the bottom-boards and thwarts. Now and again it would leap high up in the air, only to fall back again, writhing furiously, hissing and spitting and frothing at the mouth, its red eyes glaring from one to another of the terrified captors, as if saying: "Come on—just a little nearer!"

Meanwhile, Martin Bruvold was in terror that the shark would smash the boat to pieces. He drew his knife and took a step forward—a flash in the air, and the steel went in deep between the back fins, sending up a spurt of blood. "Look out!" cried the others, but Martin had already sprung back out of reach of the black tail. And

now the dance of death began anew. The knife
was fixed to the grip in the creature's back; one
gaff had buried its hook between the eyes, and
another hung on the flank—the wooden shafts
were flung this way and that at every bound, and
the boat's frame shook and groaned under the
blows.

"She'll smash the boat and we'll go to the bottom," cried Peer.

And now *his* knife flashed out and sent a stream
of blood spouting from between the shoulders, but
the blow cost him his foothold—and in a moment
the two bodies were rolling over and over together
in the bottom of the boat.

"Oh, Lord Jesus!" shrieked Klaus, clinging to
the stempost. "She'll kill him! She'll kill him!"

Peer was half up now, on his knees, but as he
reached out a hand to grasp the side, the brute's
jaws seized on his arm. The boy's face was con-
torted with pain—another moment and the sharp
teeth would have bitten through, when, swift as
thought, Peter Rönningen dropped his oars and
sent his knife straight in between the beast's eyes.
The blade pierced through to the brain, and the
grip of the teeth relaxed.

"C-c-cursed d-d-devil!" stammered Peter, as he
scrambled back to his oars. Another moment, and
Peer had dragged himself clear and was kneeling
by the forward thwart, holding the ragged sleeve
of his wounded arm, while the blood trickled
through his fingers.

When at last they were pulling homeward, the little boat overloaded with the weight of the great carcase, all at once they stopped rowing.

"Where is Klaus?" asked Peer—for the doctor's son was gone from where he had sat, clinging to the stem.

"Why—there he is—in the bottom!"

There lay the big lout of fifteen, who already boasted of his love-affairs, learned German, and was to be a gentleman like his father—there he lay on the bottom-boards in the bow in a dead faint.

The others were frightened at first, but Peer, who was sitting washing his wounded arm, took a dipper full of water and flung it in the unconscious one's face. The next instant Klaus had started up sitting, caught wildly at the gunwale, and shrieked out:

"Cut the line, and row for your lives!"

A roar of laughter went up from the rest; they dropped their oars and sat doubled up and gasping. But on the beach, before going home, they agreed to say nothing about Klaus's fainting fit. And for weeks afterwards the four scamps' exploit was the talk of the village, so that they felt there was not much fear of their getting the thrashing they deserved when the men came home.

WHEN Peer, as quite a little fellow, had been sent to live with the old couple at Tröen, he had already passed several times from one adopted home to another, though this he did not remember. He was one of the madcaps of the village now, but it was not long since he had been a solitary child, moping apart from the rest. Why did people always say "Poor child!" whenever they were speaking about his real mother? Why did they do it? Why, even Peter Rönningen, when he was angry, would stammer out: "You ba-ba-bastard!" But Peer called the pock-marked good-wife at Tröen "mother" and her bandy-legged husband "father," and lent the old man a hand wherever he was wanted—in the smithy or in the boats at the fishing.

His childhood was passed among folk who counted it sinful to smile, and whose minds were gloomy as the grey sea-fog with poverty, psalm-singing, and the fear of hell.

One day, coming home from his work at the peat bog, he found the elders snuffling and sighing over their afternoon meal. Peer wiped the sweat from his forehead, and asked what was the matter.

The eldest son shoved a spoonful of porridge

into his mouth, wiped his eyes, swallowed, and
said: "Poor Peer!"

"Aye, poor little chap," sighed the old man,
thrusting his horn spoon into a crack in the wall
that served as a rack.

"Neither father nor mother now," whimpered
the eldest daughter, looking over to the window.

"Mother? Is she——"

"Ay, dearie, yes," sighed the old woman.
"She's gone for sure—gone to meet her Judge."

Later, as the day went on, Peer tried to cry
too. The worst thing of all was that every one in
the house seemed so perfectly certain where his
mother had gone to. And to heaven it certainly
was not. But how could they be so sure about it?

Peer had seen her only once, one summer's day
when she had come out to see the place. She wore
a light dress and a big straw hat, and he thought
he had never seen anything so beautiful before.
She made no secret of it among the neighbours
that Peer was not her only child; there was a little
girl, too, named Louise, who was with some folks
away up in the inland parishes. She was in high
spirits, and told risky stories and sang songs by
no means sacred. The old people shook their
heads over her—the younger ones watched her
with sidelong glances. And when she left, she
kissed Peer, and turned round more than once to
look back at him, flushed under her big hat, and
smiling; and it seemed to Peer that she must
surely be the loveliest creature in all the world.

But now—now she had gone to a place where the ungodly dwell in such frightful torment, and no hope of salvation for her through all eternity—and Peer all the while could only think of her in a light dress and a big straw hat, all song and happy laughter.

Then came the question: Who was to pay for the boy now? True, his baptismal certificate said that he had a father—his name was Holm, and he lived in Christiania—but, from what the mother had said, it was understood that he had disappeared long ago. What was to be done with the boy?

Never till now had Peer rightly understood that he was a stranger here, for all that he called the old couple father and mother.

He lay awake night after night up in the loft, listening to the talk about him going on in the room below—the good-wife crying and saying: "No, no!", the others saying how hard the times were, and that Peer was quite old enough now to be put to service as a goat-herd on some up-country farm.

Then Peer would draw the skin-rug up over his head. But often, when one of the elders chanced to be awake at night, he could hear some one in the loft sobbing in his sleep. In the daytime he took up as little room as he could at the table, and ate as little as humanly possible; but every morning he woke up in fear that to-day—to-day he would have to bid the old foster-mother farewell and go out among strangers.

Then something new and unheard of plumped down into the little cottage by the fjord.

There came a registered letter with great dabs of sealing-wax all over it, and a handwriting so gentlemanly as to be almost unreadable. Every one crowded round the eldest son to see it opened —and out fell five ten-crown notes. "Mercy on us!" they cried in amazement, and "Can it be for us?" The next thing was to puzzle out what was written in the letter. And who should that turn out to be from but—no other than Peer's father, though he did not say it in so many words. "Be good to the boy," the letter said. "You will receive fifty crowns from me every half-year. See that he gets plenty to eat and goes dry and well shod. Faithfully your, P. Holm, Captain."

"Why, Peer—he's—he's—— Your father's a captain, an officer," stammered the eldest girl, and fell back a step to stare at the boy.

"And we're to get twice as much for him as before," said the son, holding the notes fast and gazing up at the ceiling, as if he were informing Heaven of the fact.

But the old wife was thinking of something else as she folded her hands in thankfulness—now she needn't lose the boy.

"Properly fed!" No need to fear for that. Peer had treacle with his porridge that very day, though it was only a week-day. And the eldest son

gave him a pair of stockings, and made him sit
down and put them on then and there; and the
same night, when he went to bed, the eldest girl
came and tucked him up in a new skin-rug, not
quite so hairless as the old one. His father a captain! It seemed too wonderful to be true.

From that day times were changed for Peer.
People looked at him with very different eyes. No
one said "Poor boy" of him now. The other boys
left off calling him bad names; the grown-ups said
he had a future before him. "You'll see," they
would say, "that father of yours will get you on;
you'll be a parson yet, ay, maybe a bishop, too."
At Christmas, there came a ten-crown note all for
himself, to do just as he liked with. Peer changed
it into silver, so that his purse was near bursting
with prosperity. No wonder he began to go about
with his nose in the air, and play the little prince
and chieftain among the boys. Even Klaus Brock,
the doctor's son, made up to him, and taught him
to play cards. But—"You surely don't mean to
go and be a parson," he would say.

For all this, no one could say that Peer was too
proud to help with the fishing, or make himself
useful in the smithy. But when the sparks flew
showering from the glowing iron, he could not help
seeing visions of his own—visions that flew out
into the future. Aye, he *would* be a priest. He
might be a sinner now, and a wild young scamp;
he certainly did curse and swear like a trooper at
times, if only to show the other boys that it was

all nonsense about the earth opening and swallowing you up. But a priest he would be, all the same. None of your parsons with spectacles and a pot belly: no, but a sort of heavenly messenger with snowy white robes and a face of glory. Perhaps some day he might even come so far that he could go down into that place of torment where his mother lay, and bring her up again, up to salvation. And when, in autumn evenings, he stood outside his palace, a white-haired bishop, he would lift up his finger, and all the stars should break into song.

Clang, clang, sang the anvil under the hammer's beat.

In the still summer evenings a troop of boys go climbing up the naked slopes towards the high wooded ranges to fetch home the cows for the milking. The higher they climb, the farther and farther their sight can travel out over the sea. And an hour or two later, as the sun goes down, here comes a long string of red-flanked cattle trailing down, with a faint jangle of bells, over the far-off ridges. The boys halloo them on—"Ohoo-oo-oo!"—and swing their ringed rowan staves, and spit red juice of the alder bark that they are chewing as men chew tobacco. Far below them they see the farm lands, grey in shadow, and, beyond, the waters of the fjord, yellow in the evening light, a mirror where red clouds and white sails and hills of liquid blue are shining. And away out on the farthest headland, the lonely star of the coast light over the grey sea.

On such an evening Peer came down from the hills just in time to see a gentleman in a carriole turn off from the highway and take the by-road down towards Tröen. The horse balked suddenly at a small bridge, and when the driver reined him in and gave him a cut with his whip, the beast reared, swung about, and sent the cart fairly dancing round on its high wheels. "Oh, well, then, I'll have to walk," cried the gentleman angrily, and, flinging the reins to the lad behind him, he jumped down. Just at this moment Peer came up.

"Here, boy," began the traveller, "just take this bag, will you? And——" He broke off suddenly, took a step backward, and looked hard at the boy. "What—surely it can't be—— Is it you, Peer?"

"Ye-es," said Peer, gaping a little, and took off his cap.

"Well, now, that's funny. My name is Holm. Well, well—well, well!"

The lad in the cart had driven off, and the gentleman from the city and the pale country boy with the patched trousers stood looking at each other.

The newcomer was a man of fifty or so, but still straight and active, though his hair and close-trimmed beard were sprinkled with grey. His eyes twinkled gaily under the brim of his black felt hat; his long overcoat was open, showing a gold chain across his waistcoat. With a pair of gloves and an umbrella in one hand, a light travelling bag in the other, and his beautifully polished shoes—a grand gentleman, thought Peer, if ever there was one. And this was his father!

"So that's how you look, my boy? Not very big for your age—nearly sixteen now, aren't you? Do they give you enough to eat?"

"Yes," said Peer, with conviction.

The pair walked down together, towards the grey cottage by the fjord. Suddenly the man stopped, and looked at it through half-shut eyes.

"Is that where you've been living all these years?"

"Yes."

"In that little hut there?"

"Yes. That's the place—Tröen they call it."

"Why, that wall there bulges so, I should think the whole affair would collapse soon."

Peer tried to laugh at this, but felt something like a lump in his throat. It hurt to hear fine folks talk like that of father and mother's little house.

There was a great flurry when the strange gentleman appeared in the doorway. The old wife was kneading away at the dough for a cake, the front of her all white with flour; the old man sat with his spectacles on, patching a shoe, and the two girls sprang up from their spinning wheels. "Well, here I am. My name's Holm," said the traveller, looking round and smiling. "Mercy on us! the Captain his own self," murmured the old woman, wiping her hands on her skirt.

He was an affable gentleman, and soon set them all at their ease. He sat down in the seat of honour, drumming with his fingers on the table, and talking easily as if quite at home. One of the girls had been in service for a while in a Consul's family in the town, and knew the ways of gentlefolk, and she fetched a bowl of milk and offered it with a curtsy and a: "Will the Captain please to take some milk?" "Thanks, thanks," said the visitor. "And what is your name, my dear? Come, there's nothing to blush about. Nicoline? First-rate! And you? Lusiana? That's right." He looked at the red-rimmed basin, and, taking it up, all but emptied it at a draught, then, wiping his beard, took breath. "Phu!—that was good. Well, so here I am." And he looked around the room and at each of them in turn, and smiled, and drummed with his fingers, and said, "Well, well—well, well," and seemed much amused with everything in general. "By the way, Nicoline," he said suddenly, "since you're so well up in titles, I'm not 'Captain' any more now; they've sent me up this way as Lieutenant-Colonel, and my wife has just had a house left her in your town here, so we may be coming to settle down in these parts. And perhaps you'd better send letters to me through a friend in future. But we can talk about all that by and by. Well, well—well, well." And all the time he was drumming with his fingers on the table and smiling. Peer noticed that he wore gold sleeve-links and a fine gold stud in his broad white shirt-front.

And then a little packet was produced. "Hi, Peer, come and look; here's something for you." And the "something" was nothing less than a real silver watch—and Peer was quite unhappy for the moment because he couldn't dash off at once and show it to all the other boys. "There's a father for you," said the old wife, clapping her hands, and almost in tears. But the visitor patted her on the shoulder. "Father? father? H'm—that's not a thing any one can be so sure about. Haha-ha!" And "hahaha" echoed the old man, still sitting with the awl in his hand. This was the sort of joke he could appreciate.

Then the visitor went out and strolled about the place, with his hands under his coat tails, and looked at the sky, and the fjord, and murmured, "Well, well—well, well," and Peer followed him about all the while, and gazed at him as he might have gazed at a star. He was to sleep in a neighbour's house, where there was a room that had a bed with sheets on it, and Peer went across with him and carried his bag. It was Martin Bruvold's parents who were to house the traveller, and people stood round staring at the place. Martin himself was waiting outside. "This a friend of yours, Peer? Here, then, my boy, here's something to buy a big farm with." This time it was a five-crown note, and Martin stood fingering it, hardly able to believe his eyes. Peer's father was something like a father.

It was a fine thing, too, to see a grand gentleman undress. "I'll have things like that some day," thought Peer, watching each new wonder that came out of the bag. There was a silver-backed brush, that he brushed his hair and beard with, walking up and down in his underclothes and humming to himself. And then there was another shirt, with red stripes round the collar, just to wear in bed. Peer nodded to himself, taking it all in. And when the stranger was in bed he took out a flask with a silver cork, that screwed off and turned into a cup, and had a dram for a nightcap; and then he reached for a long pipe with a beaded cord, and when it was drawing well he stretched himself out comfortably and smiled at Peer.

"Well, now, my boy—are you getting on well at school?"

Peer put his hands behind him and set one foot forward. "Yes—he says so—teacher does."

"How much is twelve times twelve?"

That was a stumper! Peer hadn't got beyond ten times ten.

"Do they teach you gymnastics at the school?"

"Gym——? What's that?"

"Jumping and vaulting and climbing ropes and drilling in squads—what?"

"But isn't it—isn't that wicked?"

"Wicked! Hahaha! Wicked, did you say? So

that's the way they look at things here, is it? Well, well—well, well! Hahaha! Hand me that match-box, my boy. H'm!'' He puffed away for a while in silence. Then, suddenly:

"See here, boy. Did you know you'd a little sister?''

"Yes, I know."

"Half-sister, that is to say. I didn't quite know how it was myself. But I may as well tell you, my boy, that I paid the same for you all along, the same as now. Only I sent the money by your mother, and she—well, she, poor girl, had another one to look after, and no father to pay for it. So she made my money do for both. Hahaha! Well, poor girl, we can't blame her for that. Anyhow, we'll have to look after that little half-sister of yours now, I suppose, till she grows up. Don't you think so yourself?''

Peer felt the tears coming. Think so!—indeed he did.

Next day Peer's father went away. He stood there, ready to start, in the living-room at Tröen, stiff felt hat and overcoat and all, and said, in a tone like the sheriff's when he gives out a public notice at the church door:

"And, by the way, you're to have the boy confirmed this year."

"Yes, to be sure we will," the old mother hastened to say.

"Then I wish him to be properly dressed, like the best of the other youngsters. And there's fifty crowns for him to give the school-teacher and the parson as a parting gift." He handed over some more notes.

"Afterwards," he went on, "I mean, of course, to look after him until he can make his own way in a respectable position. But first we must see what he has a turn for, and what he'd like to be himself. He'd better come to town and talk it over with me—but I'll write and arrange all that after he's confirmed. Then in case anything unexpected should happen to me, there's some money laid by for him in a savings bank account; he can apply to a friend of mine, who knows all about it. Well, good-bye, and very many thanks!"

And the great man smiled to right and left, and shook them all by the hand, and waved his hat and was gone.

For the next few days Peer walked on air, and found it hard to keep his footing at all on the common earth. People were for ever filling his head with talk about that savings bank account—it might be only a few thousands of crowns—but then again, it might run up to a million. A million! and here he was, eating herrings for dinner, and talking to Tom, Dick, and Harry just like any one else. A million crowns!

Late in the autumn came the confirmation, and the old wooden church, with its tarred walls, nestled among its mighty tree-tops, sent its chimes ringing and ringing out into the blue autumn air. It seemed to Peer like some kindly old grand-

mother, calling so lovingly: "Come, come—old
and young—old and young—from fjord and valley—northways and southways; come, come—this
day of all days—this day of all days—come, come,
come!" So it had stood, ringing out the chimes
for one generation after another through hundreds
of years, and now it is calling to us. And the young
folks are there, looking at one another in their
new clothes, and blowing their noses on clean
white handkerchiefs, so carefully folded. There
comes Peter Rönningen, passed by good luck this
year, but forced to turn out in a jacket borrowed
from Peer, as the tailor wasn't ready with his
own new things. The boys say "how-do-you-do"
and try to smile like grown-up folks. One or two
of them may have some little account dating from
old school-fights waiting to be settled—but, never
mind—just as well to forget old scores now. Peer
caught sight of Johan Koja, who stole a pencil
from him last summer, but, after all, even that
didn't seem worth making a fuss about. "Well,
how've you been getting on since last summer?"
they ask each other, as they move together up the
stone steps to the big church door, through which
the peal of the organ comes rolling out to meet
them.

How good it seems, and how kind, the little
church, where all you see bids you welcome!
Through the stained-glass windows with their tiny
leaded panes falls a light so soft that even poor
ugly faces seem beautiful. The organ tones are

the very light itself turned into sweet sound. On one side of the nave you can see all the boys' heads, sleek with water; on the other the little mothers to be, in grown-up dress to-day for the first time, kerchief on head and hymn-book in hand, and with careful faces. And now they all sing. The elder folks have taken their places farther back to-day, but they join in, looking up now and again from the book to those young heads in front, and wondering how they will fare in life. And the young folk themselves are thinking as they sing, "To-day is the beginning of new things. Play and frolic are over and done with; from to-day we're grown-up." But the church and all in it seemed to say: "If ever you are in heavy trouble, come hither to me." Just look at that altar-piece there—the wood-carvings are a whole Bible in themselves—but Moses with the Tables of the Law is gentle of face to-day; you can see he means no harm after all. St. Peter, with the keys, pointing upwards, looks like a kind old uncle, bringing something good home from market. And then the angels on the walls, pictured or carved in wood, have borrowed the voice of the organ and the tones of the hymn, and they widen out the vaulted roof into the dome of heaven; while light and song and worshippers melt together and soar upwards toward the infinite spaces.

Peer was thinking all the time: I don't care if I'm rich as rich, I *will* be a priest. And then perhaps with all my money I can build a church that no one ever saw the like of. And the first couple I'll marry there shall be Martin Bruvold and little sister Louise—if only he'll have her. Just wait and see!

A few days later he wrote to his father, asking if he might come into town now and go to school. A long time passed, and then at last a letter came in a strange hand-writing, and all the grown folks at Tröen came together again to read it. But what was their amazement when they read:

"You will possibly have learned by now from the newspapers that your benefactor, Colonel Holm, has met his death by a fall from a horse. I must therefore request you to call on me personally at your earliest convenience, as I have several matters to settle with you. Yours faithfully, J. Grundt, Senior Master."

They stood and looked at one another.

Peer was crying—chiefly, it must be admitted, at the thought of having to bid good-bye to all the Tröen folks and the two cows, and the calf, and the grey cat. He might have to go right on to Christiania, no later than to-morrow—to go to school there; and when he came back—why, very likely the old mother might not be there any more.

So all three of them were heavy-hearted, when the pock-marked good-wife, and the bow-legged old man, came down with him to the pier. And soon he was standing on the deck of the fjord steamer, gazing at the two figures growing smaller

and smaller on the shore. And then one hut after
another in the little hamlet disappeared behind the
ness—Tröen itself was gone now—and the hills
and the woods where he had cut ring staves and
searched for stray cattle—swiftly all known things
drew away and vanished, until at last the whole
parish was gone, and his childhood over.

As evening fell, he saw a multitude of lights spread out on every side far ahead in the darkness. And next, with his little wooden chest on his shoulder, he was finding his way up through the streets by the quay to a lodging-house for country folk, which he knew from former visits, when he had come to the town with the Lofoten boats.

Next morning, clad in his country homespun, he marched up along River Street, over the bridge, and up the hill to the villa quarter, where he had to ask the way. At last he arrived outside a white-painted wooden house standing back in a garden. Here was the place—the place where his fate was to be decided. After the country fashion he walked in at the kitchen door.

A stout servant maid in a big white apron was rattling the rings of the kitchen range into place; there was a pleasing smell of coffee and good things to eat. Suddenly a door opened, and a figure in a dressing-gown appeared—a tall red-haired man with gold spectacles astride on a long red nose, his thick hair and scrubby little moustaches touched with grey. He gasped once or twice and then started sneezing—hoc-hoc-put-putsch!—wiped his nose with a large pocket-handkerchief, and grumbled out: "Ugh!—this wretched cold—

can't get rid of it. How about my socks, Bertha,
my good girl; do you think they are quite dry
now?"

"I've had them hung up ever since I lit the
fire this morning," said the girl, tossing her
head.

"But who is this young gentleman, may I ask?"
The gold spectacles were turned full on Peer, who
rose and bowed.

"Said he wanted to speak to you, sir," put in
the maid.

"Ah. From the country, I see. Have you anything to sell, my lad?"

"No," said Peer. He had had a letter. . . .
The red head seemed positively frightened at
this—and the dressing-gown faltered backwards,
as if to find support. He cast a hurried glance at
the girl, and then beckoned with a long fore-finger
to Peer. "Yes, yes, perfectly so. Be so good as
to come this way, my lad."

Peer found himself in a room with rows of books
all round the walls, and a big writing-table in the
centre. "Sit down, my boy." The schoolmaster
went and picked out a long pipe, and filled it, clearing his throat nervously, with an occasional glance
at the boy. "H'm—so this is you. This is Peer—
h'm." He lit his pipe and puffed a little, found
himself again obliged to sneeze—but at last settled down in a chair at the writing-table, stretched
out his long legs, and puffed away again.

"So that's what you look like?" With a quick

movement he reached for a photograph in a frame.
Peer caught a glimpse of his father in uniform.
The schoolmaster lifted his spectacles, stared at
the picture, then let down his spectacles again and
fell to scrutinising Peer's face. There was a silence for a while, and then he said: "Ah, indeed—
I see—h'm." Then turning to Peer:

"Well, my lad, it was very sudden—your benefactor's end—most unexpected. He is to be buried
to-day."

"Benefactor?" thought Peer. "Why doesn't
he say 'your father'?"

The schoolmaster was gazing at the window.
"He informed me some time ago of—h'm—of all
the—all the benefits he had conferred on you—
h'm! And he begged me to keep an eye on you
myself in case anything happened to him. And
now"—the spectacles swung round towards Peer
—"now you are starting out in life by yourself,
hey?"

"Yes," said Peer, shifting a little in his seat.

"You will have to decide now what walk in life
you are to—er—devote yourself to."

"Yes," said Peer again, sitting up straighter.

"You would perhaps like to be a fisherman—
like the good people you've been brought up
among?"

"No." Peer shook his head disdainfully. Was
this man trying to make a fool of him?

"Some trade, then, perhaps?"

"No!'

"Oh, then I suppose it's to be America. Well, you will easily find company to go with. Such numbers are going nowadays—I am sorry to say. . . . "

Peer pulled himself together. "Oh, no, not that at all." Better get it out at once. "I wish to be a priest," he said, speaking with a careful town accent.

The schoolmaster rose from his seat, holding his long pipe up in the air in one hand, and pressing his ear forward with the other, as though to hear better. "What?—what did you say?"

"A priest," repeated Peer, but he moved behind his chair as he spoke, for it looked as if the schoolmaster might fling the pipe at his head.

But suddenly the red face broke into a smile, exposing such an array of greenish teeth as Peer had never seen before. Then he said in a sort of singsong, nodding: "A priest? Oh, indeed! Quite a small matter!" He rose and wandered once or twice up and down the room, then stopped, nodded, and said in a fatherly tone—to one of the bookshelves: "H'm—really—really—we're a little ambitious, are we not?"

He turned on Peer suddenly. "Look here, my young friend—don't you think your benefactor has been quite generous enough to you already?"

"Yes, indeed he has," said Peer, his voice beginning to tremble a little.

"There are thousands of boys in your position who are thrown out in the world after confirma-

tion and left to shift for themselves, without a soul
to lend them a helping hand.''

"Yes,'' gasped Peer, looking round involuntarily towards the door.

"I can't understand—who can have put these
wild ideas into your head?''

With an effort Peer managed to get out: "It's
always been what I wanted. And he—father——''

"Who? Father——? Do you mean your benefactor?''

"Well, he was my father, wasn't he?'' burst out
Peer.

The schoolmaster tottered back and sank into
a chair, staring at Peer as if he thought him a
quite hopeless subject. At last he recovered so
far as to say: "Look here, my lad, don't you
think you might be content to call him—now and
for the future—just your benefactor? Don't you
think he deserves it?''

"Oh, yes,'' whispered Peer, almost in tears.

"You are thinking, of course—you and those
who have put all this nonsense into your head—
of the money which he—h'm——''

"Yes—isn't there a savings bank account——?''

"Aha! There we are! Yes, indeed. There is
a savings bank account—in my care.'' He rose,
and hunted out from a drawer a small green-
covered book. Peer could not take his eyes from
it. "Here it is. The sum entered here to your
account amounts to eighteen hundred crowns.''

Crash! Peer felt as if he had fallen through the floor into the cellarage. All his dreams vanished into thin air—the million crowns—priest and bishop—Christiania—and all the rest.

"On the day when you are in a fair way to set up independently as an artisan, a farmer, or a fisherman—and when you seem to me, to the best of my judgment, to deserve such help—then and not till then I place this book at your disposal. Do you understand what I say?"

"Yes."

"I am perfectly sure that I am in full agreement with the wishes of the donor in deciding that the money must remain untouched in my safe keeping until then."

"Yes," whispered Peer.

"What?—are you crying?"

"N-no. Good-morning——"

"No, pray don't go yet. Sit down. There are one or two things we must get settled at once. First of all—you must trust me, my good boy. Do you believe that I wish you well, or do you not?"

"Yes, sir."

"Then it is agreed that all these fancies about going to college and so forth must be driven out of your head once for all?"

"Y-yes, sir."

"You can see yourself that, even supposing you had the mental qualifications, such a sum, generous as it is in itself, would not suffice to carry you far.''

''No-no, sir.''

''On the other hand, if you wish it, I will gladly arrange to get you an apprentice's place with a good handicraftsman here. You would have free board there, and—well, if you should want clothes the first year or so, I dare say we could manage that. You will be better without pocket-money to fling about until you can earn it for yourself.''

Peer sighed, and drooped as he stood. When he saw the green-backed book locked into its drawer again, and heard the keys rattle as they went back into a pocket under the dressing-gown, he felt as if some one were pointing a jeering finger at him, and saying, ''Yah!''

''Then there's another thing. About your name. What name have you thought of taking, my lad—surname, I mean?''

''My name is Peer Holm!'' said the boy, instinctively drawing himself up as he had done when the bishop had patted his head at the confirmation and asked his name.

The schoolmaster pursed up his lips, took off his spectacles and wiped them, put them on again, and turned to the bookshelves with a sigh. ''Ah, indeed!—yes—yes—I almost thought as much.''

Then he came forward and laid a hand kindly on Peer's shoulder.

''My dear boy—that is out of the question.''

A shiver went through Peer. Had he done something wrong again?

"See here, my boy—have you considered that there may be others of that name in this same place?"

"Yes—but——"

"Wait a minute—and that you would occasion these—others—the deepest pain and distress if it should become known that—well, how matters stand. You see, I am treating you as a grown-up man—a gentleman. And I feel sure you would not wish to inflict a great sorrow—a crushing blow— upon a widow and her innocent children. There, there, my boy, there's nothing to cry about. Life, my young friend, life has troubles that must be faced. What is the name of the farm, or house, where you have lived up to now?"

"T—Tröen."

"Tröen—a very good name indeed. Then from to-day on you will call yourself Peer Tröen."

"Y-yes, sir."

"And if any one should ask about your father, remember that you are bound in honour and con-science not to mention your benefactor's name."

"Y-yes."

"Well, then, as soon as you have made up your mind, come at once and let me know. We shall be great friends yet, you will see. You're sure you wouldn't like to try America? Well, well, come along out to the kitchen and see if we can find you some breakfast."

Peer found himself a moment after sitting on a chair in the kitchen, where there was such a good smell of coffee. "Bertha," said the schoolmaster coaxingly, "you'll find something good for breakfast for my young friend here, won't you?" He waved a farewell with his hand, took down his socks from a string above the stove, and disappeared through the door again.

Chapter IV

WHEN a country boy in blue homespun, with a
peaked cap on his blond head, goes wandering at
random through the streets of a town, it is no
particular concern of any one else. He moves
along, gazing in at shop windows, hands deep in
his pockets, whistling, looking at everything
around him—or at nothing at all. And yet—perhaps in the head under that peaked cap it seems
as if a whole little world had suddenly collapsed,
and he may be whistling hard to keep from crying in the streets for people to see. He steps
aside to avoid a cart, and runs into a man, who
drops his cigar in the gutter. "Confounded
country lout!" says the man angrily, but passes
on and has forgotten boy and all the next moment. But a little farther on a big dog comes
dashing out of a yard and unluckily upsets a fat
old woman on the pavement, and the boy with
the peaked cap, for all his troubles, cannot help
doubling up and roaring with laughter.

That afternoon, Peer sat on one of the ramparts
below the fortress, biting at a stalk of grass, and
twirling the end in his fingers. Below him lay
town and fjord in the mild October sunlight; the
rumble of traffic, the noises from workshops and

harbour, came up to him through the rust-brown
luminous haze. There he sat, while the sentry
on the wall above marched back and forth, with
his rifle on his shoulder, left—right—left.

You may climb very high up indeed, and fall
down very deep, and no such terrible harm done
after all, as long as you don't absolutely break
your neck. And gradually Peer began to realise
that he was still alive, after all. It is a bad business when the world goes against you, even though
you may have some one to turn to for advice and
sympathy. But when all the people round you
are utter strangers, there is nothing to be done
but sit down and twirl a straw, and think things
out a bit for yourself. Peer's thoughts were of
a thing in a long dressing-gown that had taken
his bank book and locked it up and rattled the
keys at him and said "Yah!" and deposed him
from his bishopric and tried to sneeze and squeeze
him into a trade, where he'd have to carry a
pressing-iron all his life and be Peer Tröen,
Tailor. But he wouldn't have that. He sat there
bracing himself up, and trying to gather together
from somewhere a thing he had never had much
need of before—to wit, a will of his own, something to set up against the whole wide world.
What was he to do now? He felt he would like
to go back to Tröen first of all, and talk things
over with the old father and mother; they would
be sorry for him there, and say "Poor boy," and
pray for him—but after a day or two, he knew,

they would begin to glance at him at meals, and
remember that there was no one to pay for him
now, and that times were hard. No, that was no
refuge for him now. But what could he do, then?
Clearly it was not such a simple matter to be all
alone in the world.

A little later he found himself on a hillside by
the Cathedral churchyard, sitting under the yellowing trees, and wondering dreamily where his
father was to be buried. What a difference between him and that schoolmaster man! No
preaching with him; no whining about what his
boy might call himself or might not. Why must
he go and die?

It was strange to think of that fine strong man,
who had brushed his hair and beard so carefully
with his silver-backed brush—to think that he was
lying still in a coffin now, and would soon be covered up with earth.

People were coming up the hill now, and passing in to the churchyard. The men wore black
clothes and tall shiny hats—but there were some
officers too, with plumes and sashes. And then a
regimental band—with its brass instruments.
Peer slipped into the churchyard with the crowd,
but kept apart from the rest, and took up his stand
a little way off, beside a big monument. "It must
be father's funeral," he thought to himself, and
was broad awake at once.

This, he guessed, must be the Cadet School,
that came marching in, and formed up in two lines

from the mortuary chapel to the open grave. The place was nearly full of people now; there were women holding handkerchiefs to their eyes, and an elderly lady in black went into the chapel, on the arm of a tall man in uniform. "That must be father's wife," thought Peer, "and the young ladies there in black are—my half-sisters, and that young lieutenant—my half-brother." How strange it all was! A sound of singing came from the chapel. And a little later six sergeants came out, carrying a coffin all heaped with flowers. "Present arms!" And the soldiers presented, and the band played a slow march and moved off in front of the coffin, between the two lines of soldiers. And then came a great following of mourners. The lady in black came out again, sobbing behind her handkerchief, and hardly able to follow, though she clung to the tall officer's arm. But in front of the pair, just behind the coffin itself, walked a tall man in splendid uniform, with gold epaulettes, plumed hat, and sword, bearing a cushion with two jewelled stars. And the long, long train of mourners moved slowly, gently on, and there—there by the grave, stood the priest, holding a spade.

Peer was anxious to hear what the priest would have to say about his father. Involuntarily he stole a little nearer, though he felt somehow that it would not do to come too close.

A hymn was sung at the graveside, the band accompanying. Peer took off his cap. He was

too taken up to notice that one of the mourners
was watching him intently, and presently left the
group and came towards him. The man wore spectacles, and a shiny tall hat, and it was not until
he began to sneeze that Peer recognised him. It
was the schoolmaster, glaring at him now with a
face so full of horror and fury that the spectacles
almost seemed to be spitting fire.

"You—you—— Are you mad?" he whispered
in Peer's face, clenching his black gloved hands.
"What are you doing here? Do you want to cause
a catastrophe to-day of all days? Go—get away
at once, do you hear me? Go! For heaven's sake,
get away from here before any one sees." Peer
turned and fled, hearing behind him as he went
a threatening "If ever you dare—again——,"
while the voices and the band, swelling higher in
the hymn, seemed to strike him in the back and
drive him on.

He was far down in the town before he could
stop and pull himself together. One thing was
clear—after this he could never face that schoolmaster again. All was lost. Could he even be
sure that what he had done wasn't so frightfully
wrong that he would have to go to prison for it?

Next day the Tröen folk were sitting at their
dinner when the eldest son looked out of the window and said: "There's Peer coming."

"Mercy on us!" cried the good-wife, as he came
in. "What is the matter, Peer? Are you ill?"

Ah, it was good that night to creep in under

the old familiar skin-rug once more. And the old mother sat on the bedside and talked to him of the Lord, by way of comfort. Peer clenched his hands under the clothes—somehow he thought now of the Lord as a sort of schoolmaster in a dressing-gown. Yet it was some comfort all the same to have the old soul sit there and talk to him.

Peer had much to put up with in the days that followed—much tittering and whispers of "Look! there goes the priest," as he went by. At table, he felt ashamed of every mouthful he took; he hunted for jobs as day-labourer on distant farms so as to earn a little to help pay for his keep. And when the winter came he would have to do as the others did—hire himself out, young and small as he was, for the Lofoten fishing.

But one day after church Klaus Brock drew him aside and got him to talk things over at length. First, Klaus told him that he himself was going away—he was to begin in one of the mechanical workshops in town, and go from there to the Technical College, to qualify for an engineer. And next he wanted to hear the whole truth about what had happened to Peer that day in town. For when people went slapping their thighs and sniggering about the young would-be priest that had turned out a beggar, Klaus felt he would like to give the lot of them a darned good hammering.

So the two sixteen-year-old boys wandered up and down talking, and in the days to come Peer

never forgot how his old accomplice in the shark-
fishing had stood by him now. "Do like me,"
urged Klaus. "You're a bit of a smith already,
man; go to the workshops, and read up in your
spare time for the entrance exam. to the Technical.
Then three years at the College—the eighteen
hundred crowns will cover that—and there you
are, an engineer—and needn't even owe any one
a halfpenny."

Peer shook his head; he was sure he would never
dare to show his face before that schoolmaster
again, much less ask for the money in the bank.
No; the whole thing was over and done with for
him.

"But devil take it, man, surely you can see
that this ape of a schoolmaster dare not keep you
out of your money. Let me come with you; we'll
go up and tackle him together, and then—then
you'll see." And Klaus clenched his fists and
thrust out one shoulder fiercely.

But when January came, there was Peer in oil-
skins, in the foc's'le of a Lofoten fishing-smack,
ploughing the long sea-road north to the fishing-
grounds, in frost and snow-storms. All through
that winter he lived the fisherman's life: on land,
in one of the tiny fisher-booths where a five-man
crew is packed like sardines in an air so thick you
can cut it with a knife; at sea, where in a fair
wind you stand half the day doing nothing and
freezing stiff the while—and a foul wind means
out oars, and row, row, row, over an endless plain

of rolling icy combers; row, row, till one's hands
are lumps of bleeding flesh. Peer lived through
it all, thinking now and then, when he could think
at all, how the grand gentlefolk had driven him
out to this life because he was impertinent enough
to exist. And when the fourteen weeks were past,
and the Lofoten boats stood into the fjord again
on a mild spring day, it was easy for Peer to
reckon out his earnings, which were just nothing
at all. He had had to borrow money for his out-
fit and food, and he would be lucky if his boy's
share was enough to cover what he owed.

A few weeks later a boy stood by the yard gate
of an engineering works in the town just as the
bell was ringing and the men came streaming out,
and asked for Klaus Brock.

"Hullo, Peer—that you? Been to Lofoten and
made your fortune?"

The two boys stood a moment taking stock of
one another: Klaus grimy-faced and in working-
clothes—Peer weather-beaten and tanned by
storm and spray.

The manager of the factory was Klaus's uncle,
and the same afternoon his nephew came into the
office with a new hand wanting to be taken on as
apprentice. He had done some smithy work before, he said; and he was taken on forthwith, at
a wage of twopence an hour.

"And what's your name?"

"Peer—er"—the rest stuck in his throat.

"Holm," put in Klaus.

"Peer Holm? Very well, that'll do."

The two boys went out with a feeling of having done something rather daring. And anyway, if trouble should come along, there would be two of them now to tackle it.

Chapter V

In a narrow alley off Sea Street lived Gorseth the job-master, with a household consisting of a lean and skinny wife, two half-starved horses, and a few ramshackle flies and sledges. The job-master himself was a hulking toper with red nose and beery-yellow eyes, who spent his nights in drinking and got home in the small hours of the morning when his wife was just about getting up. All through the morning she went about the place scolding and storming at him for a drunken ne'er-do-well, while Gorseth himself lay comfortably snoring.

When Peer arrived on the scene with his box on his shoulder, Gorseth was on his knees in the yard, greasing a pair of leather carriage-aprons, while his wife, sunken-lipped and fierce-eyed, stood in the kitchen doorway, abusing him for a profligate, a swine, and the scum of the earth. Gorseth lay there on all-fours, with the sun shining on his bald head, smearing on the grease; but every now and then he would lift his head and snarl out, "Hold your jaw, you damned old jade!"

"Haven't you a room to let?" Peer asked.

A beery nose was turned towards him, and the man dragged himself up and wiped his hands on

his trousers. "Right you are," said he, and led
the way across the yard, up some stairs, and into
a little room with two panes of glass looking on
to the street and a half-window on the yard. The
room had a bed with sheets, a couple of chairs,
and a table in front of the half-window. Six and
six a month. Agreed. Peer took it on the spot,
paid down the first month's rent, and having got
rid of the man sat down on his chest and looked
about him. Many people have never a roof to
their heads, but here was he, Peer, with a home
of his own. Outside in the yard the woman had
begun yelping her abuse again, the horses in
the stable beneath were stamping and whinnying,
but Peer had lodged in fisher-booths and peasants'
quarters and was not too particular. Here he
was for the first time in a place of his own, and
within its walls was master of the house and his
own master.

Food was the next thing. He went out and
bought in supplies, stocking his chest with plain
country fare. At dinner time he sat on the lid, as
fishermen do, and made a good solid meal of flat
bannocks and cold bacon.

And now he fell-to at his new work. There was
no question of whether it was what he wanted
or not; here was a chance of getting up in the
world, and that without having to beg any one's
leave. He meant to get on. And it was not long
before his dreams began to take a new shape from
his new life. He stood at the bottom of a ladder,

a blacksmith's boy—but up at the top sat a mighty
Chief Engineer, with gold spectacles and white
waistcoat. That was where he would be one day.
And if any schoolmaster came along and tried to
keep him back this time—well, just let him try it.
They had turned him out of a churchyard once—
he would have his revenge for that some day. It
might take him years and years to do it, but one
fine day he would be as good as the best of them,
and would pay them back in full.

In the misty mornings, as he tramped in to his
work, dinner-pail in hand, his footsteps on the
plank bridge seemed hammering out with concen-
trated will: "To-day I shall learn something new
—new—new!"

The great works down at the harbour—shipyard, foundry, and machine shops—were a whole
city in themselves. And into this world of fire
and smoke and glowing iron, steam-hammers, racing wheels, and bustle and noise, he was thrusting his way, intent upon one thing, to learn and
learn and ever learn. There were plenty of those
by him who were content to know their way
about the little corner where they stood—but they
would never get any farther. They would end
their days broken-down workmen—*he* would
carve his way through till he stood among the
masters. He had first to put in some months'
work in the smithy, then he would be passed on
to the machine shops, then to work with the carpenters and painters, and finally in the shipyard.

The whole thing would take a couple of years.
But the works and all therein were already a kind
of new Bible to him; a book of books, which he
must learn by heart. Only wait!

And what a place it was for new adventures!
Many times a day he would find himself gazing
at some new wonder; sheer miracle and revela-
tion—yet withal no creation of God's grace, but
an invention of men. Press a button, and behold, a miracle springs to life. He would stare
at the things, and the strain of understanding
them would sometimes keep him awake at night.
There was something behind this, something that
must be—spirit, even though it did not come from
God. These engineers were priests of a sort,
albeit they did not preach nor pray. It was a new
world.

One day he was put to riveting work on an
enormous boiler, and for the first time found himself working with a power that was not the power
of his own hands. It was a tube, full of compressed air, that drove home the rivets in quick
succession with a clashing wail from the boiler
that sounded all over the town. Peer's head and
ears ached with the noise, but he smiled all the
same. He was used to toil himself, in weariness
of body; now he stood here master, was mind
and soul and directing will. He felt it now for
the first time, and it sent a thrill of triumph
through every nerve of his body.

But all through the long evenings he sat alone,

reading, reading, and heard the horses stamping
in the stable below. And when he crept into bed,
well after midnight, there was only one thing that
troubled him—his utter loneliness. Klaus Brock
lived with his uncle, in a fine house, and went to
parties. And he lay here all by himself. If he
were to die that very night, there would be hardly
a soul to care. So utterly alone he was—in a
strange and indifferent world.

Sometimes it helped him a little to think of the
old mother at Tröen, or of the church at home,
where the vaulted roof had soared so high over
the swelling organ-notes, and all the faces had
looked so beautiful. But the evening prayer was
no longer what it had been for him. There was
no grey-haired bishop any more sitting at the top
of the ladder he was to climb. The Chief Engineer that was there now had nothing to do with
Our Lord, or with life in the world to come. He
would never come so far now that he could go
down into the place of torment where his mother
lay, and bring her up with him, up to salvation.
And whatever power and might he gained, he
could never stand in autumn evenings and lift up
his finger and make all the stars break into song.

Something was past and gone for Peer. It was
as if he were rowing away from a coast where red
clouds hung in the sky and dream-visions filled
the air—rowing farther and farther away, towards something quite new. A power stronger
than himself had willed it so.

One Sunday, as he sat reading, the door opened, and Klaus Brock entered whistling, with his cap on the back of his head.

"Hullo, old boy! So this is where you live?"

"Yes, it is—and that's a chair over there."

But Klaus remained standing, with his hands in his pockets and his cap on, staring about the room. "Well, I'm blest!" he said at last. "If he hasn't stuck up a photograph of himself on his table!"

"Well, did you never see one before? Don't you know everybody has them?"

"Not their own photos, you ass! If anybody sees that, you'll never hear the last of it."

Peer took up the photograph and flung it under the bed. "Well, it was a rubbishy thing," he muttered. Evidently he had made a mistake. "But what about this?"—pointing to a coloured picture he had nailed up on the wall.

Klaus put on his most manly air and bit off a piece of tobacco plug. "Ah! that!" he said, trying not to laugh too soon.

"Yes; it's a fine painting, isn't it? I got it for fourpence."

"Painting! Ha-ha! that's good! Why, you silly cow, can't you see it's only an oleograph?"

"Oh, of course you know all about it. You always do."

"I'll take you along one day to the Art Gallery," said Klaus. "Then you can see what a real painting looks like. What's that you've got there—English reader?"

"Yes," put in Peer eagerly; "hear me say a poem." And before Klaus could protest, he had begun to recite.

When he had finished, Klaus sat for a while in silence, chewing his quid. "H'm!" he said at last, "if our last teacher, Fröken Zebbelin, could have heard that English of yours, we'd have had to send for a nurse for her, hanged if we wouldn't!"

This was too much. Peer flung the book against the wall and told the other to clear out to the devil. When Klaus at last managed to get a word in, he said:

"If you are to pass your entrance at the Technical you'll have to have lessons—surely you can see that. You must get hold of a teacher."

"Easy for you to talk about teachers! Let me tell you my pay is twopence an hour."

"I'll find you one who can take you twice a week or so in languages and history and mathematics. I daresay some broken-down sot of a student would take you on for sevenpence a lesson. You could run to that, surely?"

Peer was quiet now and a little pensive. "Well, if I give up butter, and drink water instead of coffee——"

Klaus laughed, but his eyes were moist. Hard luck that he couldn't offer to lend his comrade a few shillings—but it wouldn't do.

So the summer passed. On Sundays Peer would
watch the young folks setting out in the morning
for the country, to spend the whole day wandering
in the fields and woods, while he sat indoors over
his books. And in the evening he would stick his
head out of his two-paned window that looked on
to the street, and would see the lads and girls
coming back, flushed and noisy, with flowers and
green boughs in their hats, crazy with sunshine
and fresh air. And still he must sit and read on.
But in the autumn, when the long nights set in,
he would go for a walk through the streets before
going to bed, as often as not up to the white
wooden house where the manager lived. This
was Klaus's home. Lights in the windows, and
often music; the happy people that lived here
knew and could do all sorts of things that could
never be learned from books. No mistake: he had
a goodish way to go—a long, long way. But get
there he would.

One day Klaus happened to mention, quite casually, where Colonel Holm's widow lived, and late
one evening Peer made his way out there, and cautiously approached the house. It was in River
Street, almost hidden in a cluster of great trees,
and Peer stood there, leaning against the garden
fence, trembling with some obscure emotion. The
long rows of windows on both floors were lighted
up; he could hear youthful laughter within, and
then a young girl's voice singing—doubtless they
were having a party. Peer turned up his collar

against the wind, and tramped back through the town to his lodging above the carter's stable.

For the lonely working boy Saturday evening is a sort of festival. He treats himself to an extra wash, gets out his clean underclothes from his chest, and changes. And the smell of the newly-washed underclothing calls up keenly the thought of a pock-marked old woman who sewed and patched it all, and laid it away so neatly folded. He puts it on carefully, feeling almost as if it were Sunday already.

Now and again, when a Sunday seemed too long, Peer would drift into the nearest church. What the parson said was all very good, no doubt, but Peer did not listen; for him there were only the hymns, the organ, the lofty vaulted roof, the coloured windows. Here, too, the faces of the people looked otherwise than in the street without; touched, as it were, by some reflection from all that their thoughts aspired to reach. And it was so homelike here. Peer even felt a sort of kinship with them all, though every soul there was a total stranger.

But at last one day, to his surprise, in the middle of a hymn, a voice within him whispered suddenly: "You should write to your sister. She's as much alone in the world as you are."

And one evening Peer sat down and wrote. He took quite a lordly tone, saying that if she wanted help in any way, she need only let him know. And if she would care to move in to town, she could

come and live with him. After which he remained,
her affectionate brother, Peer Holm, engineer apprentice.

A few days later there came a letter addressed
in a fine slanting hand. Louise had just been confirmed. The farmer she was with wished to keep
her on as dairymaid through the winter, but she
was afraid the work would be too heavy for her.
So she was coming in to town by the boat arriving on Sunday evening. With kind regards, his
sister, Louise Hagen.

Peer was rather startled. He seemed to have
taken a good deal on his shoulders.

On Sunday evening he put on his blue suit and
stiff felt hat, and walked down to the quay. For
the first time in his life he had some one else to
look after—he was to be a father and benefactor
from now on to some one worse off than himself.
This was something new. The thought came back
to him of the jolly gentleman who had come driving down one day to Tröen to look after his little
son. Yes, that was the way to do things; that
was the sort of man he would be. And involuntarily he fell into something of his father's look
and step, his smile, his lavish, careless air. "Well,
well—well, well—well, well," he seemed saying to
himself. He might almost, in his fancy, have
had a neat iron-grey beard on his chin.

The little green steamboat rounded the point
and lay in to the quay, the gangways were run
out, porters jumped aboard, and all the passen-

gers came bundling ashore. Peer wondered how
he was to know her, this sister whom he had never
seen.

The crowd on deck soon thinned, and people began moving off from the quay into the town.

Then Peer was aware of a young peasant-girl,
with a box in one hand and a violin-case in the
other. She wore a grey dress, with a black kerchief over her fair hair; her face was pale, and
finely cut. It was his mother's face; his mother
as a girl of sixteen. Now she was looking about
her, and now her eyes rested on him, half afraid,
half inquiring.

"Is it you, Louise?"

"Is that you, Peer?"

They stood for a moment, smiling and measur-
ing each other with their eyes, and then shook
hands.

Together they carried the box up through the
town, and Peer was so much of a townsman already that he felt a little ashamed to find himself
walking through the streets, holding one end of
a trunk, with a peasant-girl at the other. And
what a clatter her thick shoes made on the pavement! But all the time he was ashamed to feel
ashamed. Those blue arch eyes of hers, constantly glancing up at him, what were they saying? "Yes, I have come," they said—"and I've
no one but you in all the world—and here I am,"
they kept on saying.

"Can you play that?" he asked, with a glance at her violin-case.

"Oh well; my playing's only nonsense," she laughed. And she told how the old sexton she had been living with last had not been able to afford a new dress for her confirmation, and had given her the violin instead.

"Then didn't you have a new dress to be confirmed in?"

"No."

"But wasn't it—didn't you feel horrible, with the other girls standing by you all dressed up fine?"

She shut her eyes for a moment. "Oh, yes—it *was* horrid," she said.

A little farther on she asked: "Were you boarded out at a lot of places?"

"Five, I think."

"Pooh—why, that's nothing. I was at nine, I was." The girl was smiling again.

When they came up to his room she stood for a moment looking round the place. It was hardly what she had expected to find. And she had not been in town lodgings before, and her nose wrinkled up a little as she smelt the close air. It seemed so stuffy, and so dark.

"We'll light the lamp," he said.

Presently she laughed a little shyly, and asked where she was to sleep.

"Lord bless us, you may well ask!" Peer

scratched his head. "There's only one bed, you see." At that they both burst out laughing.

"The one of us'll have to sleep on the floor," suggested the girl.

"Right. The very thing," said he, delighted. "I've two pillows; you can have one. And two rugs—anyway, you won't be cold."

"And then I can put on my other dress over," she said. "And maybe you'll have an old overcoat——"

"Splendid! So we needn't bother any more about that."

"But where do you get your food from?" She evidently meant to have everything cleared up at once.

Peer felt rather ashamed that he hadn't money enough to invite her to a meal at an eating-house then and there. But he had to pay his teacher's fees the next day; and his store-box wanted refilling too.

"I boil the coffee on the stove there overnight," he said, "so that it's all ready in the morning. And the dry food I keep in that box there. We'll see about some supper now." He opened the box, fished out a loaf and some butter, and put the kettle on the stove. She helped him to clear the papers off the table, and spread the feast on it. There was only one knife, but it was really much better fun that way than if he had had two. And soon they were seated on their chairs—they had a chair each—having their first meal in their own home, he and she together.

It was settled that Louise should sleep on the floor, and they both laughed a great deal as he tucked her in carefully so that she shouldn't feel cold. It was not till afterwards, when the lamp was out, that they noticed that the autumn gales had set in, and there was a loud north-wester howling over the housetops. And there they lay, chatting to each other in the dark, before falling asleep.

It seemed a strange and new thing to Peer, this really having a relation of his own—and a girl, too—a young woman. There she lay on the floor near by him, and from now on he was responsible for what was to become of her in the world. How should he put that job through?

He could hear her turning over. The floor was hard, very likely.

"Louise?"

"Yes."

"Did you ever see mother?"

"No."

"Or your father?"

"My father?" She gave a little laugh.

"Yes, haven't you ever seen him either?"

"Why, how should I, silly? Who says that mother knew herself who it was?"

There was a pause. Then Peer brought out, rather awkwardly: "We're all alone, then—you and I."

"Yes—we are that."

"Louise! What are you thinking of taking to now?"

"What are you?"

So Peer told her all his plans. She said nothing for a little while—no doubt she was lying thinking of the grand things he had before him.

At last she spoke. "Do you think—does it cost very much to learn to be a midwife?"

"A midwife—is that what you want to be, girl?" Peer couldn't help laughing. So this was what she had been planning in these days—since he had offered to help her on in the world.

"Do you think my hands are too big?" she ventured presently—he could just hear the whisper.

Peer felt a pang of pity. He had noticed already how ill the red swollen hands matched her pale clear-cut face, and he knew that in the country, when any one has small, fine hands, people call them "midwife's hands."

"We'll manage it somehow, I daresay," said Peer, turning round to the wall. He had heard that it cost several hundred crowns to go through the course at the midwifery school. It would be years before he could get together anything like that sum. Poor girl, it looked as if she would have a long time to wait.

After that they fell silent. The north-wester roared over the housetops, and presently brother and sister were asleep.

When Peer awoke the next morning, Louise

was about already, making coffee over the little
stove. Then she opened her box, took out a yellow petticoat and hung it on a nail, placed a pair
of new shoes against the wall, lifted out some
under-linen and woollen stockings, looked at them,
and put them back again. The little box held all
her worldly goods.

As Peer was getting up: "Gracious mercy!"
she cried suddenly, "what is that awful noise
down in the yard?"

"Oh, that's nothing to worry about," said
Peer. "It's only the job-master and his wife.
They carry on like that every blessed morning;
you'll soon get used to it."

Soon they were seated once more at the little
table, drinking coffee and laughing and looking at
each other. Louise had found time to do her hair
—the two fair plaits hung down over her shoulders.

It was time for Peer to be off, and, warning
the girl not to go too far from home and get lost,
he ran down the stairs.

At the works he met Klaus Brock, and told him
that his sister had come to town.

"But what are you going to do with her?"
asked Klaus.

"Oh, she'll stay with me for the present."

"Stay with you? But you've only got one room
and one bed, man!"

"Well—she can sleep on the floor."

"She? Your sister? She's to sleep on the floor —and you in the bed!" gasped Klaus.

Peer saw he had made a mistake again. "Of course I was only fooling," he hastened to say. "Of course it's Louise that's to have the bed."

When he came home he found she had borrowed a frying-pan from the carter's wife, and had fried some bacon and boiled potatoes; so that they sat down to a dinner fit for a prince.

But when the girl's eyes fell on the coloured print on the wall, and she asked if it was a painting, Peer became very grand at once. "That—a painting? Why, that's only an oleograph, silly! No, I'll take you along to the Art Gallery one day, and show you what real paintings are like." And he sat drumming with his fingers on the table, and saying: "Well, well—well, well, well!"

They agreed that Louise had better look out at once for some work to help things along. And at the first eating-house they tried, she was taken on at once in the kitchen to wash the floor and peel potatoes.

When bedtime came he insisted on Louise taking the bed. "Of course all that was only a joke last night," he explained. "Here in town women always have the best of everything—that's what's called manners." As he stretched himself on the hard floor, he had a strange new feeling. The narrow little garret seemed to have widened out now that he had to find room in it for a guest. There was something not unpleasant even in lying

on the hard floor, since he had chosen to do it for
some one else's sake.

After the lamp was out he lay for a while, listening to her breathing. Then at last:

"Louise."

"Yes?"

"Is your father—was his name Hagen?"

"Yes. It says so on the certificate."

"Then you're Fröken Hagen. Sounds quite
fine, doesn't it?"

"Uf! Now you're making fun of me."

"And when you're a midwife, Fröken Hagen
might quite well marry a doctor, you know."

"Silly! There's no chance—with hands like
mine."

"Do you think your hands are too big for you
to marry a doctor?"

"Uf! you *are* a crazy thing. Ha-ha-ha!"

"Ha-ha-ha!"

They both snuggled down under the clothes,
with the sense of ease and peace that comes from
sharing a room with a good friend in a happy
humour.

"Well, good-night, Louise."

"Good-night, Peer."

So things went on till winter was far spent. Now that Louise, too, was a wage-earner, and could help with the expenses, they could dine luxuriously at an eating-house every day, if they pleased, on meat-cakes at fourpence a portion. They managed to get a bed for Peer that could be folded up during the day, and soon learned, too, that good manners required they should hang up Louise's big woollen shawl between them as a modest screen while they were dressing and undressing. And Louise began to drop her country speech and talk city-fashion like her brother.

One thought often came to Peer as he lay awake. "The girl is the very image of mother, that's certain—what if she were to go the same way? Well, no, that she shall not. You're surely man enough to see to that. Nothing of that sort shall happen, my dear Fröken Hagen."

They saw but little of each other during the day, though, for they were apart from early in the morning till he came home in the evening. And when he lectured her, and warned her to be careful and take no notice of men who tried to speak to her, Louise only laughed. When Klaus Brock came up one day to visit them, and made great

play with his eyes while he talked to her, Peer
felt much inclined to take him by the scruff of
the neck and throw him downstairs.

When Christmas-time was near they would
wander in the long evenings through the streets
and look in at the dazzlingly lit shop-windows,
with their tempting, glittering show of gold and
finery. Louise kept asking continually how much
he thought this thing or that cost—that lace, or
the cloak, or the stockings, or those gold brooches.
"Wait till you marry that doctor," Peer would
say, "then you can buy all those things." So
far neither of them had an overcoat, but Peer
turned up his coat-collar when he felt cold, and
Louise made the most of her thick woollen dress
and a pair of good country gloves that kept her
quite warm. And she had adventured on a hat
now, in place of her kerchief, and couldn't help
glancing round, thinking people must notice how
fine she was.

On Christmas Eve he carried up buckets of
water from the yard, and she had a great scrub-
bing-out of the whole room. And then they in
their turn had a good wash, helping each other in
country fashion to scrub shoulders and back.

Peer was enough of a townsman now to have
laid in a few little presents to give his sister; but
the girl, who had not been used to such doings,
had nothing for him, and wept a good deal when
she realised it. They ate cakes from the confec-
tioner's with syrup over them, and drank choco-

late, and then Louise played a hymn-tune, in her
best style, on her violin, and Peer read the Christmas lessons from the prayer-book—it was all just
like what they used to do at Tröen on Christmas
Eve. And that night, after the lamp was put out,
they lay awake talking over plans for the future.
They promised each other that when they had
got well on in the world, he in his line and she
in hers, they would manage to live near each other,
so that their children could play together and
grow up good friends. Didn't she think that was
a good idea? Yes, indeed she did. And did he
really mean it? Yes, of course he meant it, really.

But later on in the winter, when she sat at home
in the evenings waiting for him—he often worked
overtime—she was sometimes almost afraid.
There was his step on the stairs! If it was hurried and eager she would tremble a little. For
the moment he was inside the door he would burst
out: "Hurrah, my girl! I've learnt something
new to-day, I tell you!" "Have you, Peer?"
And then out would pour a torrent of talk about
motors and power and pressures and cylinders
and cranes and screws, and such-like. She would
sit and listen and smile, but of course understood
not a word of it all, and as soon as Peer discovered
this he would get perfectly furious, and call her
a little blockhead.

Then there were the long evenings when he sat
at home reading, by himself or with his teacher,
and she had to sit so desperately still that she

hardly dared take a stitch with her needle. But one day he took it into his head that his sister ought to be studying too; so he set her a piece of history to learn by the next evening. But time to learn it—where was that to come from? And then he started her writing to his dictation, to improve her spelling—and all the time she kept dropping off to sleep. She had washed so many floors and peeled so many potatoes in the daytime that now her body felt like lead.

"Look here, my fine girl!" he would storm at her, raging up and down the room, "if you think you can get on in the world without education, you're most infernally mistaken." He succeeded in reducing her to tears—but it wasn't long before her head had fallen forward on the table again and she was fast asleep. So he realised there was nothing for it but to help her to bed— as quietly as possible, so as not to wake her up.

Some way on in the spring Peer fell sick. When the doctor came, he looked round the room, sniffed, and frowned. "Do you call this a place for human beings to live in?" he asked Louise, who had taken the day off. "How can you expect to keep well?"

He examined Peer, who lay coughing, his face a burning red. "Yes, yes—just as I expected. Inflammation of the lungs." He glanced round the room once more. "Better get him off to the hospital at once," he said.

Louise sat there in terror at the idea that Peer

was to be taken away. And then, as the doctor was going, he looked at her more closely, and said: "You'd do well to be a bit careful yourself, my good girl. You look as if you wanted a change to a decent room, with a little more light and air, pretty badly. Good-morning."

Soon after he was gone the hospital ambulance arrived. Peer was carried down the stairs on a stretcher, and the green-painted box on wheels opened its door and swallowed him up; and they would not even let her go with him. All through the evening she sat in their room alone, sobbing.

The hospital was one of the good old-fashioned kind that people don't come near if they can help it, because the walls seem to reek of the discomfort and wretchedness that reign inside. The general wards—where the poor folks went—were always so overcrowded that patients with all sorts of different diseases had to be packed into the same rooms, and often infected each other. When an operation was to be performed, things were managed in the most cheerfully casual way: the patient was laid on a stretcher and carried across the open yard, often in the depth of winter, and as he was always covered up with a rug, the others usually thought he was being taken off to the dead-house.

When Peer opened his eyes, he was aware of a man in a white blouse standing by the foot of his bed. "Why, I believe he's coming-to," said the man, who seemed to be a doctor. Peer found out

afterwards from a nurse that he had been unconscious for more than twenty-four hours.

He lay there, day after day, conscious of nothing but the stabbing of a red-hot iron boring
through his chest and cutting off his breathing.
Some one would come every now and then and
pour port wine and naphtha into his mouth; and
morning and evening he was washed carefully
with warm water by gentle hands. But little by
little the room grew lighter, and his gruel began
to have some taste. And at last he began to dis-
tinguish the people in the beds near by, and to
chat with them.

On his right lay a black-haired, yellow-faced
dock labourer with a broken nose. His disease,
whatever it might be, was clearly different from
Peer's. He plagued the nurse with foul-mouthed
complaints of the food, swearing he would report
about it. On the other side lay an emaciated cobbler with a soft brown beard like the Christ pictures, and cheeks glowing with fever. He was
dying of cancer. At right angles with him lay
a man with the face and figure of a prophet—a
Moses—all bushy white hair and beard; he was
in the last stage of consumption, and his cough
was like a riveting machine. "Huh!" he would
groan, "if only I could get across to Germany
there'd be a chance for me yet." Beside him was
a fellow with short beard and piercing eyes, who
was a little off his head, and imagined himself a
corporal of the Guards. Often at night the others

would be wakened by his springing upright in bed
and calling out: "Attention!"

One man lay moaning and groaning all the time,
turning from side to side of a body covered with
sores. But one day he managed to swallow some
of the alcohol they used as lotion, and after that
lay singing and weeping alternately. And there
was a red-bearded man with glasses, a commercial traveller; he had put a bullet into his head,
but the doctors had managed to get it out again,
and now he lay and praised the Lord for his
miraculous deliverance.

It was strange to Peer to lie awake at night in
this great room in the dim light of the night-lamp;
it seemed as if beings from the land of the dead
were stirring in those beds round about him. But
in the daytime, when friends and relations of the
patients came a-visiting, Peer could hardly keep
from crying. The cobbler had a wife and a little
girl who came and sat beside him, gazing at him
as if they could never let him go. The prophet,
too, had a wife, who wept inconsolably—and all
the rest seemed to have some one or other to
care for them. But where was Louise—why did
Louise never come?

The man on the right had a sister, who came
sweeping in, gorgeous in her trailing soiled silk
dress. Her shoes were down at heel, but her hat
was a wonder, with enormous plumes. "Hallo,
Ugly! how goes it?" she said; and sat down and
crossed her legs. Then the pair would talk mys-

teriously of people with strange names: "The
Flea," "Cockroach," "The Galliot," "King
Ring," and the like, evidently friends of theirs.
One day she managed to bring in a small bottle
of brandy, a present from "The Hedgehog," and
smuggle it under the bedclothes. As soon as she
had gone, and the coast was clear, Peer's neighbour drew out the bottle, managed to work the
cork out, and offered him a drink. "Here's luck,
sonny; do you good." No—Peer would rather
not. Then followed a gurgling sound from the
docker's bed, and soon he too was lying singing
at the top of his voice.

At last one day Louise came. She was wearing
her neat hat, and had a little bundle in her hand,
and as she came in, looking round the room, the
close air of the sick-ward seemed to turn her a
little faint. But then she caught sight of Peer,
and smiled, and came cautiously to him, holding
out her hand. She was astonished to find him so
changed. But as she sat down by his pillow she
was still smiling, though her eyes were full of
tears.

"So you've come at last, then?" said Peer.

"They wouldn't let me in before," she said with
a sob. And then Peer learned that she had come
there every single day, but only to be told that
he was too ill to see visitors.

The man with the broken nose craned his head
forward to get a better view of the modest young
girl. And meanwhile she was pulling out of the

bundle the offering she had brought—a bottle of lemonade and some oranges.

But it was a day or two later that something happened which Peer was often to remember in the days to come.

He had been dozing through the afternoon, and when he woke the lamp was lit, and a dull yellow half-light lay over the ward. The others seemed to be sleeping; all was very quiet, only the man with the sores was whimpering softly. Then the door opened, and Peer saw Louise glide in, softly and cautiously, with her violin-case under her arm. She did not come over to where her brother lay, but stood in the middle of the ward, and, taking out her violin, began to play the Easter hymn: "The mighty host in white array." [1]

The man with the sores ceased whimpering; the patients in the beds round about opened their eyes. The docker with the broken nose sat up in bed, and the cobbler, roused from his feverish dream, lifted himself on his elbow and whispered: "It is the Redeemer. I knew Thou wouldst come." Then there was silence. Louise stood there with eyes fixed on her violin, playing her simple best. The consumptive raised his head and forgot to cough; the corporal slowly stiffened his body to attention; the commercial traveller folded his hands and stared before him. The simple tones of the hymn seemed to be giving

---

[1] "Den store hvide Flok vi se."

new life to all these unfortunates; the light of it was in their faces. But to Peer, watching his sister as she stood there in the half-light, it seemed as if she grew to be one with the hymn itself, and that wings to soar were given her.

When she had finished, she came softly over to his bed, stroked his forehead with her swollen hand, then glided out and disappeared as silently as she had come.

For a long time all was silent in the dismal ward, until at last the dying cobbler murmured: "I thank Thee. I knew—I knew Thou wert not far away."

When Peer left the hospital, the doctor said he had better not begin work again at once; he should take a holiday in the country and pick up his strength. "Easy enough for you to talk," thought Peer, and a couple of days later he was at the workshop again.

But his ways with his sister were more considerate than before, and he searched about until he had found her a place as seamstress, and saved her from her heavy floor-scrubbing.

And soon Louise began to notice with delight that her hands were much less red and swollen than they had been; they were actually getting soft and pretty by degrees.

Next winter she sat at home in the evenings while he read, and made herself a dress and cloak and trimmed a new hat, so that Peer soon had quite an elegant young lady to walk out with.

But when men turned round to look at her as she passed, he would scowl and clench his fists. At last one day this was too much for Louise, and she rebelled. "Now, Peer, I tell you plainly I won't go out with you if you go on like that."

"All right, my girl," he growled. "I'll look after you, though, never fear. We're not going to have mother's story over again with you."

"Well, but, after all, I'm a grown-up-girl, and you can't prevent people looking at me, idiot!"

Klaus Brock had been entered at the Technical College that autumn, and went about now with the College badge in his cap, and sported a walking-stick and a cigarette. He had grown into a big, broad-shouldered fellow, and walked with a little swing in his step; a thick shock of black hair fell over his forehead, and he had a way of looking about him as if to say: "Anything the matter? All right, I'm ready!"

One evening he came in and asked Louise to go with him to the theatre. The young girl blushed red with joy, and Peer could not refuse; but he was waiting for them outside the yard gate when they came back. On a Sunday soon after Klaus was there again, asking her to come out for a drive. This time she did not even look to Peer for leave, but said "yes" at once. "Just you wait," said Peer to himself. And when she came back that evening he read her a terrific lecture.

Soon he could not help seeing that the girl was going about with half-shut eyes, dreaming dreams

of which she would never speak to him. And as
the days went on her hands grew whiter, and she
moved more lightly, as if to the rhythm of unheard music. Always as she went about the
room on her household tasks she was crooning
some song; it seemed that there was some joy
in her soul that must find an outlet.

One Saturday in the late spring she had just
come home, and was getting the supper, when
Peer came tramping in, dressed in his best and
carrying a parcel.

"Hi, girl! Here you are! We're going to have
a rare old feast to-night."

"Why—what is it all about?"

"I've passed my entrance exam. for the Technical—hurrah! Next autumn—next autumn—I'll
be a student!"

"Oh, splendid! I *am* so glad!" And she dried
her hand and grasped his.

"Here you are—sausages, anchovies—and
here's a bottle of brandy—the first I ever bought
in my life. Klaus is coming up later on to have
a glass of toddy. And here's cheese. We'll
make things hum to-night."

Klaus came, and the two youths drank toddy
and smoked and made speeches, and Louise played
patriotic songs on her violin, and Klaus gazed at
her and asked for "more—more."

When he left, Peer went with him, and as the
two walked down the street, Klaus took his
friend's arm, and pointed to the pale moon rid-

ing high above the fjord, and vowed never to
give him up, till he stood at the very top of the
tree—never, never! Besides, he was a Socialist
now, he said, and meant to raise a revolt against
all class distinctions. And Louise—Louise was
the most glorious girl in all the world—and now
—and now—Peer might just as well know it
sooner as later—they were as good as engaged
to be married, he and Louise.

Peer pushed him away, and stood staring at
him. "Go home now, and go to bed," he said.

"Ha! You think I'm not man enough to defy
my people—to defy the whole world!"

"Good-night," said Peer.

Next morning, as Louise lay in bed—she had
asked to have her breakfast there for once in a
way—she suddenly began to laugh. "What *are*
you about now?" she asked teasingly.

"Shaving," said Peer, beginning operations.

"Shaving! Are you so desperate to be grand
to-day that you must scrape all your skin off?
You know there's nothing else to shave."

"You hold your tongue. Little do you know
what I've got in front of me to-day."

"What can it be? You're not going courting
an old widow with twelve children, are you?"

"If you want to know, I'm going to that schoolmaster fellow, and going to wring my savings-
bank book out of him."

Louise sat up at this. "My great goodness!"
she said.

Yes; he had been working himself up to this for a year or more, and now he was going to do it. To-day he would show what he was made of—whether he was a snivelling child, or a man that could stand up to any dressing-gown in the world. He was shaving for the first time—quite true. And the reason was that it was no ordinary day, but a great occasion.

His toilet over, he put on his best hat with a flourish, and set out.

Louise stayed at home all the morning, waiting for his return. And at last she heard him on the stairs.

"Puh!" he said, and stood still in the middle of the room.

"Well? Did you get it?"

He laughed, wiped his forehead, and drew a green-covered book from his coat-pocket. "Here we are, my girl—there's fifty crowns a month for three years. It's going to be a bit of a pinch, with fees and books, and living and clothes into the bargain. But we'll do it. Father was one of the right sort, I don't care what they say."

"But how did you manage it? What did the schoolmaster say?"

" 'Do you suppose that you—you with your antecedents—could ever pass into the Technical College?' he said. And I told him I *had* passed. 'Good heavens! How could you possibly qualify?' and he shifted his glasses down his nose. And then: 'Oh, no! it's no good coming here with tales

of that sort, my lad.' Well, then I showed him
the certificate, and he got much meeker. 'Really!'
he said, and 'Dear me!' and all that. But I say,
Louise—there's another Holm entered for the
autumn term.''

"Peer, you don't mean—your half-brother?''

"And old Dressing-gown said it would never
do—never! But I said it seemed to me there must
be room in the world for me as well, and I'd like
that bank book now, I said. 'You seem to fancy
you have some legal right to it,' he said, and got
perfectly furious. Then I hinted that I'd rather
ask a lawyer about it and make sure, and at that
he regularly boiled with rage and waved his arms
all about. But he gave in pretty soon all the
same—said he washed his hands of the whole
thing. 'And besides,' he said, 'your name's
Tröen, you know—Peer Tröen.' Ho-ho-ho—Peer
Tröen! Wouldn't he like it! Tra-la-la-la!—I say,
let's go out and get a little fresh air.''

Peer said nothing then or after about Klaus
Brock, and Klaus himself was going off home for
the summer holidays. As the summer wore on
the town lay baking in the heat, reeking of drains,
and the air from the stable came up to the couple
in the garret so heavy and foul that they were
sometimes nearly stifled.

"I'll tell you what," said Peer one day, "we
really must spend a few shillings more on house
rent and get a decent place to live in.''

And Louise agreed. For till the time came for

him to join the College in the autumn, Peer was
obliged to stick to the workshops; he could not
afford a holiday just now.

One morning he was just starting with a working gang down to Stenkjær to repair some damage in the engine-room of a big Russian grain boat,
when Louise came and asked him to look at her
throat. "It hurts so here," she said.

Peer took a spoon and pressed down her tongue,
but could not see anything wrong. "Better go and
see the doctor, and make sure," he said.

But the girl made light of it. "Oh, nonsense!"
she said; "it's not worth troubling about."

Peer was away for over a week, sleeping on
board with the rest. When he came back, he hurried home, suddenly thinking of Louise and her
sore throat. He found the job-master greasing
the wheels of a carriage, while his wife leaned out
of a window scolding at him. "Your sister," repeated the carter, turning round his face with its
great red lump of nose—"she's gone to hospital—
diphtheria hospital—she has. Doctor was here
over a week ago and took her off. They've been
here since poking round and asking who she was
and where she belonged—well, we didn't know.
And asking where you were, too—and we didn't
know either. She was real bad, if you ask
me——"

Peer hastened off. It was a hot day, and the
air was close and heavy. On he went—all down
the whole length of Sea Street, through the fisher-

men's quarter, and a good way further out round the bay. And then he saw a cart coming towards him, an ordinary work-cart, with a coffin on it. The driver sat on the cart, and another man walked behind, hat in hand. Peer ran on, and at last came in sight of the long yellow building at the far end of the bay. He remembered all the horrible stories he had heard about the treatment of diphtheria patients—how their throats had to be cut open to give them air, or something burned out of them with red-hot irons—oh! When at last he had reached the high fence and rung the bell, he stood breathless and dripping with sweat, leaning against the gate.

There was a sound of steps within, a key was turned, and a porter with a red moustache and freckles about his hard blue eyes thrust out his head.

"What d'you want to go ringing like that for?"

"Fröken Hagen—Louise Hagen—is she better? How—how is she?"

"Lou—Louise Hagen? A girl called Louise Hagen? Is it her you've come to ask about?"

"Yes. She's my sister. Tell me—or—let me in to see her."

"Wait a bit. You don't mean a girl that was brought in here about a week ago?"

"Yes, yes—but let me in."

"We've had no end of bother and trouble about that girl, trying to find out where she came from, and if she had people here. But, of course, this weather, we couldn't possibly keep her any longer. Didn't you meet a coffin on a cart as you came along?"

"What—what—you don't mean——?"

"Well, you should have come before, you know. She did ask a lot for some one called Peer. And she got the matron to write somewhere—wasn't it to Levanger? Were you the fellow she was asking for? So you came at last! Oh, well—she died four or five days ago. And they're just gone now to bury her, in St. Mary's Churchyard."

Peer turned round and looked out over the bay at the town, that lay sunlit and smoke-wreathed beyond. Towards the town he began to walk, but his step grew quicker and quicker, and at last he took off his cap and ran, panting and sobbing as he went. Have I been drinking? was the thought that whirled through his brain, or why can't I wake? What is it? What is it? And still he ran. There was no cart in sight as yet; the little streets of the fisher-quarter were all twists and turns. At last he reached Sea Street once more, and there —there far ahead was the slow-moving cart. Almost at once it turned off to the right and disappeared, and when Peer reached the turning, it was not to be seen. Still he ran on at haphazard. There seemed to be other people in the streets— children flying red balloons, women with baskets, men with straw hats and walking-sticks. But Peer marked his line, and ran forward, thrusting people aside, upsetting those in his way, and dashing on again. In King Street he came in sight of the cart once more, nearer this time. The man walking behind it with his hat in his hand had red curling hair, and walked with a curtsying gait, giving at the knees and turning out his toes. No doubt he made his living as mourner at funerals to which no other mourners came. As the cart turned into the churchyard Peer came up with it, and tried to follow at a walk, but stumbled and could hardly keep his feet. The man behind the cart looked at him. "What's the matter with you?" he asked. The driver looked round, but drove on again at once.

The cart stopped, and Peer stood by, leaning against a tree for support. A third man came up —he seemed to be the gravedigger—and he heard the three discussing how long they might have to wait for the parson. "The time's just about up, isn't it?" said the driver, taking out his watch. "Ay, the clerk said he'd be here by now," agreed the gravedigger, and blew his nose.

Soon the priest came in sight, wearing his black robe and white ruff; there were doubtless to be other funerals that day. Peer sank down on a bench and looked stupidly on while the coffin was lifted from the cart, carried to the grave, and lowered down. A man with spectacles and a red nose came up with a hymn-book, and sang something over the grave. The priest lifted the spade—and at the sound of the first spadeful of earth falling on Louise's coffin, Peer started as if struck, and all but fell from his seat.

When he looked up again, the place was deserted. The bell was ringing, and a crowd was collecting in another part of the churchyard. Peer sat where he was, quite still.

In the evening, when the gravedigger came to lock the gates, he had to take the young man by the shoulder and shake him to his senses. "Locking-up time," he said. "You must go now."

Peer rose and tried to walk, and by and by he was stumbling blindly out through the gate and down the street. And after a time he found himself climbing a flight of stairs above a stable-yard. Once in his room, he flung himself down on the bed as he was, and lay there still.

The close heat of the day had broken in a downpour of rain, which drummed upon the roof above his head, and poured in torrents through the gutters. Instinctively Peer started up: Louise was out in the rain—she would need her cloak. He was on his feet in a moment, as if to find it—then he stopped short, and sank slowly back upon the bed.

He drew up his feet under him, and buried his head in his arms. His brain was full of changing, hurrying visions, of storm and death, of human beings helpless in a universe coldly and indifferently ruled by a will that knows no pity.

Then for the first time it was as if he lifted up

his head against Heaven itself and cried: "There
is no sense in all this. I will not bear it."

Later in the night, when he found himself mechanically folding his hands for the evening prayer
he had learnt to say as a child, he suddenly burst
out laughing, and clenched his fists, and cried
aloud: "No, no, no—never—never again."

Once more it came to him that there was something in God like the schoolmaster—He took the
side of those who were well off already. "Yes,
they who have parents and home and brothers and
sisters and worldly goods—them I protect and
care for. But here's a boy alone in the world,
struggling and fighting his way on as best he can
—from him I will take the only thing he has. That
boy is nothing to any one. Let him be punished
because he is poor, and cast down to the earth,
for there is none to care for him. That boy is
nothing to any one—nothing." Oh, oh, oh!—he
clenched his fists and beat them against the wall.

His whole little world was broken to pieces.
Either God did not exist at all, or He was cold
and pitiless—one way of it was as bad as the
other. The heavenly country dissolved into cloud
and melted away, and above was nothing but
empty space. No more folding of your hands, like
a fool! Walk on the earth, and lift up your head,
and defy Heaven and fate, as you defied the schoolmaster. Your mother has no need of you to save
her—she is not anywhere any more. She is dead
—dead and turned to clay; and more than that

there is not, for her or for you or any other being in this world.

Still he lay there. He would fain have slept, but seemed instead to sink into a vague far-away twilight that rocked him—rocked him on its dark and golden waves. And now he heard a sound—what was it? A violin. "The mighty host in white array." Louise—is it you—and playing? He could see her now, out there in the twilight. How pale she was! But still she played. And now he understood what that twilight was.

It was a world beyond the consciousness of daily life—and that world belonged to him. "Peer, let me stay here." And something in him answered: "Yes, you shall stay, Louise. Even though there is no God and no immortality, you shall stay here." And then she smiled. And still she played. And it was as though he were building a little vaulted chapel for her in defiance of Heaven and of God—as though he were ringing out with his own hands a great eternal chime for her sake. What was happening to him? There was none to comfort him, yet it ended, as he lay there, with his pouring out something of his innermost being, as an offering to all that lives, to the earth and the stars, until all seemed rocking, rocking with him on the stately waves of the psalm. He lay there with fast-closed eyes, stretching out his hands as though afraid to wake, and find it all nothing but a beautiful dream.

Chapter VII

THE two-o'clock bell at the Technical College had just begun to ring, and a stream of students appeared out of the long straggling buildings and poured through the gate, breaking up then into little knots and groups that went their several ways into the town.

It was a motley crowd of young men of all ages from seventeen to thirty or more. Students of the everlasting type, sent here by their parents as a last resource, for—"he can always be an engineer"; young sparks who paid more attention to their toilet than their books, and hoped to "get through somehow" without troubling to work; and stiff youths of soldierly bearing, who had been ploughed for the Army, but who likewise could "always be engineers." There were peasant-lads who had crammed themselves through their Intermediate at a spurt, and now wore the College cap above their rough grey homespun, and dreamed of getting through in no time, and turning into great men with starched cuffs and pince-nez. There were pale young enthusiasts, too, who would probably end as actors; and there were also quondam actors, killed by the critics, but still sufficiently alive, it seemed, "to be engineers." And as the young fellows hurried on their gay and careless way through the town, an older man here and there might look round after them with a smile of some sadness. It was easy to say what fate awaited most of them. College ended, they would be scattered like birds of passage throughout the wide world, some to fall by sunstroke in Africa, or be murdered by natives in China, others to become mining kings in the mountains of Peru, or heads of great factories in Siberia, thousands of miles from home and friends. The whole planet was their home. Only a few of them—not always the shining lights—would stay at home, with a post on the State railways, to sit in an office and watch their salaries mount by increments of £12 every fifth year.

"That's a devil of a fellow, that brother of yours that's here," said Klaus Brock to Peer one day, as they were walking into town together with their books under their arms.

"Now, look here, Klaus, once for all, be good enough to stop calling him my brother. And another thing—you're never to say a word to any one about my father having been anything but a farmer. My name's Holm, and I'm called so after my father's farm. Just remember that, will you?"

"Oh, all right. Don't excite yourself."

"Do you suppose I'd give that coxcomb the triumph of thinking I want to make up to him?"

"No, no, of course not." Klaus shrugged his shoulders and walked on, whistling.

"Or that I want to make trouble for that fine family of his? No, I may find a way to take it out of him some day, but it won't be that way."

"Well, but, damn it, man! you can surely stand hearing what people say about him." And Klaus went on to tell his story. Ferdinand Holm, it seemed, was the despair of his family. He had thrown up his studies at the Military Academy, because he thought soldiers and soldiering ridiculous. Then he had made a short experiment with theology, but found that worse still; and finally, having discovered that engineering was at any rate an honest trade, he had come to anchor at the Technical College. "What do you say to that?" asked Klaus.

"I don't see anything so remarkable about it."

"Wait a bit, the cream of the story's to come. A few weeks ago he thrashed a policeman in the street—said he'd insulted a child, or something. There was a fearful scandal—arrest, the police-court, fine, and so forth. And last winter what must he do but get engaged, formally and publicly engaged, to one of his mother's maids. And when his mother sent the girl off behind his back, he raised the standard of revolt and left home altogether. And now he does nothing but breathe fire and slaughter against the upper classes and all their works. What do you say to that?"

"My good man, what the deuce has all this got to do with me?"

"Well, I think it's confoundedly plucky of him,

anyhow," said Klaus. "And for my part I shall get to know him if I can. He's read an awful lot, they say, and has a damned clever head on his shoulders."

On his very first day at the College, Peer had learned who Ferdinand Holm was, and had studied him with interest. He was a tall, straight-built fellow with reddish-blond hair and freckled face, and wore a dark tortoiseshell pincenez. He did not wear the usual College cap, but a stiff grey felt hat, and he looked about four or five and twenty.

"Wait!" thought Peer to himself—"wait, my fine fellow! Yes, you were there, no doubt, when they turned me out of the churchyard that day. But all that won't help you here. You may have got the start of me at first, and learned this, that, and the other, but—you just wait."

But one morning, out in the quadrangle, he noticed that Ferdinand Holm in his turn was looking at him, in fact was putting his glasses straight to get a better view of him—and Peer turned round at once and walked away.

Ferdinand, however, had been put into a higher class almost at once, on the strength of his matriculation. Also he was going in for a different branch of the work—roads and railway construction—so that it was only in the quadrangle and the passages that the two ever met.

But one afternoon, soon after Christmas, Peer was standing at work in the big designing-room, when he heard steps behind him, and, turning round, saw Klaus Brock and—Ferdinand Holm.

"I wanted to make your acquaintance," said Holm, and when Klaus had introduced them, he held out a large white hand with a red seal-ring on the first finger. "We're namesakes, I understand, and Brock here tells me you take your name from a country place called Holm."

"Yes. My father was a plain country farmer," said Peer, and at once felt annoyed with himself for the ring of humility the words seemed to have.

"Well, the best is good enough," said the other with a smile. "I say, though, has the first-term class gone as far as this in projection drawing? Excuse my asking. You see, we had a good deal of this sort of thing at the Military Academy, so that I know a little about it."

Thought Peer: "Oh, you'd like to give me a little good advice, would you, if you dared?" Aloud he said: "No, the drawing was on the blackboard —the senior class left it there—and I thought I'd like to see what I could make out of it."

The other sent him a sidelong glance. Then he nodded, said, "Good-bye—hope we shall meet again," and walked off, his boots creaking slightly as he went. His easy manners, his gait, the tone of his voice, all seemed to irritate and humiliate Peer. Never mind—just let him wait!

Days passed, and weeks. Peer soon found another object to work for than getting the better of Ferdinand Holm. Louise's dresses hung still untouched in his room, her shoes stood under the bed; it still seemed to him that some day she must open the door and walk in. And when he lay there alone at night, the riddle was always with him: Where is she now?—why should she have died?—would he never meet her again? He saw her always as she had stood that day playing to the sick folks in the hospital ward. But now she was dressed in white. And it seemed quite natural now that she had wings. He heard her music too —it cradled and rocked him. And all this came to be a little world apart, where he could take refuge for Sunday peace and devotion. It had nothing to do with faith or religion, but it was there. And sometimes in the midst of his work in the daytime he would divine, as in a quite separate conscious-ness, the tones of a fiddle-bow drawn across the strings, like reddish waves coming to him from far off, filling him with harmony, till he smiled with-out knowing it.

Often, though, a sort of hunger would come upon him to let his being unfold in a great wide wave of organ music in the church. But to church he never went any more. He would stride by a church door with a kind of defiance. It might in-deed be an Almighty Will that had taken Louise from him, but if so he did not mean to give thanks to such a Will or bow down before it. It was as though he had in view a coming reckoning—his reckoning with something far out in eternity—and

he must see to it that when that time came he could
feel free—free.

On Sunday mornings, when the church bells began to ring, he would turn hastily to his books, as
if to find peace in them. Knowledge—knowledge
—could it stay his hunger for the music of the
hymn? When he had first started work at the
shops, he had often and often stood wide-eyed before some miracle—now he was gathering the
power to work miracles himself. And so he read
and read, and drank in all that he could draw from
teacher or book, and thought and thought things
out for himself. Fixed lessons and set tasks were
all well enough, but Peer was for ever looking
farther; for him there were questions and more
questions, riddles and new riddles—always new,
always farther and farther on, towards the unknown. He had made as yet but one step forward in physics, mathematics, chemistry; he di-
vined that there were worlds still before him, and
he must hasten on, on, on. Would the day ever
come when he should reach the end? What is
knowledge? What use do men make of all that
they have learned? Look at the teachers, who
knew so much—were they greater, richer, brighter
beings than the rest? Could much study bring a
man so far that some night he could lift up a finger
and make the stars themselves break into song?
Best drive ahead, at any rate. But, again, could
knowledge lead on to that ecstasy of the Sunday
psalm, that makes all riddles clear, that bears a

man upwards in nameless happiness, in which his soul expands till it can enfold the infinite spaces? Well, at any rate the best thing was to drive ahead, drive ahead both early and late.

One day that spring, when the trees in the city avenues were beginning to bud, Klaus Brock and Ferdinand Holm were sitting in a café in North Street. "There goes your friend," said Ferdinand; and looking from the window they saw Peer Holm passing the post-office on the other side of the road. His clothes were shabby, his shoes had not been cleaned, he walked slowly, his fair head with its College cap bent forward, but seemed nevertheless to notice all that was going on in the street.

"Wonder what he's going pondering over now," said Klaus.

"Look there—I suppose that's a type of carriage he's never seen before. Why, he has got the driver to stop——"

"I wouldn't mind betting he'll crawl in between the wheels to find out whatever he's after," laughed Klaus, drawing back from the window so as not to be seen.

"He looks pale and fagged out," said Ferdinand, shifting his glasses. "I suppose his people aren't very well off?"

Klaus opened his eyes and looked at the other. "He's not overburdened with cash, I fancy."

They drank off their beer, and sat smoking and talking of other things, until Ferdinand remarked casually: "By the way—about your friend—are his parents still alive?"

Klaus was by no means anxious to go into Peer's family affairs, and answered briefly—No, he thought not.

"I'm afraid I'm boring you with questions, but the fact is the fellow interests me rather. There is something in his face, something—arresting. Even the way he walks—where is it I've seen some one walk like that before? And he works like a steam-engine, I hear?"

"Works!" repeated Klaus. "He'll ruin his health before long, the way he goes on grinding. I believe he's got an idea that by much learning he can learn at last to—— Ha-ha-ha!"

"To do what?"

"Why—to understand God!"

Ferdinand was staring out of the window. "Funny enough," he said.

"I ran across him last Sunday, up among the hills. He was out studying geology, if you please. And if there's a lecture anywhere about anything —whether it's astronomy or a French poet—you can safely swear he'll be sitting there, taking notes. You can't compete with a fellow like that! He'll run across a new name somewhere—Aristotle, for instance. It's something new, and off he must go to the library to look it up. And then he'll lie awake for nights after, stuffing his head with translations from the Greek. How the deuce can any one keep up with a man who goes at things that way? There's one thing, though, that he knows nothing about.''

"And that is?"

"Well, wine and women, we'll say—and fun in general. One thing he isn't, by Jove!—and that's *young.*"

"Perhaps he's not been able to afford that sort of thing," said Ferdinand, with something like a sigh.

The two sat on for some time, and every now and then, when Klaus was off his guard, Ferdinand would slip in another little question about Peer. And by the time they had finished their second glass, Klaus had admitted that people said Peer's mother had been a—well—no better than she should be.

"And what about his father?" Ferdinand let fall casually.

Klaus flushed uncomfortably at this. "Nobody —no—nobody knows much about him," he stammered. "I'd tell you if I knew, hanged if I wouldn't. No one has an idea who it was. He— he's very likely in America.''

"You're always mighty mysterious when you get on the subject of his family, I've noticed," said Ferdinand with a laugh. But Klaus thought his companion looked a little pale.

A few days later Peer was sitting alone in his room above the stables, when he heard a step on the stairs, the door opened, and Ferdinand Holm walked in.

Peer rose involuntarily and grasped at the back of his chair as if to steady himself. If this young coxcomb had come—from the schoolmaster, for instance—or to take away his name—why, he'd just throw him downstairs, that was all.

"I thought I'd like to look you up, and see where you lived," began the visitor, laying down his hat and taking a seat. "I've taken you unawares, I see. Sorry to disturb you. But the fact is there's something I wanted to speak to you about."

"Oh, is there?" and Peer sat down as far as conveniently possible from the other.

"I've noticed, even in the few times we've happened to meet, that you don't like me. Well, you know, that's a thing I'm not going to put up with."

"What do you mean?" asked Peer, hardly knowing whether to laugh or not.

"I want to be friends with you, that's all. You probably know a good deal more about me than I do about you, but that need not matter. Hullo—do you always drum with your fingers on the table like that? Ha-ha-ha! Why, that was a habit of my father's, too."

Peer stared at the other in silence. But his fingers stopped drumming.

"I rather envy you, you know, living as you do. When you come to be a millionaire, you'll have an effective background for your millions. And then, you must know a great deal more about life than we do; and the knowledge that comes out of books must have quite another spiritual value for you than for the rest of us, who've been stuffed mechanically with 'lessons' and 'education' and so forth since we were kids. And now you're going in for engineering?"

"Yes," said Peer. His face added pretty clearly, "And what concern is it of yours?"

"Well, it does seem to me that the modern technician is a priest in his way—or no, perhaps I should rather call him a descendant of old Prometheus. Quite a respectable ancestry, too, don't you think? But has it ever struck you that with every victory over nature won by the human spirit, a fragment of their omnipotence is wrested from the hands of the gods? I always feel as if we were using fire and steel, mechanical energy and human thought, as weapons of revolt against the Heavenly tyranny. The day will come when we shall no longer need to pray. The hour will strike when the Heavenly potentates will be forced to capitulate, and in their turn bend the knee to us. What do you think yourself? Jehovah doesn't like engineers—that's *my* opinion."

"Sounds very well," said Peer briefly. But he had to admit to himself that the other had put into words something that had been struggling for expression in his own mind.

"Of course for the present we two must be content with smaller things," Ferdinand went on. "And I don't mind admitting that laying out a bit of road, or a bit of railway, or bridging a ditch

or so, isn't work that appeals to me tremendously.
But if a man can get out into the wide world,
there are things enough to be done that give him
plenty of chance to develop what's in him—if
there happens to be anything. I used to envy the
great soldiers, who went about to the ends of the
earth, conquering wild tribes and founding em-
pires, organising and civilising where they went.
But in our day an engineer can find big jobs too,
once he gets out in the world—draining thousands
of square miles of swamp, or regulating the Nile,
or linking two oceans together. That's the sort
of thing I'm going to take a hand in some day.
As soon as I've finished here, I'm off. And we'll
leave it to the engineers to come, say in a couple
of hundred years or so, to start in arranging tourist routes between the stars. Do you mind my
smoking?''

"No, please do,'' said Peer. "But I'm sorry I
haven't——''

"I have—thanks all the same.'' Ferdinand
took out his cigar-case, and when Peer had de-
clined the offered cigar, lit one himself.

"Look here,'' he said, "won't you come out and
have dinner with me somewhere?''

Peer started at his visitor. What did all this
mean?

"I'm a regular Spartan, as a rule, but they've
just finished dividing up my father's estate, so
I'm in funds for the moment, and why shouldn't
we have a little dinner to celebrate? If you want

to change, I can wait outside—but come just as you are, of course, if you prefer.''

Peer was more and more perplexed. Was there something behind all this? Or was the fellow simply an astonishingly good sort? Giving it up at last, he changed his collar and put on his best suit and went.

For the first time in his life he found himself in a first-class restaurant, with small tables covered with snow-white tablecloths, flowers in vases, napkins folded sugar-loaf shape, cut-glass bowls, and coloured wine-glasses. Ferdinand seemed thoroughly at home, and treated his companion with a friendly politeness. And during the meal he managed to make the talk turn most of the time on Peer's childhood and early days.

When they had come to the coffee and cigars, Ferdinand leaned across the table towards him, and said: ''Look here, don't you think we two ought to say thee and thou [1] to each other?''

''Oh, yes!'' said Peer, really touched now.

''We're both Holms, you know.''

''Yes. So we are.''

''And, after all, who knows that there mayn't be some sort of connection? Come, now, don't look like that! I only want you to look on me as your good friend, and to come to me if ever there's anything I can do. We needn't live in each other's pockets, of course, when other people are by—but

---

[1] ''Tutoyer,'' the mode of address of intimate friendship or relationship.

we must take in Klaus Brock along with us, don't
you think?''

Peer felt a strong impulse to run away. Did
the other know everything? If so, why didn't he
speak straight out?

As the two walked home in the clear light of
the spring evening, Ferdinand took his companion's arm, and said: ''I don't know if you've
heard that I'm not on good terms with my people
at home. But the very first time I saw you, I had
a sort of feeling that we two belonged together.
Somehow you seemed to remind me so of—well,
to tell the truth, of my father. And he, let me tell
you, was a gallant gentleman——''

Peer did not answer, and the matter went no
farther then.

But the next few days were an exciting time
for Peer. He could not quite make out how much
Ferdinand knew, and nothing on earth would have
induced him to say anything more himself. And
the other asked no questions, but was just a first-
rate comrade, behaving as if they had been friends
for years. He did not even ask Peer any more
about his childhood, and never again referred to
his own family. Peer was always reminding himself to be on his guard, but could not help feeling glad all the same whenever they were to meet.

He was invited one evening, with Klaus, to a
wine-party at Ferdinand's lodging, and found
himself in a handsomely furnished room, with pictures on the walls, and photographs of his host's

parents. There was one of his father as a young
man, in uniform; another of his grandfather, who
had been a Judge of the Supreme Court. "It's
very good of you to be so interested in my people," said Ferdinand with a smile. Klaus Brock
looked from one to the other, wondering to himself how things really stood between the two.

The summer vacation came round, and the students prepared to break up and go their various
ways. Klaus was to go home. And one day Ferdinand came to Peer and said: "Look here, old
man. I want you to do me a great favour. I'd
arranged to go to the seaside this summer, but
I've a chance of going up to the hills, too. Well,
I can't be in two places at once—couldn't you take
on one of them for me? Of course I'd pay all expenses." "No, thank you!" said Peer, with a
laugh. But when Klaus Brock came just before
leaving and said: "See here, Peer. Don't you
think you and I might club together and put a
marble slab over—Louise's grave?", Peer was
touched, and clapped him on the shoulder. "What
a good old fellow you are, Klaus," he said.

Later in the summer Peer set out alone on a
tramp through the country, and whenever he saw
a chance, he would go up to one of the farms and
say: "Would you like to have a good map of the
farm? It'll cost ten crowns and my lodging while
I'm at it." It made a very pleasant holiday for
him, and he came home with a little money in his
pocket to boot.

His second year at the school was much like the first. He plodded along at his work. And now and then his two friends would come and drag him off for an evening's jollification. But after he had been racketing about with the others, singing and shouting through the sleeping town—and at last was alone and in his bed in the darkness, another and a very different life began for him, face to face with his innermost self. Where are you heading for, Peer? What are you aiming at in all your labours? And he would try to answer devoutly, as at evening prayers: Where? Why, of course, I am going to be a great engineer. And then? I will be one of the sons of Prometheus, that head the revolt against the tyranny of Heaven. And then? I will help to raise the great ladder on which men can climb aloft—higher and higher, up towards the light, and the spirit, and mastery over nature. And then? Live happily, marry and have children, and a rich and beautiful home. And then? Oh, well, one fine day, of course, one must grow old and die. And then? And then? Aye, what then?

At these times he found a shadowy comfort in taking refuge in the world where Louise stood—playing, as he always saw her—and cradling himself on the smooth red billows of her music. But why was it that here most of all he felt that hunger for—for something more?

Ferdinand finished his College course, and went out, as he had said, into the great world, and

Klaus went with him. And so throughout his third year Peer was mostly to be seen alone, always with books under his arm, and head bent forward.

Just as he was getting ready to go up for his final examination, a letter from Ferdinand arrived, written from Egypt. "Come over here, young fellow," he wrote. "We have got good billets at last with a big British firm—Brown Bros., of London—a firm that's building railways in Canada, bridges in India, harbour works in Argentina, and canals and barrages here in Egypt. We can get you a nice little post as draughtsman to begin with, and I enclose funds for the passage out. So come along."

But Peer did not go at once. He stayed on another year at the College, as assistant to the lecturer on mechanics, while himself going through the road and railway construction course, as his half-brother had done. Some secret instinct urged him not to be left behind even in this.

As the year went on the letters from his two comrades became more and more pressing and tempting. "Out here," wrote Klaus, "the engineer is a missionary, proclaimer, not Jehovah, but the power and culture of Europe. You're bound to take a hand in that, my boy. There's work worthy of a great general waiting for you here."

At last, one autumn day, when the woods stood yellow all around the town, Peer drove away from his home with a big new travelling-trunk strapped to the driver's seat. He had been up to the churchyard before starting, with a little bunch of flowers for Louise's grave. Who could say if he would ever see it again?

At the station he stood for a moment looking back over the old city with its cathedral, and the ancient fortress, where the sentry was pacing back and forth against the skyline. Was this the end of his youth? Louise—the room above the stables—the hospital, the lazarette, the College. . . . And there lay the fjord, and far out somewhere on the coast there stood no doubt a little grey fisher-hut, where a pock-marked goodwife and her bow-legged goodman had perhaps even now received the parcel of coffee and tobacco sent them as a parting gift.

And so Peer journeyed to the capital, and from there out into the wide world.

BOOK II

Chapter I

SOME years had passed—a good many years—and once more summer had come, and June. A passenger steamer, bound from Antwerp to Christiania, was ploughing her way one evening over a sea so motionlessly calm that it seemed a single vast mirror filled with a sky of grey and pink-tinged clouds. There were plenty of passengers on board, and no one felt inclined for bed; it was so warm, so beautiful on deck. Some artists, on their way home from Paris or Munich, cast about for amusements to pass the time; some ordered wine, others had unearthed a concertina, and very soon, no one knew how, a dance was in full swing. "No, my dear," said one or two cautious mothers to their girls, "certainly not." But before long the mothers were dancing themselves. Then there was a doctor in spectacles, who stood up on a barrel and made a speech; and presently two of the artists caught hold of the grey-bearded captain and chaired him round the deck. The night was so clear, the skies so ruddily beautiful, the air so soft, and out here on the open sea all hearts were light and happy.

"Who's that wooden-faced beggar over there that's too high and mighty for a little fun?" asked

Storaker the painter, of his friend the sculptor
Praas.

"That fellow? Oh, he's the one that was so
infernally instructive at dinner, when we were
talking about Egyptian vases."

"So it is, by Jove! Schoolmaster abroad, I
should think. When we got on to Athens and
Greek sculpture he condescended to set us right
about that, too."

"I heard him this morning holding forth to the
doctor on Assyriology. No wonder he doesn't
dance!"

The passenger they were speaking of was a man
of middle height, between thirty and forty apparently, who lay stretched in a deck-chair a little
way off. He was dressed in grey throughout,
from his travelling-cap to the spats above his
brown shoes. His face was sallow, and the short
brown beard was flecked with grey. But his eyes
had gay little gleams in them as they followed the
dancers. It was Peer Holm.

As he sat there watching, it annoyed him to feel
that he could not let himself go like the others.
But it was so long since he had mixed with his
own countrymen, that he felt insecure of his footing and almost like a foreigner among them. Besides, in a few hours now they should sight the
skerries on the Norwegian coast; and the thought
awoke in him a strange excitement—it was a moment he had dreamed of many and many a time
out there in the wide world.

After a while stillness fell on the decks around him, and he too went below, but lay down in his cabin without undressing. He thought of the time when he had passed that way on the outward voyage, poor and unknown, and had watched the last island of his native land sink below the sea-rim. Much had happened since then—and now that he had at last come home, what life awaited him there?

A little after two in the morning he came on deck again, but stood still in astonishment at finding that the vessel was now boring her way through a thick woolly fog. The devil! thought he, beginning to tramp up and down the deck impatiently. It seemed that his great moment was to be lost—spoiled for him! But suddenly he stopped by the railing, and stood gazing out into the east.

What was that? Far out in the depths of the woolly fog a glowing spot appeared; the grey mass around grew alive, began to move, to redden, to thin out as if it were streaming up in flames. Ah! now he knew! It was the globe of the sun, rising out of the sea. On board, every point where the night's moisture had lodged began to shine in gold. Each moment it grew clearer and lighter, and the eye reached farther. And before he could take in what was happening, the grey darkness had rolled itself up into mounds, into mountains, that grew buoyant and floated aloft and melted away. And there, all revealed, lay the fresh bright morning, with a clear sun-filled sky over the blue sea.

It was time now to get out his field-glasses. For a long time he stood motionless, gazing intently through them.

There! Was it his fancy? No, there far ahead he can see clearly now a darker strip between sky and sea. It's the first skerry. It is Norway, at last!

Peer felt a sudden catch in his breath; he could hardly stand still, but he stopped again and again in his walk to look once more at the far-off strip of grey. And now there were seabirds too, with long necks and swiftly-beating wings. Welcome home!

And now the steamer is ploughing in among the skerries, and a world of rocks and islets unfolds on every side. There is the first red fisher-hut. And then the entrance to Christiansand, between wooded hills and islands, where white cottages shine out, each with its patch of green grassland and its flagstaff before it.

Peer watched it all, drinking it in like nourishment. How good it all tasted—he felt it would be long before he had drunk his fill.

Then came the voyage up along the coast, all through a day of brilliant sunshine and a luminous night. He saw the blue sounds with swarms of white gulls hovering above them, the little coast-towns with their long white-painted wooden houses, and flowers in the windows. He had never passed this way before, and yet something in him seemed to nod and say: "I know myself again here." All the way up the Christiania Fjord there was the scent of leaves and meadows; big farms stood by the shore shining in the sun. This was what a great farm looked like. He nodded again. So warm and fruitful it all seemed, and dear to him as home—though he knew that, after all, he would be little better than a tourist in his own country. There was no one waiting for him, no one to take him in. Still, some day things might be very different.

As the ship drew alongside the quay at Christiania, the other passengers lined the rail, friends and relations came aboard, there were tears and laughter and kisses and embraces. Peer lifted his hat as he passed down the gangway, but no one had time to notice him just now. And when he had found a hotel porter to look after his luggage, he walked up alone through the town, as if he were a stranger.

The light nights made it difficult to sleep—he had actually forgotten that it was light all night long. And this was a capital city—yet so touchingly small, it seemed but a few steps wherever he went. These were his countrymen, but he knew no one among them; there was no one to greet him. Still, he thought again, some day all this might be very different.

At last, one day as he stood looking at the window of a bookseller's shop, he heard a voice behind him: "Why, bless me! surely it's Peer Holm!" It was one of his fellow-students at the Technical College, Reidar Langberg, pale and thin now as ever. He had been a shining light at the College, but now—now he looked shabby, worn and aged.

"I hardly knew you again," said Peer, grasping the other's hand.

"And you're a millionaire, so they say—and famous, out in the big world?"

"Not quite so bad as that, old fellow. But what about you?"

"I? Oh, don't talk about me." And as they walked down the street together, Langberg poured out his tale, of how times were desperately bad, and conditions at home here simply strangled a man. He had started ten or twelve years ago as a draughtsman in the offices of the State Railways, and was still there, with a growing family —and "such pay—such pay, my dear fellow!" He threw up his eyes and clasped his hands despairingly.

"Look here," said Peer, interrupting him. "Where is the best place in Christiania to go and have a good time in the evening?"

"Well, St. Hans Hill, for instance. There's music there."

"Right—will you come and dine with me there, to-night—shall we say eight o'clock?"

"Thanks. I should think I would!"

Peer arrived in good time, and engaged a table

on a verandah. Langberg made his appearance
shortly after, dressed in his well-saved Sunday
best—faded frock-coat, light trousers bagged at
the knees, and a straw hat yellow with age.

"It's a pleasure to have someone to talk to
again," said Peer. "For the last year or so I've
been knocking about pretty much by myself."

"Is it as long as that since you left Egypt?"

"Yes; longer. I've been in Abyssinia since
then."

"Oh, of course, I remember now. It was in the
papers. Building a railway for King Menelik,
weren't you?"

"Oh, yes. But the last eighteen months or so
I've been idling—running about to theatres and
museums and so forth. I began at Athens and
finished up with London. I remember one day
sitting on the steps of the Parthenon declaiming
the Antigone—and a moment with some meaning
in it seemed to have come at last."

"But, dash it, man, you're surely not compar-
ing such trifles with a thing like the great Nile
Barrage? You were on that for some years,
weren't you? Do let's hear something about that.
Up by the first cataract, wasn't it? And hadn't
you enormous quarries there on the spot? You
see, even sitting at home here, I haven't quite lost
touch. But you—good Lord! what things you
must have seen! Fancy living at—what was the
name of the town again?"

"Assuan," answered Peer indifferently, look-

ing out over the gardens, where more and more
visitors kept arriving.

"They say the barrage is as great a miracle as
the Pyramids. How many sluice-gates are there
again—a hundred and . . . ?"

"Two hundred and sixteen," said Peer.
"Look!" he broke off. "Do you know those girls
over there?" He nodded towards a party of girls
in light dresses who were sitting down at a table
close by.

Langberg shook his head. He was greedy for
news from the great world without, which he had
never had the luck to see.

"I've often wondered," he went on, "how you
managed to come to the front so in that sort of
work—railways and barrages, and so forth—when
your original line was mechanical engineering.
Of course you did do an extra year on the roads
and railway side; but . . ."

Oh, this shining light of the schools!

"What do you say to a glass of champagne?"
said Peer. "How do you like it? Sweet or dry?"

"Why, is there any difference? I really didn't
know. But when one's a millionaire, of
course . . ."

"I'm not a millionaire," said Peer with a smile,
and beckoned to a waiter.

"Oh! I heard you were. Didn't you invent a
new motor-pump that drove all the other types
out of the field? And besides—that Abyssinian
railway. Oh well, well!" he sighed, "it's a good

thing somebody's lucky. The rest of us shouldn't complain. But how about the other two—Klaus Brock and Ferdinand Holm? What are they doing now?"

"Klaus is looking after the Khedive's estates at Edfina. Agriculture by steam power; his own railway lines to bring in the produce, and so on. Yes, Klaus has ended up in a nice little place of his own. His district's bigger than the kingdom of Denmark."

"Good heavens!" Langberg nearly fell off his chair. "And Ferdinand Holm; what about him?"

"Oh, he's got bigger things on hand. Went nosing about the Libyan desert, and found that considerable tracts of it have water-veins only a few yards beneath the surface. If so, of course, it's only a question of proper plant to turn an enormous area into a paradise for corn-growing."

"Good gracious! What a discovery!" gasped the other, almost breathless now.

Peer looked out over the fjord, and went on: "Last year he managed at last to get the Khedive interested, and they've started a joint-stock company now, with a capital of some millions. Ferdinand is chief engineer."

"And what's his salary? As much as fifty thousand crowns?"

"His pay is two hundred thousand francs a year," said Peer, not without some fear that his companion might faint. "Yes, he's an able fellow, is Ferdinand."

It took Langberg some time to get his breath again. At last he asked, with a sidelong glance:

"And you and Klaus Brock—I suppose you've put your millions in his company?"

Peer smiled as he sat looking out over the garden. Lifting his glass, "Your good health," he said, for all answer.

"Have you been in America, too?" went on the other. "No, I suppose not!"

"America? Yes, a few years back, when I was with Brown Bros., they sent me over one time to buy plant. Nothing so surprising in that, is there?"

"No, no, of course not. I was only thinking—you went about there, I daresay, and saw all the wonderful things—the miracles of science they're always producing."

"My dear fellow, if you only knew how deadly sick I am of miracles of science! What I'm longing for is a country watermill that takes twenty-four hours to grind a sack of corn."

"What? What do you say?" Langberg bounced in his chair. "Ha-ha-ha! You're the same old man, I can see."

"I'm perfectly serious," said Peer, lifting his glass towards the other. "Come. Here's to our old days together!"

"Aye—thanks, a thousand thanks—to our old days together!—Ah, delicious! Well, then, I suppose you've fallen in love away down there in the

land of the barbarians? Haven't you? Ha-ha-
ha!"

"Do you call Egypt a land of barbarians?"

"Well, don't the fellahs still yoke their wives
to their ploughs?"

"A fellah will sit all night long outside his hut
and gaze up at the stars and give himself time to
dream. And a merchant prince in Vienna will
dictate business letters in his automobile as he's
driving to the theatre, and write telegrams as he
sits in the stalls. One fine day he'll be sitting in
his private box with a telephone at one ear and
listening to the opera with the other. That's what
the miracles of science are doing for us. Awe-
inspiring, isn't it?"

"And you talk like that—a man that's helped
to harness the Nile, and has built railways through
the desert?"

Peer shrugged his shoulders, and offered the
other a cigar from his case. A waiter appeared
with coffee.

"To help mankind to make quicker progress—
is that nothing?"

"Lord! What I'd like to know is, where mankind are making for, that they're in such a hurry."

"That the Nile Barrage has doubled the production of corn in Egypt—created the possibilities
of life for millions of human beings—is that nothing?"

"My good fellow, do you really think there
aren't enough fools on this earth already? Have

we too little wailing and misery and discontent
and class-hatred as it is? Why must we go about
to double it?''

"But hang it all, man—what about European
culture? Surely you felt yourself a sort of missionary of civilisation, where you have been.''

"The spread of European civilisation in the
East simply means that half a dozen big financiers
in London or Paris take a fancy to a certain strip
of Africa or Asia. They press a button, and out
come all the ministers and generals and mission-
aries and engineers with a bow: At your service,
gentlemen!

"Culture! One wheel begets ten new ones.
Brr-rrr! And the ten again another hundred.
Brr-rr-rrr—more speed, more competition—and
all for what? For culture? No, my friend, for
money. Missionary! I tell you, as long as West-
ern Europe with all its wonders of modern science
and its Christianity and its political reforms
hasn't turned out a better type of humanity than
the mean ruck of men we have now—we'd do best
to stay at home and hold our counfounded jaw.
Here's ourselves!'' and Peer emptied his glass.

This was a sad hearing for poor Langberg.
For he had been used to comfort himself in his
daily round with the thought that even he, in his
modest sphere, was doing his share in the great
work of civilising the world.

At last he leaned back, watching the smoke
from his cigar, and smiling a little.

"I remember a young fellow at the College," he said, "who used to talk a good deal about Prometheus, and the grand work of liberating humanity, by stealing ne wand ever new fire from Olympus."

"That was me—yes," said Peer with a laugh. "As a matter of fact, I was only quoting Ferdinand Holm."

"You don't believe in all that now?"

"It strikes me that fire and steel are rapidly turning men into beasts. Machinery is killing more and more of what we call the godlike in us."

"But, good heavens, man! Surely a man can be a Christian even if . . ."

"Christian as much as you like. But don't you think it might soon be time we found something better to worship than an ascetic on a cross? Are we to keep on for ever singing Hallelujah because we've saved our own skins and yet can haggle ourselves into heaven? Is that religion?"

"No, no, perhaps not. But I don't know . . ."

"Neither do I. But it's all the same; for anyhow no such thing as religious feeling exists any longer. Machinery is killing our longings for eternity, too. Ask the good people in the great cities. They spend Christmas Eve playing tunes from *The Dollar Princess* on the gramophone."

Langberg sat for a while watching the other attentively. Peer sat smoking slowly; his face was flushed with the wine, but from time to time his eyes half-closed, and his thoughts seemed to be wandering in other fields than these.

"And what do you think of doing now you are home again?" asked his companion at last.

Peer opened his eyes. "Doing? Oh, I don't know. Look about me first of all. Then perhaps I may find a cottar's croft somewhere and settle down and marry a dairymaid. Here's luck!"

The gardens were full now of people in light summer dress, and in the luminous evening a constant ripple of laughter and gay voices came up to them. Peer looked curiously at the crowd, all strangers to him, and asked his companion the names of some of the people. Langberg pointed out one or two celebrities—a Cabinet Minister sitting near by, a famous explorer a little farther off. "But I don't know them personally," he added. "Can't afford society on that scale, of course."

"How beautiful it is here!" said Peer, looking out once more at the yellow shimmer of light above the fjord. "And how good it is to be home again!"

Chapter II

HE sat in the train on his way up-country, and from the carriage window watched farms and meadows and tree-lined roads slide past. Where was he going? He did not know himself. Why should not a man start off at haphazard, and get out when the mood takes him? At last he was able to travel through his own country without having to think of half-pennies. He could let the days pass over his head without care or trouble, and give himself good leisure to enjoy any beauty that came in his way.

There is Mjösen, the broad lake with the rich farmlands and long wooded ridges on either side. He had never been here before, yet it seemed as if something in him nodded a recognition to it all. Once more he sat drinking in the rich, fruitful landscape—the wooded hills, the fields and meadows seemed to spread themselves out over empty places in his mind.

But later in the day the landscape narrowed and they were in Gudbrandsdalen, where the sun-burned farms are set on green slopes between the river and the mountains. Peer's head was full of pictures from abroad, from the desert sands with their scorched palm-trees to the canals of Venice.

But here—he nodded again. Here he was at home, though he had never seen the place before; just this it was which had been calling to him all through his long years of exile.

At last on a sudden he gathered up his traps and got out, without the least idea even of the name of the station. A meal at the hotel, a knapsack on his back, and hey!—there before him lies the road, up into the hills.

Alone? What matter, when there are endless things that greet him from every side with "Welcome home!" The road is steep, the air grows lighter, the homesteads smaller. At last the huts look like little matchboxes—from the valley, no doubt, it must seem as if the people up here were living among the clouds. But many and many a youth must have followed this road in the evenings, going up to court his Mari or his Kari at the sæter-hut, the same road and the same errand one generation after another. To Peer it seemed as if all those lads now bore him company—aye, as if he discovered in himself something of wanton youth that had managed to get free at last.

Puh! His coat must come off and his cap go into the knapsack. Now, as the valley sinks and sinks farther beneath him, the view across it widens farther and farther out over the uplands beyond. Brown hills and blue, ridges livid or mossy-grey in the setting sun, rising and falling wave behind wave, and beyond all a great snow-field, like a sea of white breakers foaming against the sky. But surely he had seen all this before?

Ah! now he knew; it was the Lofoten Sea over again—with its white foam-crested combers and long-drawn, heavy-breathing swell—a rolling ocean turned to rock. Peer halted a moment leaning on his stick, and his eyes half-closed. Could he not feel that same ocean-swell rising and sinking in his own being? Did not the same waves surge through the centuries, carrying the generations away with them upon great wanderings? And in daily life the wave rolls us along in the old familiar rhythm, and not one in ten thousand lifts his head above it to ask: whither and why! Even now just such a little wave has hold of him, taking him—whither and why? Well, the coming days might show; meanwhile, there beyond was the sea of stone rolling its eternal cadence under the endless sky.

He wiped his forehead and turned and went his way.

But what is that far off in the north-east? three sisters in white shawls, lifting their heads to heaven—that must be Rondanë. And see how the evening sun is kindling the white peaks to purple and gold.

Puh!—only one more hill now, and here is the top at last. And there ahead lie the great uplands, with marsh and mound and gleaming tarns. Ah, what a relief! What wonder that his step grows lighter and quicker? Before he knows it he is singing aloud in mere gaiety of heart. Ah, dear

God, what if after all it were not too late to be
young!

A sæter. A little hut, standing on a patch of
green, with split-stick fence and a long cow-house
of rough planks—it must be a sæter! And listen
—isn't that a girl singing? Peer slipped softly
through the gate and stood listening against the
wall of the byre. "Shap, shap, shap," went the
streams of milk against the pail. It must be a
fairy sitting milking in there. Then came the
voice:

> Oh, Sunday eve, oh, Sunday eve,
> Ever wast thou my dearest eve!

"Shap, shap, shap!" went the milk once more
in the pail—and suddenly Peer joined in:

> Oh bright, oh gentle Sunday eve—
> Wilt ever be my dearest eve!

The milking stopped, a cowbell tinkled as the
cow turned her inquiring face, and a girl's light-
brown head of hair was thrust out of the doorway
—soon followed by the girl herself, slender, eighteen, red-cheeked, fresh and smiling.

"Good evening," said Peer, stretching out his
hand.

The girl looked at him for a moment, then cast
a glance at her own clothes—as women will when
they see a man who takes their fancy.

"An' who may you be?" she asked.

"Can you cook me some cream-porridge?"

"A' must finish milking first, then."

Here was a job that Peer could help with. He took off his knapsack, washed his hands, and was soon seated on a stool in the close sweet air of the shed, milking busily. Then he fetched water, and chopped some wood for the fire, the girl gazing at him all the time, no doubt wondering who this crazy person could be. When the porridge stood ready on the table, he insisted on her sitting down close to him and sharing the meal. They ate a little, and then laughed a little, and then chatted, and then ate and then laughed again. When he asked what he had to pay, the girl said: "Whatever you like"—and he gave her two crowns and then bent her head back and kissed her lips. "What's the man up to?" he heard her gasp behind him as he passed out; when he had gone a good way and turned to look back, there she was in the doorway, shading her eyes and watching him.

Whither away now? Well, he was pretty sure to reach some other inhabited place before night. This, he felt, was not his abiding-place. No, it was not here.

It was nearly midnight when he stood by the shore of a broad mountain lake, beneath a snow-flecked hill-side. Here were a couple of sæters, and across the lake, on a wooded island, stood a small frame house that looked like some city people's summer cottage. And see—over the lake, that still mirrored the evening red, a boat appeared moving towards the island, and two white-sleeved girls sat at the oars, singing as they rowed. A strange feeling came over him. Here—here he would stay.

In the sæter-hut stood an enormously fat woman, with a rope round her middle, evidently ready to go to bed. Could she put him up for the night? Why, yes, she supposed so—and she rolled off into another room. And soon he was lying in a tiny chamber, in a bed with a mountainous mattress and a quilt. There was a fresh smell from the juniper twigs strewed about the newly-washed floor, and the cheeses, which stood in rows all round the shelf-lined walls. Ah! he had slept in many places and fashions—at sea in a Lofoten boat; on the swaying back of a camel; in tents out in the moonlit desert; and in palaces of the Arabian Nights, where dwarfs fanned him with palm-leaves to drive away the heat, and called him *pasha*. But here, at last, he had found a place where it was good to be. And he closed his eyes, and lay listening to the murmur of a little stream outside in the light summer night, till he fell asleep.

Late in the forenoon of the next day he was awakened by the entry of the old woman with coffee. Then a plunge into the blue-green water of the mountain lake, a short swim, and back to find grilled trout and new-baked waffles and thick cream for lunch.

Yes, said the old woman, if he could get along with the sort of victuals she could cook, he might stay here a few days and welcome. The bed was standing there empty, anyway.

Chapter III

So Peer stays on and goes fishing. He catches little; but time goes leisurely here, and the summer lies soft and warm over the brown and blue hillsides. He has soon learned that a merchant named Uthoug, from Ringeby, is living in the house on the island, with his wife and daughter. And what of it?

Often he would lie in his boat, smoking his pipe, and giving himself up to quiet dreams that came and passed. A young girl in a white boat, moving over red waters in the evening—a secret meeting on an island—no one must know just yet. . . . Would it ever happen to him? Ah, no.

The sun goes down, there come sounds of cowbells nearing the sæters, the musical cries and calls of the sæter-girls, the lowing of the cattle. The mountains stand silent in the distance, their snowclad tops grown golden; the stream slides rippling by, murmuring on through the luminous nights.

Then at last came the day of all days.

He had gone out for a long tramp at random over the hills, making his way by compass, and noting landmarks to guide him back. Here was a marsh covered with cloudberries—the taste

brought back his own childhood. He wandered
on up a pale-brown ridge flecked with red heather
—and what was that ahead? Smoke? He made
towards it. Yes, it was smoke. A ptarmigan
fluttered out in front of him, with a brood of tiny
youngsters at her heels—Lord, what a shave!—
he stopped short to avoid treading on them. The
smoke meant someone near—possibly a camp of
Lapps. Let's go and see.

He topped the last mound, and there was the
fire just below. Two girls jumped to their feet;
there was a bright coffee-kettle on the fire, and
on the moss-covered ground close by bread and
butter and sandwiches laid out on a paper table-
cloth.

Peer stopped short in surprise. The girls gazed
at him for a moment, and he at them, all three
with a hesitating smile.

At last Peer lifted his hat and asked the way to
Rustad sæter. It took them some time to explain
this, and then they asked him the time. He told
them exactly to the minute, and then showed them
his watch so that they might see for themselves.
All this took more time. Meanwhile, they had
inspected each other, and found no reason to part
company just yet. One of the girls was tall, slender of figure, with a warm-coloured oval face and
dark brown hair. Her eyebrows were thick and
met above the nose, delightful to look at. She
wore a blue serge dress, with the skirt kilted up a
little, leaving her ankles visible. The other was a

blonde, smaller of stature, and with a melancholy
face, though she smiled constantly. "Oh," she
said suddenly, "have you a pocket-knife by any
chance?"

"Oh yes!" Peer was just moving off, but
gladly seized the opportunity to stay a while.

"We've a tin of sardines here, and nothing to
open it with," said the dark one.

"Let me try," said Peer. As luck would have
it, he managed to cut himself a little, and the two
girls tumbled over each other to tie up the wound.
It ended, of course, with their asking him to join
their coffee-party.

"My name is Merle Uthoug," said the dark one,
with a curtsy.

"Oh, then, it's your father who has the place
on the island in the lake?"

"My name's only Mörk—Thea Mörk. My
father is a lawyer, and we have a little cottage
farther up the lake," said the blonde.

Peer was about to introduce himself, when the
dark girl interrupted: "Oh, we know you already," she said. "We've seen you out rowing on
the lake so often. And we had to find out who
you were. We have a good pair of glasses . . ."

"Merle!" broke in her companion warningly.

". . . and then, yesterday, we sent one of the
maids over reconnoitring, to make inquiries and
bring us a full report."

"Merle! How can you say such things?"

It was a cheery little feast. Ah! how young

they were, these two girls, and how they laughed
at a joke, and what quantities of bread and butter and coffee they all three disposed of! Merle
now and again would give their companion a sidelong glance, while Thea laughed at all the wild
things her friend said, and scolded her, and looked
anxiously at Peer.

And now the sun was nearing the shoulder of a
hill far in the west, and evening was falling. They
packed up their things, and Peer was loaded up
with a big bag of cloud-berries on his back, and a
tin pail to carry in his hand. "Give him some
more," said Merle. "It'll do him good to work
for a change."

"Merle, you really are too bad!"

"Here you are," said the girl, and slid the handle of a basket into his other hand.

Then they set out down the hill. Merle sang
and yodelled as they went; then Peer sang, and
then they all three sang together. And when they
came to a heather-tussock or a puddle, they did
not trouble to go round, but just jumped over it,
and then gave another jump for the fun of the
thing.

They passed the sæter and went on down to the
water's edge, and Peer proposed to row them
home. And so they rowed across. And the whole
time they sat talking and laughing together as if
they had known each other for years.

The boat touched land just below the cottage,
and a broad-shouldered man with a grey beard

and a straw hat came down to meet them. "Oh,
father, are you back again?" cried Merle, and,
springing ashore, she flung her arms round his
neck. The two exchanged some whispered words,
and the father glanced at Peer. Then, taking off
his hat, he came towards him and said politely,
"It was very kind of you to help the girls down."

"This is Herr Holm, engineer and Egyptian,"
said Merle, "and this is father."

"I hear we are neighbours," said Uthoug.
"We're just going to have tea, so if you have
nothing better to do, perhaps you will join us."

Outside the cottage stood a grey-haired lady
with a pale face, wearing spectacles. She had a
thick white woollen shawl over her shoulders, but
even so she seemed to feel cold. "Welcome,"
she said, and Peer thought there was a tremor
in her voice.

There were two small low rooms with an open
fireplace in the one, and in it there stood a table
ready laid. But from the moment Merle entered
the house, she took command of everything, and
whisked in and out. Soon there was the sound
of fish cooking in the kitchen, and a moment later
she came in with a plate full of lettuce, and said:
"Mr. Egyptian—you can make us an Arabian
salad, can't you?"

Peer was delighted. "I should think so," he
said.

"You'll find salt and pepper and vinegar and
oil on the table there, and that's all we possess in

the way of condiments. But it must be a real Arabian salad all the same, if you please!'' And out she went again, while Peer busied himself with the salad.

''I hope you will excuse my daughter,'' said Fru Uthoug, turning her pale face towards him and looking through her spectacles. ''She is not really so wild as she seems.''

Uthoug himself walked up and down the room, chatting to Peer and asking a great many questions about conditions in Egypt. He knew something about the Mahdi, and General Gordon, and Khartoum, and the strained relations between the Khedive and the Sultan. He was evidently a diligent reader of the newspapers, and Peer gathered that he was a Radical, and a man of some weight in his party. And he looked as if there was plenty of fire smouldering under his reddish eyelids: ''A bad man to fall out with,'' thought Peer.

They sat down to supper, and Peer noticed that Fru Uthoug grew less pale and anxious as her daughter laughed and joked and chattered. There even came a slight glow at last into the faded cheeks; the eyes behind the spectacles seemed to shine with a light borrowed from her daughter's. But her husband seemed not to notice anything, and tried all the time to go on talking about the Mahdi and the Khedive and the Sultan.

So for the first time for many years Peer sat down to table in a Norwegian home—and how

good it was! Would he ever have a home of his
own, he wondered.

After the meal, a mandolin was brought out,
and they sat round the fire in the great fireplace
and had some music. Until at last Merle rose
and said: "Now, mother, it's time you went to
bed."

"Yes, dear," came the answer submissively,
and Fru Uthoug said good-night, and Merle led
her off.

Peer had risen to take leave, when Merle came
in again. "Why," she said, "you're surely not
going off before you've rowed Thea home?"

"Oh, Merle, please . . ." put in the other.

But when the two had taken their places in the
boat and were just about to start up the lake,
Merle came running down and said she might just
as well come too.

Half an hour later, having seen the young girl
safely ashore at her father's place, Merle and
Peer were alone, rowing back through the still
night over the waters of the lake, golden in the
light and dark blue in the shadows. Merle leaned
back in the stern, silent, trailing a small branch
along the surface of the water behind. After
a while Peer laid in his oars and let the boat
drift.

"How beautiful it is!" he said.

The girl lifted her head and looked round.
"Yes," she answered, and Peer fancied her voice
had taken a new tone.

It was past midnight. Heights and woods and
sæters lay lifeless in the soft suffused reddish
light. The lake-trout were not rising any more,
but now and again the screech of a cock-ptarmi-
gan could be heard among the withies.

"What made you come just here for your holiday, I wonder," she asked suddenly.

"I leave everything to chance, Fröken Uthoug.
It just happened so. It's all so homelike here,
wherever one goes. And it is so wonderful to be
home in Norway again."

"But haven't you been to see your people—
your father and mother—since you came home?"

"I——! Do you suppose I have a father and
mother?"

"But near relations—surely you must have a
brother or sister somewhere in the world?"

"Ah, if one only had! Though, after all, one
can get on without."

She looked at him searchingly, as if trying to
see whether he spoke in earnest. Then she said:

"Do you know that mother dreamed of you
before you came?"

"Of me?" Peer's eyes opened wide. "What
did she dream about me?"

A sudden flush came to the girl's face, and she
shook her head. "It's foolish of me to sit here
and tell you all this. But you see that was why
we wanted so much to find out about you when
you came. And it gives me a sort of feeling of
our having known each other a long time."

"You appear to have a very constant flow of high spirits, Fröken Uthoug!"

"I? Why do you think——? Oh, well, yes. One can come by most things, you know, if one has to have them."

"Even high spirits?"

She turned her head and looked towards the shore. "Some day perhaps—if we should come to be friends—I'll tell you more about it."

Peer bent to his oars and rowed on. The stillness of the night drew them nearer and nearer together, and made them silent; only now and then they would look at each other and smile.

"What mysterious creature is this I have come upon?" thought Peer. She might be about one- or two-and-twenty. She sat there with bowed head, and in this soft glow the oval face had a strange light of dreams upon it. But suddenly her glance came back and rested on him again, and then she smiled, and he saw that her mouth was large and her lips full and red.

"I wish I had been all over the world, like you," she said.

"Have you never been abroad, Fröken Uthoug?" he asked.

"I spent a winter in Berlin, once, and a few months in South Germany. I played the violin a little, you see; and I hoped to take it up seriously abroad and make something of it—but——"

"Well, why shouldn't you?"

She was silent for a little, then at last she said:

"I suppose you are sure to know about it some day, so I may just as well tell you now. Mother has been out of her mind."

"My dear Fröken——"

"And when she's at home my—high spirits are needed to help her to be more or less herself."

He felt an impulse to rise and go to the girl, and take her head between his hands. But she looked up, with a melancholy smile; their eyes met in a long look, and she forgot to withdraw her glance.

"I must go ashore now," she said at last.

"Oh, so soon! Why, we have hardly begun our talk!"

"I must go ashore now," she repeated; and her voice, though still gentle, was not to be gainsaid.

At last Peer was alone, rowing back to his sæter. As he rowed he watched the girl going slowly up towards the cottage. When she reached the door she turned for the first time and waved to him. Then she stood for a moment looking after him, and then opened the door and disappeared. He gazed at the door some time longer, as if expecting to see it open again, but no sign of life was to be seen.

The sun's rim was showing now above the distant ranges in the east, and the white peaks in the north and west kindled in the morning glow. Peer laid in his oars again, and rested, with his elbows on his knees and his head in his hands.

What could this thing be that had befallen him to-day?

How could those peaks stand round so aloof and indifferent, and leave him here disconsolate and alone?

What was it, this new rushing in his ears; this new rhythm of his pulse? He lay back at last in the bottom of the boat, with hands clasped behind his head, and let boat and all things drift.

And when the glare of the rising sun came slanting into the boat and beat dazzlingly in his face, he only turned his head a little and let it shine full upon him.

Now she is lying asleep over there, the morning streaming red through her window—of whom is she dreaming as she sleeps?

Have you ever seen such eyebrows before? To press one's lips to them—to take her head between one's hand . . . and so it is to save your mother that you give up your own dreams, and to warm her soul that you keep that flame of gladness burning in you? Is that the sort you are?

Merle—was ever such a name? Are you called Merle?

Day spreads over the heavens, kindling all the night-clouds, great and small, to gold and scarlet. And here he lies, rocking, rocking, on no lake, but on a red stately-heaving ocean swell.

Ah! till now your mind has been so filled with cold mechanics, with calculations, with steel and fire. More and more knowledge, ever more striving to understand all things, to know all, to master all. But meanwhile, the tones of the hymn died within you, and the hunger for that which lies beyond all things grew ever fiercer and fiercer. You thought it was Norway that you needed—and now you are here. But is it enough?

Merle—is your name Merle?

There is nothing that can be likened to the first day of love. All your learning, your travel, and deeds and dreams—all has been nothing but dry firewood that you have dragged and heaped together. And now has come a spark, and the whole heap blazes up, casting its red glow over earth and heaven, and you stretch out your cold hands, and warm them, and shiver with joy that a new bliss has come upon the earth.

And all that you could not understand—the relation between the spark of eternity in your soul and the Power above, and the whole of endless space—has all of a sudden become so clear that you lie here trembling with joy at seeing to the very bottom of the infinite enigma.

You have but to take her by the hand, and "Here are we two," you say to the powers of life and death. "Here is she and here am I—we two" —and you send the anthem rolling aloft—a strain from little Louise's fiddle-bow mingling with it— not to the vaultings of any church, but into endless space itself. And Thou, Power above, now I understand Thee. How could I ever take seriously a Power that sat on high playing with Sin and Grace—but now I see Thee, not the blood-thirsty Jehovah, but a golden-haired youth, the Light itself. We two worship Thee; not with a wail of prayer, but with a great anthem, that has the World-All in it. All our powers, our knowledge, our dreams—all are there. And each has its own instrument, its own voice in the mighty chorus. The dawn reddening over the hills is with us. The goat grazing on that northern hillside, dazzled with sun-gold when it turns its head to the east—it is with us, too. The waking birds are with us. A frog, crawling up out of a puddle and stopping to wonder at the morning—it is there. Even the little insect with diamonds on its wings—and the grass-blade with its pearl of dew, trying to mirror as much of the sky as it can—it is there, it is there, it is there. We are standing amid Love's first day, and there is no more talk of grace or doubt or faith or need of aid; only a rushing sound of music rising to heaven from all the golden rivers in our hearts.

The sæters were beginning to wake. Musical cries came echoing as the sæter-girls chid on the cattle, that moved slowly up to the northern heights, with lowings and tinkling of bells. But Peer lay still where he was—and presently the dairy-maid at the sæter caught sight of what seemed an empty boat drifting on the lake, and was afraid some accident had happened.

"Merle," thought Peer, still lying motionless. "Is your name Merle?"

The dairy-maid was down by the waterside now, calling across toward the boat. And at last she saw a man sit up, rubbing his eyes.

"Mercy on us!" she cried. "Lord be thanked that you're there. And you haven't been in the whole blessed night!"

A goat with a broken leg, set in splints, had been left to stray at will about the cattle-pens and in and out of the house, while its leg-bones were setting. Peer must needs pick up the creature and carry it round for a while in his arms, though it at once began chewing at his beard. When he sat down to the breakfast-table, he found something so touching in the look of the cream and butter, the bread and the coffee, that it seemed a man would need a heart of stone to be willing to eat such things. And when the old woman said he really ought to get some food into him, he sprang up and embraced her, as far as his arms would go round. "Nice carryings on!" she cried, struggling to free herself. But when he went so far as to imprint a sounding kiss on her forehead, she fetched him a mighty push. "Lord!" she said, "if the gomeril hasn't gone clean out of his wits this last night!"

Chapter IV

RINGEBY lay on the shore of a great lake; and was one of those busy commercial towns which have sprung up in the last fifty years from a nucleus consisting of a saw-mill and a flour-mill by the side of a waterfall. Now quite a number of modern factories had spread upwards along the river, and the place was a town with some four thousand inhabitants, with a church of its own, a monster of a school building, and numbers of yellow workmen's dwellings scattered about at random in every direction. Otherwise Ringeby was much like any other little town. There were two lawyers, who fought for scraps of legal business, and the editors of two local papers, who were constantly at loggerheads before the Conciliation Board. There was a temperance lodge and Workers' Union and a chapel and a picture palace. And every Sunday afternoon the good citizens of Ringeby walked out along the fjord, with their wives on their arms. On these occasions most of the men wore frock coats and grey felt hats; but Enebak, the tanner, being hunchbacked, preferred a tall silk hat, as better suited to eke out his height.

On Saturday evenings, when twilight began to

fall, the younger men would meet at the corner outside Hammer's store, to discuss the events of the week.

"Have you heard the latest news?" asked Lövli, the bank cashier, of his friend the telegraphist, who came up.

"News? Do you tell me that there's ever any news in this accursed hole?"

"Merle Uthoug has come back from the mountains—engaged to be married."

"The devil she is! What does the old man say to that?"

"Oh, well, the old man will want an engineer if he's to get the new timber-mills into his clutches."

"Is the man an engineer?"

"From Egypt. A Muhammadan, I daresay. Brown as a coffee-berry, and rolling in money."

"Do you hear that, Fröken Bull? Stop a minute, here's some news for you."

The girl addressed turned aside and joined them. "Oh, the same piece of news that's all over the town, I suppose. Well, I can tell you, he's most tremendously nice."

"Sh!" whispered the telegraphist. Peer Holm was just coming out of the Grand Hotel, dressed in a grey suit, and with a dark coat over his arm. He was trying to get a newly-lit cigar to draw, as he walked with a light elastic step past the group at the corner. A little farther up the street he encountered Merle, and took her arm, and the two walked off together, the young people at the corner watching them as they went.

"And when is it to be?" asked the telegraphist.

"He wanted to be married immediately, I believe," said Fröken Bull, "but I suppose they'll have to wait till the banns are called, like other people."

Lorentz D. Uthoug's long, yellow-painted wooden house stood facing the market square; the office and the big ironmonger's shop were on the ground floor, and the family lived in the upper storeys. "That's where he lives," people would say. Or "There he goes," as the broad, grey-bearded man passed down the street. Was he such a big man, then? He could hardly be called really rich, though he had a saw-mill and a machine-shop and a flour-mill, and owned a country place some way out of the town. But there was something of the chieftain, something of the prophet, about him. He hated priests. He read deep philosophical works, forbade his family to go to church, and had been visited by Björnson himself. It was good to have him on your side; to have him against you was fatal—you might just as well clear out of the town altogether. He had a finger in everything that went on; it was as if he owned the whole town. He had been known to meet a youth he had never spoken to before in the street and accost him with a peremptory "Understand me, young man; you will marry that girl." Yet for all this, Lorentz

Uthoug was not altogether content. True, he was head and shoulders above all the Ringeby folks, but what he really wanted was to be the biggest man in a place a hundred times as large.

And now that he had found a son-in-law, he seemed as it were to be walking quietly round this stranger from the great world, taking his measure, and asking in his thoughts: "Who are you at bottom? What have you seen? What have you read? Are you progressive or reactionary? Have you any proper respect for what I have accomplished here, or are you going about laughing in your sleeve and calling me a whale among the minnows?"

Every morning when Peer woke in his room at the hotel he rubbed his eyes. On the table beside his bed stood a photograph of a young girl. What? Is it really you, Peer, that have found someone to stand close to you at last? Someone in the world who cares about you. When you have a cold, there'll be people to come round and be anxious about you, and ask how you are getting on. And this to happen to you!

He dined at the Uthougs' every day, and there were always flowers beside his plate. Often there would be some little surprise—a silver spoon or fork, or a napkin-ring with his initials on. It was like gathering the first straws to make his new nest. And the pale woman with the spectacles looked kindly at him, as if to say: "You are taking her from me, but I forgive you."

One day he was sitting in the hotel, reading, when Merle came in.

"Will you come for a walk?" she asked.

"Good idea. Where shall we go to-day?"

"Well, we haven't been to see Aunt Marit at Bruseth yet. We really ought to go, you know. I'll take you there to-day."

Peer found these ceremonial visits to his new relatives quite amusing; he went round, as it were, collecting uncles and aunts. And to-day there was a new one. Well, why not?

"But—my dear girl, have you been crying?" he asked suddenly, taking her head in his hands.

"Oh, it's nothing. Come—let's go now." And she thrust him gently away as he tried to kiss her. But the next moment she dropped into a chair, and sat looking thoughtfully at him through half-closed eyes, nodding her head very slightly. She seemed to be asking herself: "Who is this man? What is this I am taking on me? A fortnight ago he was an utter stranger——"

She passed her hand across her brow. "It's mother—you know," she said.

"Is anything special wrong to-day?"

"She's so afraid you're going to carry me off into the wide world at a moment's notice."

'But I've told her we're going to live here for the present."

The girl drew up one side of her mouth in a smile, and her eyelids almost closed. "And what

about me, then? After living here all these years
crazy to get out into the world?"

"And I, who am crazy to stay at home!" said
Peer with a laugh. "How delicious it will be to
have a house and a family at last—and peace and
quiet!"

"But what about me?"

"You'll be there, too. I'll let you live with me."

"Oh! how stupid you are to-day. If you only
knew what it means, to throw away the best years
of one's youth in a hole like this! And besides—
I could have done somthing worth while in
music——"

"Why, then, let's go abroad, by all means,"
said Peer, wrinkling up his forehead as if to
laugh.

"Oh, nonsense! you know it's quite impossible
to go off and leave mother now. But you certainly
came at a very critical time. For anyway I was
longing and longing just then for someone to come
and carry me off."

"Aha! so I was only a sort of ticket for the
tour." He stepped over and pinched her nose.

"Oh! you'd better be careful. I haven't really
promised yet to have you, you know."

"Haven't promised? When you practically
asked me yourself."

She clapped her hands together. "Why, what
shameless impudence! After my saying No, No,
No, for days together. I won't, I won't, I won't—
I said it ever so many times. And you said it

didn't matter—for *you would*. Yes, you took me most unfairly off my guard; but now look out for yourself."

The next moment she flung her arms round his neck. But when he tried to kiss her, she pushed him away again. "No," she said, "you mustn't think I did it for that!"

Soon they were walking arm-in-arm along the country road, on their way to Aunt Marit at Bruseth. It was September, and all about the wooded hills stood yellow, and the cornfields were golden and the rowan berries blood-red. But there was still summer in the air.

"Ugh! how impossibly fast you walk," exclaimed Merle, stopping out of breath.

And when they came to a gate they sat down in the grass by the wayside. Below them was the town, with its many roofs and chimneys standing out against the shining lake, that lay framed in broad stretches of farm and field.

"Do you know how it came about that mother is—as she is?" asked Merle suddenly.

"No. I didn't like to ask you about it."

She drew a stalk of grass between her lips.

"Well, you see—mother's father was a clergyman. And when—when father forbade her to go to church, she obeyed him. But she couldn't sleep after that. She felt—as if she had sold her soul."

"And what did your father say to that?"

"Said it was hysteria. But, hysteria or not,

mother couldn't sleep. And at last they had to take her away to a home."

"Poor soul!" said Peer, taking the girl's hand.

"And when she came back from there she was so changed, one would hardly have known her. And father gave way a little—more than he ever used to do—and said: 'Well, well, I suppose you must go to church if you wish, but you mustn't mind if I don't go with you.' And so one Sunday she took my hand and we went together, but as we reached the church door, and heard the organ playing inside, she turned back. 'No—it's too late now,' she said. 'It's too late, Merle.' And she has never been since."

"And she has always been—strange—since then?"

Merle sighed. "The worst of it is she sees so many evil things compassing her about. She says the only thing to do is to laugh them away. But she can't laugh herself. And so I have to. But when I go away from her—oh! I can't bear to think of it."

She hid her face against his shoulder, and he began stroking her hair.

"Tell me, Peer"—she looked up with her one-sided smile—"who is right—mother or father?"

"Have you been trying to puzzle that out?"

"Yes. But it's so hopeless—so impossible to come to any sort of certainty. What do you think? Tell me what you think, Peer."

They sat there alone in the golden autumn day,

her head pressed against his shoulder. Why
should he play the superior person and try to
put her off with vague phrases?

"Dear Merle, I know, of course, no more than
you do. There was a time when I saw God standing with a rod in one hand and a sugar-cake in
the other—just punishment and rewards to all
eternity. Then I thrust Him from me, because
He seemed to me so unjust—and at last He vanished, melting into the solar systems on high, and
all the infinitesimal growths here on the earth
below. What was my life, what were my dreams,
my joy or sorrow, to these? Where was I making for? Ever and always there was something
in me saying: He *is*! But where? Somewhere
beyond and behind the things you know—it is
there He is. And so I determined to know more
things, more and more and more—and what wiser
was I? A steam-hammer crushes my skull one
day—and what has become of my part in progress
and culture and science? Am I as much of an
accident as a fly on an ant? Do I mean no more?
Do I vanish and leave as little trace? Answer
me that, little Merle—what do *you* think?"

The girl sat motionless, breathing softly, with
closed eyes. Then she began to smile—and her
lips were full and red, and at last they shaped
themselves to a kiss.

Bruseth was a large farm lying high above the
town, with its garden and avenues and long ve-

randahs round the white dwelling-house. And what a view out over the lake and the country far around! The two stood for a moment at the gate, looking back.

Merle's aunt—her father's sister—was a widow, rich and a notable manager, but capricious to a degree, capable of being generous one day and grasping the next. It was the sorrow of her life that she had no children of her own, but she had not yet decided who was to be her heir.

She came sailing into the room where the two young people were waiting, and Peer saw her coming towards them, a tall, full-bosomed woman with grey hair and florid colour. Oho! here's an aunt for you with a vengeance, he thought. She pulled off a blue apron she was wearing and appeared dressed in a black woollen gown, with a gold chain about her neck and long gold earrings.

"So you thought you'd come over at last," she said. "Actually remembered my existence, after all, did you, Merle?" She turned towards Peer, and stood examining him, with her hands on her hips. "So that's what you look like, is it, Peer? And you're the man that was to catch Merle? Well, you see I call you Peer at once, even though you *have* come all the way from—Arabia, is it? Sit down, sit down."

Wine was brought in, and Aunt Marit of Bruseth lifted a congratulatory glass toward the pair with the following words:

"You'll fight, of course. But don't overdo it,

that's all. And mark my words, Peer Holm, if
you aren't good to her, I'll come round one fine
day and warm your ears for you. Your healths,
children!"

The two went homewards arm-in-arm, dancing
down the hillsides, and singing gaily as they went.
But suddenly, when they were still some way
from the town, Merle stopped and pointed.
"There," she whispered—"there's mother!"

A solitary woman was walking slowly in the
twilight over a wide field of stubble, looking
around her. It was as if she were lingering here
to search out the meaning of something—of many
things. From time to time she would glance up
at the sky, or at the town below, or at people
passing on the road, and then she would nod her
head. How infinitely far off she seemed, how utterly a stranger to all the noisy doings of men!
What was she seeing now? What were her
thoughts?

"Let us go on," whispered Merle, drawing him
with her. And the young girl suddenly began to
sing, loudly, as if in an overflow of spirits; and
Peer guessed that it was for her mother's sake.
Perhaps the lonely woman stood there now in
the twilight smiling after them.

One Sunday morning Merle drove up to the hotel
in a light cart with a big brown horse; Peer came
out and climbed in, leaving the reins to her. They
were going out along the fjord to look at her

father's big estate which in olden days had been the County Governors' official residence.

It is the end of September. The sun is still warm, but the waters of the lake are grey and all the fields are reaped. Here and there a strip of yellowing potato-stalks lies waiting to be dug up. Up on the hillsides horses tethered for grazing stand nodding their heads slowly, as if they knew that it was Sunday. And a faint mist left by the damps of the night floats about here and there over the broad landscape.

They passed through a wood, and came on the other side to an avenue of old ash trees, that turned up from the road and ran uphill to a big house where a flag was flying. The great white dwelling-house stood high, as if to look out far over the world; the red farm-buildings enclosed the wide courtyard on three sides, and below were gardens and broad lands, sloping down towards the lake. Something like an estate!

"What's the name of that place?" cried Peer, gazing at it.

"Loreng."

"And who owns it?"

"Don't know," answered the girl, cracking her whip.

Next moment the horse turned in to the avenue, and Peer caught involuntarily at the reins. "Hei! Brownie—where are you going?" he cried.

"Why not go up and have a look?" said Merle.

"But we were going out to look at your father's place."

"Well, that is father's place."

Peer stared at her face and let go the reins. "What? What? You don't mean to say your father owns that place there?"

A few minutes later they were strolling through the great, low-ceiled rooms. The whole house was empty now, the farm-bailiff living in the servants' quarters. Peer grew more and more enthusiastic. Here, in these great rooms, there had been festive gatherings enough in the days of the old Governors, where cavaliers in uniform or with elegant shirt-frills and golden spurs had kissed the hands of ladies in sweeping silk robes. Old mahogany, pot-pourri, convivial song, wit, grace— Peer saw it all in his mind's eye, and again and again he had to give vent to his feelings by seizing Merle and embracing her.

"Oh, but look here, Merle—you know, this is a fairy-tale."

They passed out into the old neglected garden with its grass-grown paths and well-filled carp-ponds and tumble-down pavilions. Peer rushed about it in all directions. Here, too, there had been fêtes, with coloured lamps festooned around, and couples whispering in the shade of every bush. "Merle, did you say your father was going to sell all this to the State?"

"Yes, that's what it will come to, I expect," she answered. "The place doesn't pay, he says, when he can't live here himself to look after it."

"But what use can the State make of it?"

"Oh, a Home for Imbeciles, I believe."

"Good Lord! I might have guessed it! An idiot asylum—to be sure." He tramped about, fairly jumping with excitement. "Merle, look here—will you come and live here?"

She threw back her head and looked at him. "I ask you, Merle. Will you come and live here?"

"Do you want me to answer this moment, on the spot?"

"Yes. For I want to buy it this moment, on the spot."

"Well, aren't you——"

"Look, Merle, just look at it all. That long balcony there, with the doric columns—nothing shoddy about that—it's the real thing. Empire. I know something about it."

"But it'll cost a great deal, Peer." There was some reluctance in her voice. Was she thinking of her violin? Was she loth to take root too firmly?

"A great deal?" he said. "What did your father give for it?"

"The place was sold by auction, and he got it cheap. Fifty thousand crowns, I think it was."

Peer strode off towards the house again. "We'll buy it. It's the very place to make into a home. . . . Horses, cattle, sheep, goats, cottars—ah! it'll be grand."

Merle followed him more slowly. "But, Peer,

remember you've just taken over father's ma-
chine-shops in town.''

"Pooh!" said Peer scornfully. "Do you think
I can't manage to run that village smithy and
live here too! Come along, Merle." And he took
her hand and drew her into the house again.

It was useless to try to resist. He dragged her
from room to room, furnishing as he went along.
"This room here is the dining-room—and that's
the big reception-room; this will be the study—
that's a boudoir for you. . . . Come now; to-morrow we'll go into Christiania and buy the furniture.''

Merle gasped for breath. He had got so far
by this time that the furnishing was complete
and they were installed. They had a governess
already, and he was giving parties too. Here
was the ballroom. He slipped an arm round her
waist and danced round the room with her, till
she was carried away by his enthusiasm, and
stood flushed and beaming, while all she had
dreamed of finding some day out in the wide world
seemed suddenly to unfold around her here in
these empty rooms. Was this really to be her
home? She stopped to take breath and to look
around her.

Late that evening Peer sat at the hotel with a
note-book, working the thing out. He had bought
Loreng; his father-in-law had been reasonable,
and had let him have the place, lands and woods
and all, for the ridiculous price he had paid him-

self. There was a mortgage of thirty thousand crowns on the estate. Well, that might stand as it was, for the bulk of Peer's money was tied up in Ferdinand Holm's company.

A few days after he carried Merle off to the capital, leaving the carpenters and painters hard at work at Loreng.

One day he was sitting alone at the hotel in Christiania—Merle was out shopping—when there was a very discreet knock at the door.

"Come in," called Peer. And in walked a middle-sized man, of thirty or more, dressed in a black frock-coat with a large-patterned vest, and his dark hair carefully combed over a bald patch on the crown. He had a red, cheery face; his eyes were of the brightest blue, and the whole man breathed and shone with good humour.

"I am Uthoug junior," said the new-comer, with a bow and a laugh.

"Oh—that's capital."

"Just come across from Manchester—beastly voyage. Thanks, thanks—I'll find a seat." He sat down, and flung one striped trouser-leg over the other.

Peer sent for some wine, and in half an hour the two were firm allies. Uthoug junior's life-story to date was quickly told. He had run away from home because his father had refused to let him go on the stage—had found on trial that in these days there weren't enough theatres to go round—then had set up in business for himself,

and now had a general agency for the sale of
English tweeds. "Freedom, freedom," was his
idea; "lots of elbow-room—room to turn about in
—without with your leave or by your leave to
father or anyone! Your health!"

A week later the street outside Lorentz D.
Uthoug's house in Ringeby was densely crowded
with people, all gazing up at the long rows of
lighted windows. There was feasting to-night in
the great man's house. About midnight a carriage drove up to the door. "That's the bride-
groom's," whispered a bystander. "He got those
horses from Denmark!"

The street door opened, and a white figure,
thickly cloaked, appeared on the steps. "The
bride!" whispered the crowd. Then a slender man
in a dark overcoat and silk hat. "The bride-
groom!" And as the pair passed out, "Hip-hip-
hip——" went the voice of the general agent for
English tweeds, and the hurrahs came with a will.

The carriage moved off, and Peer sat, with his
arm round his bride, driving his horses at a sharp
trot out along the fjord. Out towards his home,
towards his palace, towards a new and untried
future.

Chapter V

A LITTLE shaggy, grey-bearded old man stood chopping and sawing in the wood-shed at Loreng. He had been there longer than anyone could remember. One master left, another took his place —what was that to the little man? Didn't the one need firewood—and didn't the other need firewood just the same? In the evening he crept up to his den in the loft of the servants' wing; at meal-times he sat himself down in the last seat at the kitchen-table, and it seemed to him that there was always food to be had. Nowadays the master's name was Holm—an engineer he was— and the little man blinked at him with his eyes, and went on chopping in the shed. If they came and told him he was not wanted and must go— why, thank heaven, he was stone deaf, as everyone knew. Thud, thud, went his axe in the shed; and the others about the place were so used to it that they heeded it no more than the ticking of a clock upon the wall.

In the kitchen of the big house two girls stood by the window peeping out into the garden and giggling.

"There he is again," said Laura. "Sh! don't laugh so loud. There! now he's stopping again!"

"He's whistling to a bird," said Oliana. "Or talking to himself perhaps. Do you think he's quite right in his head?"

"Sh! The mistress'll hear."

It was no less a person than the master of Loreng himself whose proceedings struck them as so comic.

Peer it was, wandering about in the great neglected garden, with his hands in the pockets of his knickerbockers and his cap on the back of his head, stopping here and there, and moving on again as the fancy took him. Sometimes he would hum a snatch of a song, and again fall to whistling; here he would pick up a twig and look at it, or again it might be a bird, or perhaps an old neglected apple-tree that seemed worth stopping to talk to. The best of it was that these were his own lands and his own woods that lay there in the rusty October sunshine. Was all that nothing? And the hill over on the farther shore, standing on its head in the dark lake-mirror, clothed in a whole world of colour—yellow leaves and green leaves, and light red and dark red, and golden and blood-red patches, with the dark green of the pines between. His eyes had all this to rest on. Did he really live here? What abundant fruitfulness all around him! What a sky, so wide, so golden that it seemed to ring again. The potato-stalks lay uprooted, scattered on the fields; the corn was safely housed. And here he stood. He seemed again to be drawing in nourish-

ment from all he saw, drinking it greedily. The
empty places in his mind were filled; the sight of
the rich soft landscape worked on his being, giving it something of its own abundant fruitfulness,
its own wide repose.

And—what next?

"What next?" he mimicked in his thoughts,
and started again tramping up and down the garden paths. What next—what next? Could he not
afford now to take his time—to rest a little?
Every man must have an end in view—must strive
to reach this goal or that. And what was his
object now? What was it he had so toiled for,
from those hard years in the loft above the stable
even until now? What was it? Often it seemed
as if everything were going smoothly, going of
itself; as if one day, surely, he would find his
part in a great, happy world-harmony. But had
he not already found it? What more would he
have? Of course he had found it.

But is this all, then? What is there behind and
beyond? Hush! have done with questioning.
Look at the beauty around you. Here is peace,
peace and rest.

He hurried up to the house, and in—it might
help matters if he could take his wife in his arms;
perhaps get her to come out with him a while.

Merle was in the pantry, with a big apron on,
ranging jars of preserves on the shelves.

"Here, dearest little wife," cried Peer, throwing his arms about her, "what do you say to a little run?"

"Now? Do you suppose a housewife has nothing better to do than gad about? Uf! my hair! you'll make it come down."

Peer took her arm and led her over to a window looking out on the lake. "There, dearest! Isn't it lovely here?"

"Peer, you've asked me that twenty times a day ever since we came."

"Yes, and you never answer. And you've never once yet run and thrown your arms round my neck and said how happy you were. And it's never yet come to pass that you've given me a single kiss of your own accord."

"I should think not, when you steal such a lot." And she pushed him aside, and slipped under his arm, and ran out of the room. "I must go in and see mother again to-day," she said as she went.

"Huit! Of course!" He paced up and down the room, his step growing more and more impatient. "In to mother—in to mother! Always and everlastingly mother and mother and nothing else. Huit!" and he began to whistle.

Merle put her head in at the door. "Peer—have you such a terrible lot of spare time?"

"Well, yes and no. I'm busy enough looking about in every corner here for something or another. But I can't find it, and I don't even know exactly what it is. Oh well, yes—I have plenty of time to spare."

"But what about the farm?"

"Well, there's the dairy-woman in the cow-house, and the groom in the stables, and the bailiff to worry the tenants and workpeople. What am I to do—poke around making improvements?"

"But what about the machine-shop?"

"Don't I go in twice a day—cycle over to see how things are going? But with Rode for manager—that excellent and high-principled engineer——"

"Surely you could help him in some way?"

"He's got to go on running along the line of rails he's used to—nothing else for it, my darling. And four or five thousand crowns a year, net profit—why, it's magnificent!"

"But couldn't you extend the business?"

He raised his eyebrows, and his mouth pursed itself up.

"Extend—did you say extend? Extend a—a doll's house!"

"Oh, Peer, you shouldn't laugh at it—a thing that father took so much pains to set going!"

"And *you* shouldn't go worrying me to get to work again in earnest, Merle. You shouldn't really. One of these days I might discover that there's no way to be happy in the world but to drag a plough and look straight ahead and forget that there's anything else in existence. It may come to that one day—but give me a little breathing-space first, and you love me. Well, good-bye for a while."

Merle, busying herself again in her pantry, glanced out of the window and saw him disappear into the stables. At first she had gone with him when he wandered about like this, touching and feeling all his possessions. In the cattle-stalls, it might be, stroking and patting, getting himself covered with hairs, and chattering away in childish glee. "Look, Merle—this cow is mine, child! Dagros her name is—and she's mine. We have forty of them—and they're all mine. And that nag there—what a sight he is! We have eight of them. They're mine. Yours too, of course. But you don't care a bit about it. You haven't even hugged any of them yet. But when a man's been as poor as I've been—and suddenly wakened up one day and found he owned all this—— No, wait a minute, Merle—come and kiss old Brownie." She knew the ritual now—he could go over it all again and again, and each time with the same happy wonder. Was it odious of her that she was beginning to find it a little comic? And how did it come about that often, when she might be filled with the deepest longing for him, and he burst in upon her boisterously, hungry for her caresses, she would grow suddenly cold, and put him aside? What was the matter? Why did she behave like this?

Perhaps it was because he was so much the stronger, so overwhelming in his effect on her that she had to keep a tight hold on herself to avoid being swept clean away and losing her iden-

tity. At one moment they might be sitting in the
lamplight, chatting easily together, and so near
in heart and mind; and the next it would be over
—he would suddenly have started up and be pacing up and down the room, delivering a sort of
lecture. Merle—isn't it marvellous, the spiritual
life of plants? And then would come a torrent of
talk about strange plant-growths in the north and
in the south, plants whose names she had never
even heard—their struggle for existence, their
loves and longings, their heroism in disease, the
divine marvel of their death. Their inventions,
their wisdom, aye, their religious sense—is it not
marvellous, Merle? From this it was only a step
to the earth's strata, fossils, crystals—a fresh
lecture. And finally he would sum up the whole
into one great harmony of development, from
the primary cell-life to the laws of gravitation
that rule the courses of the stars. Was it not
marvellous? One common rhythm beating through
the universe—a symphony of worlds!—And then
he must have a kiss!

But she could only draw back and put him gently aside. It was as if he came with all his stored-
up knowledge—his lore of plants and fossils,
crystals and stars—and poured it all out in a
caress. She could almost have cried out for help.
And after hurrying her through the wonders of
the universe in this fashion, he would suddenly
catch her up in his arms, and whirl her off in a
passionate intoxication of the senses till she woke

at last like a castaway on an island, hardly knowing where or what she was. She laughed, but she could have found it in her heart to weep. Could this be love? In this strong man, whose life till now had been all study and work, the stored-up feeling burst vehemently forth, now that it had found an outlet. But why did it leave her so cold?

When Peer came in from the stables, humming a tune, he found her in the sitting-room, dressed in a dark woollen dress with a red ribbon round her throat.

He stopped short: "By Jove—how that suits you, Merle!"

She let her eyes linger on him for a moment, and then came up and threw her arms round his neck.

"Did he have to go to the stables all alone to-day?"

"Yes; I've been having a chat with the young colt."

"Am I unkind to you, Peer?"

"You?—you!"

"Not even if I ask you to drive me in to see mother?"

"Why, that's the very thing. The new horse I bought yesterday from Captain Myhre should be here any minute—I'm just waiting for it."

"A new horse—to ride?"

"Yes. Hang it—I must get some riding. I had to handle Arab horses for years. But we'll try this one in the gig first."

Merle was still standing with her arms round his neck, and now she pressed her warm rich lips to his, close and closer. It was at such moments that she loved him—when he stood trembling with a joy unexpected, that took him unawares. She too trembled, with a blissful thrill through soul and body; for once and at last it was she who gave.

"Ah!" he breathed at last, pale with emotion. "I—I'd be glad to die like that."

A little later they stood on the balcony looking over the courtyard, when a bearded farm-hand came up with a big light-maned chestnut horse prancing in a halter. The beast stood still in the middle of the yard, flung up its head, and neighed, and the horses in the stable neighed in answer.

"Oh, what a beauty!" exclaimed Merle, clapping her hands.

"Put him into the gig," called Peer to the stable-boy who had come out to take the horse.

The man touched his cap. "Horse has never been driven before, sir, I was to say."

"Everything must have a beginning," said Peer.

Merle glanced at him. But they were both dressed to go out when the chestnut came dancing up before the door with the gig. The white hoofs pawed impatiently, the head was high in the air, and the eyes flashed fire—he wasn't used to having shafts pressing on his sides and wheels rumbling just behind him. Peer lit a cigar.

"You're not going to smoke?" Merle burst out.
"Just to show him I'm not excited," said Peer.
No sooner had they taken their seats in the gig
than the beast began to snort and rear, but the
long lash flicked out over its neck, and a minute
later they were tearing off in a cloud of dust towards the town.

Winter came—and a real winter it was. Peer
moved about from one window to another, calling
all the time to Merle to come and look. He had
been away so long—the winter of Eastern Norway
was all new to him. Look—look! A world of
white—a frozen white tranquillity—woods, plains,
lakes all in white, a fairy-tale in sunlight, a dream-
land at night under the great bright moon. There
was a ringing of sleigh-bells out on the lake, and
up in the snow-powdered forest; the frost stood
thick on the horses' manes and the men's beards
were hung with icicles. And in the middle of the
night loud reports of splitting ice would come from
the lake—sounds to make one sit up in bed with a
start.

Driving's worth while in weather like this—
come, Merle. The new stallion from Gudbrandsdal
wants breaking in—we'll take him. Hallo! and
away they go in their furs, swinging out over the
frozen lake, whirling on to the bare glassy ice,
where they skid and come near capsizing, and
Merle screams—but they get on to snow, and hoofs
and runners grip again. None of your galloping

—trot now, trot! And Peer cracks his whip. The black, long-maned Gudbrandsdaler lifts his head and trots out. And the evening comes, and under the wide and starry sky they dash up again to Loreng—Loreng that lies there lighting them home with its long rows of glowing windows. A glorious day, wife!

Or they would go out on ski over the hills to the woodmen's huts in the forest, and make a blazing fire in the big chimney and drink steaming coffee. Then home again through one of those pale winter evenings with a violet twilight over woods and fields and lake, over white snow and blue. Far away on the brown hillside in the west stands a farmhouse, with all its windows flaming with the reflection from a golden cloud. Here they come rushing, the wind of their passing shaking the snow from the pines; on, on, over deep-rutted woodcutters' roads, over stumps and stones —falling, bruising themselves, burying their faces deep in the snow, but dragging themselves up again, smiling to each other and rushing on again. Then, reaching home red and dripping, they lean the ski up against the wall, and stamp the snow off their boots.

"Merle," said Peer, picking the ice from his beard, "we must have a bottle of Burgundy at dinner to-night."

"Yes—and shall we ring up and ask someone to come over?"

"Someone—from outside? Can't we two have a little jollification all to ourselves?"

"Yes, yes, of course, if you like."

A shower-bath—a change of underclothes—how delicious! And—an idea! He'll appear at dinner in evening dress, just for a surprise. But as he entered the room he stopped short. For there stood Merle herself in evening dress—a dress of dark red velvet, with his locket round her neck and the big plaits of hair rolled into a generous knot low on her neck. Flowers on the table—the wine set to warm—the finest glass, the best silver—ptarmigan—how splendid! They lift their glasses filled with the red wine and drink to each other.

The frozen winter landscape still lingered in their thoughts, but the sun had warmed their souls; they laughed and jested, held each other's hands long, and sat smiling at each other in long silences.

"A glorious day to-day, Merle. And to-morrow we die."

"What do you say!—to-morrow!"

"Or fifty years hence. It comes to the same thing." He pressed her hand and his eyes half closed.

"But this evening we're together—and what could we want more?"

Then he fell to talking of his Egyptian experiences. He had once spent a month's holiday in visiting ruined cities with Maspero, the great Maspero himself, going with him to Luxor, to Karnak,

with its great avenues of sphinxes, to El Amarna
and Shubra. They had looked on ancient cities of
temples and king's mausoleums, where men thousands of years dead lay as if lost in thought, with
eyes wide open, ready at any moment to rise and
call out: Slave, is the bath ready? There in the
middle of a cornfield rises an obelisk. You ask
what it is—it is all that is left of a royal city.
There, too, a hundred thousand years ago maybe,
young couples have sat together, drinking to each
other in wine, revelling in all the delights of love
—and where are they now? Aye, where are they,
can you tell me?

"When that journey was over, Merle, I began
to think that it was not mere slime of the Nile
that fertilised the fields; it was the mouldered
bodies of the dead. I rode over dust that had
been human fingers, lips that had clung in kisses.
Millions and millions of men and women have
lived on those river-banks, and what has become
of them now? Geology. And I thought of the
millions of prayers wailed out there to the sun
and stars, to stone idols in the temples, to croco-
diles and snakes and the river itself, the sacred
river. And the air, Merle—the air received them,
and vibrated for a second—and that was all. And
even so our prayers go up, to this very day. We
press our warm lips to a cold stone, and think to
leave an impression. *Skaal!*"

But Merle did not touch her glass; she sat still,
with her eyes on the yellow lampshade. She had

not yet given up all her dreams of going forth and conquering the world with her music—and he sat there rolling out eternity itself before her, while he and she herself, her parents, all, all became as chaff blown before the wind and vanished.

"What, won't you drink with me? Well, well—then I must pledge you by myself. *Skaal!*"

And being well started on his travellers' tales he went on with them, but now in a more cheerful vein, so that she found it possible to smile. He told of the great lake-swamps, with their legions of birds, ibis, pelicans, swans, flamingos, herons, and storks—a world of long beaks and curved breasts and stilt-like legs and shrieking and beating of wings. Most wonderful of all it was to stand and watch and be left behind when the birds of passage flew northward in their thousands in the spring. My love to Norway, he would say, as they passed. And in the autumn to see them return, grey goose, starling, wagtail, and all the rest. "How goes it now at home?" he would think—and "Next time I'll go with you," he would promise himself year after year.

"And here I am at last! *Skaal!*"

"Welcome home," said Merle, lifting her glass with a smile.

He rang the bell. "What do you want?" her eyes asked.

"Champagne," said Peer to the maid, who appeared and vanished again.

"Are you crazy, Peer?"

He leaned back, flushed and in happy mood,
lit a cigarette and told of his greatest triumph out
there; it was after he had finished his work at the
cataracts, and had started again with a branch of
the English firm in Alexandria. One morning in
walked the Chief and said: "Now, gentlemen,
here's a chance for a man that has the stuff in him
to win his spurs—who's ready?" And half a
score of voices answered "I." "Well, here's the
King of Abyssinia suddenly finds he must be in
the fashion and have a railway—couple of hundred miles of it—what do you say to that?"
"Splendid," we cried in chorus. "Well, but we've
got to compete with Germans, and Swiss, and
Americans—and we've got to win." "Of course"
—a louder chorus still. "Now, I'm going to take
two men and give them a free hand. They'll go
up there and survey and lay out lines, and work
out the whole project thoroughly, both from the
technical and the financial side—and a project
that's better and cheaper than the opposition ones.
Eight months' work for a good man, but I must
have it done in four. Take along assistants and
equipment—all you need—and a thousand pounds
premium to the man who puts it through so that
we get the job."

"Peer—were you sent?" Merle half rose from
her seat in her excitement.

"I—and one other."

"Who was that?"

"His name was Ferdinand Holm."

Merle smiled her one-sided smile, and looked at him through her long lashes. She knew it had been the dream of his life to beat that half-brother of his in fair fight. And now!

"And what came of it?" she asked, with a seeming careless glance at the lamp.

Peer flung away his cigarette. "First an expedition up the Nile, then a caravan journey, camels and mules and assistants and provisions and instruments and tents and quinine—heaps of quinine. Have you any idea, I wonder, what a job like that means? The line was to run through forests and tunnels, over swamps and torrents and chasms, and everything had to be planned and estimated at top speed—material, labour, time, cost and all. It was all very well to provide for the proper spans and girders for a viaduct, and estimate for thoroughly sound work in casting and erecting—but even then it would be no good if the Germans could come along and say their bridge looked handsomer than ours. It was a job that would take a good man eight months, and I had to get it done in four. There are just twelve hours in a day, it's true—but then there are twelve more hours in the night. Fever? Well, yes. And sunstroke—yes, both men and beasts went down with that. Maps got washed out by the rain. I lost my best assistant by snakebite. But such things didn't count as hindrances, they couldn't be allowed to delay the work. If I lost a man, it simply meant so much more work for me. After a

couple of months a blacksmith's hammer started
thumping in the back of my head, and when I
closed my eyes for a couple of hours at night, little
fiery snakes went wriggling about in my brain.
Tired out? When I looked in the glass, my eyes
were just two red balls in my head. But when the
four months were up, I was back in the Chief's
office."

"And—and Ferdinand Holm?"

"Had got in the day before."

Merle shifted a little in her seat. "And so—he
won?"

Peer lit another cigarette. "No," he said—the
cigarette seemed to draw rather badly—"I won.
And that's how I came to be building railways in
Abyssinia."

"Here's the champagne," said Merle. And as
the wine foamed in the glasses, she rose and drank
to him. She said nothing, only looked at him with
eyes half veiled, and smiled. But a wave of fire
went through him from head to foot.

"I feel like playing to-night," she said.

It was rarely that she played, though he had
often begged her to. Since they had been married
she had seemed loth to touch her violin, feeling
perhaps some vague fear that it would disturb her
peace and awaken old longings.

Peer sat on the sofa, leaning forward with his
head in his hands, listening. And there she stood,
at the music-stand, in her red dress, flushed and

warm, and shining in the yellow lamplight, playing.

Then suddenly the thought of her mother came to her, and she went to the telephone. "Mother—are you there, mother? Oh, we've had such a glorious day." And the girl ran on, as if trying to light up her mother's heart with some rays of the happiness her own happy day had brought her.

A little later Peer lay in bed, while Merle flitted about the room, lingering over her toilet.

He watched her as she stood in her long white gown before the toilet-table with the little green-shaded lamps, doing her hair for the night in a long plait. Neither of them spoke. He could see her face in the glass, and saw that her eyes were watching him, with a soft, mysterious glance—the scent of her hair seemed to fill the place with youth.

She turned round towards him and smiled. And he lay still, beckoning her towards him with shining eyes. All that had passed that evening—their outing, and the homeward journey in the violet dusk, their little feast, and his story, the wine—all had turned to love in their hearts, and shone out now in their smile.

It may be that some touch of the cold breath of the eternities was still in their minds, the remembrance of the millions on millions that die, the flight of the æons towards endless darkness; yet in spite of all, the minutes now to come, their warm embrace, held a whole world of bliss, that outweighed all, and made Peer, as he lay there, long to send out a hymn of praise into the universe, because it was so wonderful to live.

He began to understand why she lingered and took so long. It was a sign that she wanted to surprise him, that her heart was kind. And her light breathing seemed even now to fill the room with love.

Outside in the night the lake-ice, splitting into new crevices, sent up loud reports; and the winter sky above the roof that sheltered them was lit with all its stars.

For the next few years Peer managed his estate and his workshop, without giving too much of his time to either. He had his bailiff and his works-manager, and the work went on well enough in its accustomed grooves. If anyone had asked him what he actually did himself all the time, he would have found it hard to answer. He seemed to be going round gathering up something not clearly defined. There was something wanting—something missed that now had to be made good. It was not knowledge now, but life—life in his native land, the life of youth, that he reached out to grasp. The youth in him, that had never had free play in the years of early manhood, lay still dammed up, and had to find an outlet.

There were festive gatherings at Loreng. Long rows of sleighs drove in the winter evenings up from the town and back again. Tables were spread and decked with glass and flowers, the rooms were brightly lit, and the wine was good. And some-times in the long moonlit nights respectable citizens would be awakened by noisy mirth in the streets of the little town, and, going to the window in their night-shirts, would see sleighs come galloping down, with a jangle of bells, full of laughing, singing young people, returning from some excursion far up in the hills, where there had been feasting and dancing. Here a young lawyer—newly married and something of a privileged buffoon—was sitting on the lap of somebody else's wife, playing a concertina, and singing at the top of his voice. "Some of that Loreng man's doings again," people would say. "The place has never been the same since he came here." And they would get back to bed again, shaking their heads and wondering what things were coming to.

Peer drove out, too, on occasion, to parties at the big country houses round, where they would play cards all night and have champagne sent up to their rooms next morning, the hosts being men who knew how to do things in style. This was glorious. Not mathematics or religion any more—what he needed now was to assimilate something of the country life of his native land. He was not going to be a stranger in his own country. He wanted to take firm root and be able to feel, like others, that he had a spot in the world where he was at home.

Then came the sunny day in June when he stood by Merle's bed, and she lay there smiling faintly her one-sided smile, with a newborn girl on her arm.

"What are we to call her, Peer?"

"Why, we settled that long ago. After your mother, of course."

"Of course her name's to be Louise," said

Merle, turning the tiny red face towards her breast.

This came as a fresh surprise. She had been planning it for weeks perhaps, and now it took him unawares like one of her spontaneous caresses, but this time a caress to his inmost soul.

He made a faint attempt at a joke. "Oh well, I never have any say in my own house. I suppose you must have it your own way." He stroked her forehead; and when she saw how deeply moved he was, she smiled up at him with her most radiant smile.

On one of the first days of the hay-harvest, Peer lay out on a sunny hillside with his head resting on a haycock, watching his people at work. The mowing machine was buzzing down by the lake, the spreader at work on the hill-slopes, the horses straining in front, the men sitting behind driving. The whole landscape lay around him breathing summer and fruitfulness. And he himself lay there sunk in his own restful quiet.

A woman in a light dress and a yellow straw hat came down the field road, pushing a child's cart before her. It was Merle, and Merle was looking round her, and humming as she came. Since the birth of her child her mind was at peace; it was clear that she was scarcely dreaming now of conquering the world with her music—there was a tiny being in the little cart that claimed all her dreams. Never before had her skin been so dazzling, her smile so red; it was as if her youth now first blossomed out in all its fullness; her eyes seemed opened wide in a dear surprise.

After a while Peer went down and drove the mowing machine himself. He felt as if he must get to work somehow or other to provide for his wife and child.

But suddenly he stopped, got down, and began to walk round the machine and examine it closely. His face was all alert now, his eyes keen and piercing. He stared at the mechanism of the blades, and stood awhile thinking.

What was this? A happy idea was beginning to work in his mind. Vague only as yet—there was still time to thrust it aside. Should he?

Warm mild days and luminous nights. Sometimes he could not sleep for thinking how delicious it was to lie awake and see the sun come up.

On one such night he got up and dressed. A few minutes later there was a trampling of hoofs in the stable-yard and the chestnut stallion appeared, with Peer leading him. He swung himself into the saddle, and trotted off down the road, a white figure in his drill suit and cork helmet.

Where was he going? Nowhere. It was a change, to be up at an unusual hour and see the day break on a July morning.

He trotted along at an easy pace, rising lightly in the stirrups, and enjoying the pleasant warmth the rider feels. All was quiet around him, the homesteads still asleep. The sky was a pearly white, with here and there a few golden clouds, reflected in the lake below. And the broad meadows still spread their many-coloured flower-carpet abroad; there was a scent in the air of leaf and meadow-grass and pine, he drew in deep breaths of it and could have sung aloud.

He turned into the by-road up the hill, dismounting now and again to open a gate; past farms and little cottages, ever higher and higher, till at last he reached the topmost ridge, and halted in a clearing. The chestnut threw up his head and sniffed the air; horse and rider were wet with the dewdrip from the trees, that were now just flushing in the first glow of the coming sun. Far below was the lake, reflecting sky and hills and farmsteads, all asleep. And there in the east were the red flames—the sun—the day.

The horse pawed impatiently at the ground, eager to go on, but Peer held him back. He sat there gazing under the brim of his helmet at the sunrise, and felt a wave of strange feeling passing through his mind.

It seemed to him impossible that he should ever reach a higher pitch of sheer delight in life. He was still young and strong; all the organs of his body worked together in happy harmony. No cares to weigh upon his mind, no crushing responsibilities; the future lying calm and clear in the light of day, free from dizzy dreams. His hunger after knowledge was appeased; he felt that what he had learned and seen and gathered was beginning to take living organic form in his mind.

But then—what then?

The great human type of which you dreamed—have you succeeded in giving it life in yourself?

You know what is common knowledge about the progress of humanity; its struggle towards higher forms, its gropings up by many ways toward the infinite which it calls God.

You know something of the life of plants; the nest of a bird is a mystery before which you could kneel in worship. A rock shows you the marks of a glacier that scraped over it thousands of years ago, and looking on it you have a glimpse of the gigantic workings of the solar system. And on autumn evenings you look up at the stars, and the light and the death and the dizzy abysses of space above you send a solemn thrill through your soul.

And this has become a part of yourself. The joy of life for you is to grasp all you can compass of the universe, and let it permeate your thought and sense on every side.

But what then? Is this enough? Is it enough to rest thus in yourself?

Have you as yet raised one stepping-stone upon which other men can climb and say: Now we can see farther than before?

What is your inner being worth, unless it be mirrored in action?

If the world one day came to be peopled with

none but supermen—what profit in that, as long
as they must die?

What is your faith?

Ah, this sense of exile, of religious homeless-
ness! How many times have you and Merle lain
clasping each other's hands, your thoughts wandering together hand in hand, seeking over earth
or among the stars for some being to whom you
might send up a prayer; no slavish begging cry
for grace and favour, but a jubilant thanksgiving
for the gift of life.

But where was He?

He is not. And yet—He is.

But the ascetic on the cross is a God for the
sick and aged. What of us others? When shall
the modern man, strong, scientifically schooled,
find a temple for the sacred music, the anthem of
eternity in his soul?

The sun rose up from behind a distant hill-
crest, scattering gold over the million spires of the
pine-forest. Peer bent forward, with red-gleam-
ing dewdrops on his hand and his white sleeve, and
patted the neck of his restless beast.

It was two o'clock. The fires of morning were
lit in the clouds and in all the waters over the
earth. The dew in the meadows and the pearls on
the wings of butterflies began to glisten.

"Now then, Bijou!—now for home!"

And he dashed off down the grass-grown forest
paths, the chestnut snorting as he galloped.

"Hei, Merle; We're going to have distinguished visitors—where in the world have you got to!" Peer hurried through the rooms with an open telegram in his hand, and at last came upon his wife in the nursery. "Oh, is it here you are?"

"Yes—but you shout so, I could hear you all through the house. Who is it that's coming?"

"Ferdinand Holm and Klaus Brock. Coming to the christening after all. Great Cæsar!—what do you say to that, Merle?"

Merle was pale, and her cheeks a little sunken. Two years more had passed, and she had her second child now on her knee—a little boy with big wondering eyes.

"How fine for you, Peer!" she said, and went on undressing the child.

"Yes; but isn't it splendid of them to set off and come all that way, just because I asked them? By Jove, we must look sharp and get the place smartened up a bit."

And sure enough the whole place was soon turned upside-down—cartloads of sand coming in for the garden walks and the courtyard, and painters hard at work repainting the houses. And poor Merle knew very well that there would be serious trouble if anything should be amiss with the entertainment indoors.

At last came the hot August day when the flags were hoisted in honour of the expected guests. Once more the hum of mowing machines and hay-rakes came from the hill-slopes, and the air was so still that the columns of smoke from the chimneys of the town rose straight into the air. Peer had risen early, to have a last look round, inspecting everything critically, from the summer dress Merle was to wear down to the horses in the stable, groomed till their coats shone again. Merle understood. He had been a fisher-boy beside the well-dressed son of the doctor, and something meaner yet in relation to the distinguished Holm family. And there was still so much of the boy in him that he wanted to show now at his very best.

A crowd of inquisitive idlers had gathered down on the steamboat landing when the boat swung in and lay by the pier. The pair of bays in the Loreng carriage stood tossing their heads and twitching and stamping as the flies tormented them; but at last they got their passengers and were given their heads, setting off with a wild bound or two that scattered those who had pressed too near. But in the carriage they could see the two strangers and the engineer, all three laughing and gesticulating, and talking all at once. And in a few moments they vanished in a cloud of dust, whirling away beside the calm waters of the fjord.

Some way behind them a cart followed, driven

by one of the stable-boys from Loreng, and loaded with big brass-bound leather trunks and a huge chest, apparently of wood, but evidently containing something frightfully heavy.

Merle had finished dressing, and stood looking at herself in the glass. The light summer dress was pretty, she thought, and the red bows at neck and waist sat to her satisfaction. Then came the roll of wheels outside, and she went out to receive her guests.

"Here they are," cried Peer, jumping down. "This is Ferdinand Pasha, Governor-General of the new Kingdom of Sahara—and this is His Highness the Khedive's chief pipe-cleaner and body-eunuch."

A tall, stooping man with white hair and a clean-shaven, dried-up face advanced towards Merle. It was Ferdinand Holm. "How do you do, Madam?" he said, giving her a dry, bony hand.

"Why, this is quite a baronial seat you have here," he added, looking round and settling his pince-nez.

His companion was a round, plump gentleman, with a little black goatee beard and dark eyes that blinked continually. But his smile was full of mirth, and the grip of his hand felt true. So this was Klaus Brock.

Peer led his two friends in through the rooms, showing them the view from the various windows. Klaus broke into a laugh at last, and turned to Merle: "He's just the same as ever," he said—

"a little stouter, to be sure—it's clear you've been treating him well, madam." And he bowed and kissed her hand.

There was hock and seltzer ready for them—this was Merle's idea, as suitable for a hot day—and when the two visitors had each drunk off a couple of glasses, with an: "Ah! delicious!", Peer came behind her, stroked her hand lightly and whispered, "Thanks, Merle—first-rate idea of yours."

"By the way," exclaimed Ferdinand Holm suddenly, "I must send off a telegram. May I use the telephone a moment?"

"There he goes—can't contain himself any longer!" burst out Klaus Brock with a laugh. "He's had the telegraph wires going hard all the way across Europe—but you might let us get inside and sit down before you begin again here."

"Come along," said Peer. "Here's the telephone."

When the two had left the room, Klaus turned to Merle with a smile. "Well, well—so I'm really in the presence of Peer's wife—his wife in flesh and blood. And this is what she looks like! That fellow always had all the luck." And he took her hand again and kissed it. Merle drew it away and blushed.

"You are not married, then, Mr. Brock?"

"I? Well, yes and no. I did marry a Greek girl once, but she ran away. Just my luck." And he blinked his eyes and sighed with an expression so comically sad that Merle burst out laughing.

"And your friend, Ferdinand Holm?" she asked.

"He, dear lady—he—why, saving your presence, I have an idea there's a select little harem attached to that palace of his."

Merle turned towards the window and shook her head with a smile.

An hour later the visitors came down from their rooms after a wash and a change of clothes, and after a light luncheon Peer carried them off to show them round the place. He had added a number of new buildings, and had broken new land. The farm had forty cows when he came, now he had over sixty. "Of course, all this is a mere nothing for fellows like you, who bring your harvest home in railway trains," he said. "But, you see, I have my home here." And he waved his hand towards the house and the farmstead round.

Later they drove over in the light trap to look at the workshop, and here he made no excuses for its being small. He showed off the little foundry as if it had been a world-famous seat of industry, and maintained his serious air while his companions glanced sideways at him, trying hard not to smile.

The workmen touched their caps respectfully, and sent curious glances at the strangers.

"Quite a treat to see things on the Norwegian

scale again," Ferdinand Holm couldn't resist saying at last.

"Yes, isn't it charming!" cried Peer, putting on an air of ingenuous delight. "This is just the size a foundry should be, if its owner is to have a good time and possess his soul in peace."

Ferdinand Holm and Brock exchanged glances. But next moment Peer led them through into a side-room, with tools and machinery evidently having no connection with the rest.

"Now look out," said Klaus. "This is the holy of holies, you'll see. He's hard at it working out some new devilry here, or I'm a Dutchman."

Peer drew aside a couple of tarpaulins, and showed them a mowing machine of the ordinary type, and beside it another, the model of a new type he had himself devised.

"It's not quite finished yet," he said. "But I've solved the main problem. The old single knife-blade principle was clumsy; dragged, you know. But with two blades—a pair of shears, so to speak—it'll work much quicker." And he gave them a little lecture, showing how much simpler his mechanism was, and how much lighter the machine would be.

"And there you are," said Klaus. "It's Columbus's egg over again."

"The patent ought to be worth a million," said Ferdinand Holm, slowly, looking out of the window.

"Of course the main thing is, to make the work

easier and cheaper for the farmers," said Peer, with a rather sly glance at Ferdinand.

Dinner that evening was a festive meal. When the liqueur brandy went round, Klaus greeted it with enthusiasm. "Why, here's an old friend, as I live! Real Lysholmer!—well, well; and so you're still in the land of the living? You remember the days when we were boys together?" He lifted the little glass and watched the light play in the pale spirit. And the three old friends drank together, singing "The first full glass," and then "The second little nip," with the proper ceremonial observances, just as they had done in the old days, at their student wine-parties.

The talk went merrily, one good story calling up another. But Merle could not help noticing the steely gleam of Ferdinand Holm's eyes, even when he laughed.

The talk fell on new doings in Egypt, and as Peer heard more and more of these, it seemed to her that his look changed. His glance, too, seemed to have that glint of steel, there was something strange and absent in his face; was he feeling, perhaps, that wife and children were but a drag on a man, after all? He seemed like an old war-horse waking suddenly at the sound of trumpets.

"There's a nice little job waiting for you, by the way," said Ferdinand Holm, lifting his glass to Peer.

"Very kind of you, I'm sure. A sub-directorship under you?"

"You're no good under any one. You belong on top." Ferdinand illustrated his words with a downward and an upward pointing of the finger. "The harnessing of the Tigris and Euphrates will have to be taken in hand. It's only a question of time."

"Thanks very much!" said Peer, his eyes wide open now.

"The plan's simply lying waiting for the right man. It will be carried out, it may be next year, it may be in ten years—whenever the man comes along. I would think about it, if I were you."

All looked at Peer; Merle fastened her eyes on him, too. But he laughed. "Now, what on earth would be the satisfaction to me of binding in bands those two ancient and honourable rivers?"

"Well, in the first place, it would mean an increase of many millions of bushels in the corn production of the world. Wouldn't you have any satisfaction in that?"

"No," said Peer, with a touch of scorn.

"Or regular lines of communication over hundreds of thousands of square miles of the most fertile country on the globe?"

"Don't interest me," said Peer.

"Ah!" Ferdinand Holm lifted his glass to Merle. "Tell me, dear lady, how does it feel to be married to an anachronism?"

"To—to what?" stammered Merle.

"Yes, your husband's an anachronism. He

might, if he chose, be one of the kings, the prophets, who lead the van in the fight for civilisation. But he will not; he despises his own powers, and one day he will start a revolution against himself. Mark my words. Your health, dear lady!"

Merle laughed, and lifted her glass, but hesitatingly, and with a side-glance towards Peer.

"Yes, your husband is no better now than an egoist, a collector of happy days."

"Well, and is that so very wicked?"

"He sits ravelling out his life into a multitude of golden threads," went on Ferdinand with a bow, his steely eyes trying to look gentle.

"But what is wrong in that?" said the young wife stoutly.

"It is wrong. It is wasting his immortal soul. A man has no right to ravel out his life, even though the threads are of gold. A man's days of personal happiness are forgotten—his work endures. And your husband in particular—why the deuce should *he* be so happy? The world-evolution uses us inexorably, either for light or for fuel. And Peer—your husband, dear lady—is too good for fuel."

Merle glanced again at her husband. Peer laughed, but then suddenly compressed his lips and looked down at his plate.

Then the nurse came in with little Louise, to say good-night, and the child was handed round from one to the other. But when the little fair-haired girl came to Ferdinand Holm, he seemed

loth to touch her, and Merle read his glance at
Peer as meaning: "Here is another of the bonds
you've tied yourself up with."

"Excuse me," he said suddenly, looking at his
watch, "I'm afraid I must ask for the use of the
telephone again. Pardon me, Fru Holm." And
he rose and left the room. Klaus looked at the
others and shook his head. "That man would
simply expire if he couldn't send a telegram once
an hour," he said with a laugh.

Coffee was served out on the balcony, and the
men sat and smoked. It was a dusky twilight of
early autumn; the hills were dark blue now and
distant; there was a scent of hay and garden flowers. After a while Merle rose and said good-
night. And in her thoughts, when she found herself alone in her bedroom, she hardly knew
whether to be displeased or not. These strange
men were drawing Peer far away from all that
had been his chief delight since she had known
him. But it was interesting to see how different
his manner was towards the two friends. Klaus
Brock he could jest and laugh with, but with Ferdinand Holm he seemed always on his guard, ready
to assert himself, and whenever he contradicted
him it was always with a certain deference.

The great yellow disc of the moon came up over
the hills in the east, drawing a broad pillar of
gold across the dark water. And the three comrades on the balcony sat watching it for a while in
silence.

"So you're really going to go on idling here?" asked Ferdinand at last, sipping his liqueur.

"Is it me you mean?" asked Peer, bending slightly forward.

"Well, I gather you're going round here simply being happy from morning to night. I call that idling."

"Thanks."

"Of course, you're very *un*happy in reality. Everyone is, as long as he's neglecting his powers and aptitudes."

"Very many thanks," said Peer, with a laugh. Klaus sat up in his chair, a little anxious as to what was coming.

Ferdinand was still looking out over the lake. "You seem to despise your own trade—as engineer?"

"Yes," said Peer.

"And why?"

"Why, I feel the lack of some touch of beauty in our ceaseless craving to create something new, something new, always something new. More gold, more speed, more food—are these things not all we are driving at?"

"My dear fellow, gold means freedom. And food means life. And speed carries us over the dead moments. Double the possibilities of life for men, and you double their numbers."

"And what good will it do to double their numbers? Two thousand million machine-made souls —is that what you want?"

"But hang it all, man," put in Klaus Brock eagerly, "think of our dear Norway at least. Surely you don't think it would be a misfortune if our population increased so far that the world could recognise our existence."

"I do," said Peer, looking away over the lake.

"Ah, you're a fanatic for the small in size and in numbers."

"I am loth to see all Norway polluted with factories and proletariat armies. Why the devil can't we be left in peace?"

"The steel will not have it," said Ferdinand Holm, as if speaking to the pillar of moonlight on the water.

"What? Who did you say?" Peer looked at him with wide eyes.

Ferdinand went on undisturbed: "The steel will not have peace. And the fire will not. And Prometheus will not. The human spirit has still too many steps to climb before it reaches the top. Peace? No, my friend—there are powers outside you and me that determine these things."

Peer smiled, and lit a new cigar. Ferdinand Holm leaned back in his chair and went on, addressing himself apparently to the moon. "Tigris and Euphrates—Indus and Ganges—and all the rest of this planet—regulate and cultivate the whole, and what is it after all? It's only a question of a few years. It is only a humble beginning. In a couple of centuries or so there will be nothing left to occupy us any more on this little globe of ours. And then we'll have to set about colonising other worlds."

There was silence for a moment. Then Peer spoke.

"And what do we gain by it all?" he asked.

"Gain? Do you imagine there will ever be any 'thus far and no farther' for the spirit of man? Half a million years hence, all the solar systems we know of now will be regulated and ordered by the human spirit. There will be difficulties, of course. Interplanetary wars will arise, planetary patriotism, groups of planetary powers in alliances and coalitions against other groups. Little worlds will be subjugated by the bigger ones, and so on. Is there anything in all this to grow dizzy over? Great heavens—can anyone doubt that man must go on conquering and to conquer for millions of years to come? The world-will goes its way. We cannot resist. Nobody asks whether we are happy. The will that works towards the infinite asks only whom it can use for its ends, and who is useless. *Violà tout.*"

"And when I die," asked Peer—"what then?"

"You! Are you still going about feeling your own pulse and wanting to live for ever? My dear fellow, *you* don't exist. There is just one person on our side—the world-will. And that includes us all. That's what I mean by 'we.' And we are working towards the day when we can make God respect us in good earnest. The spirit of man will hold a Day of Judgment, and settle accounts with

Olympus—with the riddle, the almighty power beyond. It will be a great reckoning. And mark
my words—that is the one single religious idea
that lives and works in each and every one of us
—the thing that makes us hold up our heads and
walk upright, forgetting that we are slaves and
things that die.''

Suddenly he looked at his watch. "Excuse me
a moment. If the telegraph office is open . . .''
and he rose and went in.

When he returned, Klaus and Peer were talking of the home of their boyhood and their early
days together.

"Remember that time we went shark-fishing?''
asked Klaus.

"Oh yes—that shark. Let me see—you were a
hero, weren't you, and beat it to death with your
bare fists—wasn't that it?'' And then "Cut the
line, cut the line, and row for your lives,'' he
mimicked, and burst out laughing.

"Oh, shut up now and don't be so witty,'' said
Klaus. "But tell me, have you ever been back
there since you came home?''

Peer told him that he had been to the village
last year. His old foster-parents were dead, and
Peter Rönningen too; but Martin Bruvold was
there still, living in a tiny cottage with eight children.

"Poor devil!'' said Klaus.

Ferdinand Holm had sat down again, and now
he nodded towards the moon. "An old chum

of yours? Well, why don't we send him a thousand crowns?"

There was a little pause. "I hope you'll let me join you," went on Ferdinand, taking a note for five hundred crowns from his waistcoat pocket. "You don't mind, do you?"

Peer glanced at him and took the note. "I'm delighted for poor old Martin's sake," he said, putting the note in his waistcoat pocket. "That'll make fifteen hundred for him."

Klaus Brock looked from one to the other and smiled a little. The talk turned on other things for a while, and then he asked:

"By the way, Peer, have you seen that advertisement of the British Carbide Company's?"

"No, what about?"

"They want tenders for the damming and harnessing of the Besna River, with its lake system and falls. That should be something in your line."

"No," said Ferdinand sharply. "I told you before—that job's too small for him. Peer's going to the Euphrates."

"What would it amount to, roughly?" said Peer, addressing no one in particular.

"As far as I could make out, it should be a matter of a couple of million crowns or thereabout," said Klaus.

"That's not a thing for Peer," said Ferdinand, rising and lifting his hand to hide a yawn. "Leave trifles like that to the trifling souls. Good-night, gentlemen."

A couple of hours later, when all was silent throughout the house, Peer was still up, wandering to and fro in soft felt slippers in the great hall. Now and again he would stop, and look out of the window. Why could he not sleep? The moon was paling, the day beginning to dawn.

THE next morning Merle was alone in the pantry when she heard steps behind her, and turned her head. It was Klaus Brock.

"Good-morning, madam—ah! so this is what you look like in morning dress. Why, morning *négligé* might have been invented for you, if I may say so. You might be a Ghirlandajo. Or no, better still, Aspasia herself."

"You are up early," said Merle drily.

"Am I? What about Ferdinand Holm then? He has been up since sunrise, sitting over his letters and accounts. Anything I can help you with? May I move that cheese for you?—Well, well! you *are* strong. But there, I'm always *de trop* where women are concerned."

"Always *de trop?*" repeated Merle, watching him through her long lashes.

"Yes—my first and only love—do you know who she was?"

"No, indeed. How should I?"

"Well, it was Louise—Peer's little sister. I wish you could have known her."

"And since then?" Merle let her eyes rest on this flourishing gentleman, who looked as if he could never have had a trouble in the world.

"Since then, dear lady?—since then? Let me see. Why, at this moment I really can't remember ever having met any other woman except . . ."

"Except . . . ?"

"Except yourself, madam." And he bowed.

"You are *too* kind!"

"And, that being so, don't you think it's your plain duty, as a hospitable hostess, to grant me . . ."

"Grant you—what? A piece of cheese?"

"Why, no, thanks. Something better. Something much better than that."

"What, then?"

"A kiss. I might as well have it now." As he took a step nearer, she looked laughingly round for a way of escape, but he was between her and the door.

"Well," said Merle, "but you must do something to make yourself useful first. Suppose you ran up that step-ladder for me."

"Delighted. Why, this is great fun!" The slight wooden ladder creaked under the weight of his solid form as he climbed. "How high am I to go?"

"To reach the top shelf—that's it. Now, you see that big brown jar? Careful—it's cranberries."

"Splendid—I do believe we're to have cranberry preserve at dinner." By standing on tiptoe he managed to reach and lift the heavy jar, and stood holding it, his face flushed with his exertions.

"And now, little lady?"

"Just stay there a moment and hold it carefully; I have to fetch something." And she hurried out.

Klaus stood at the top of the ladder, holding the heavy jar. He looked round. What was he to do with it? He waited for Merle to return—but she did not appear. Someone was playing the piano in the next room. Should he call for help? He waited on, getting redder and redder in the face. And still no Merle came.

With another mighty effort he set the jar back in its place, and then climbed down the ladder and walked into the drawing-room, very red and out of breath. In the doorway he stopped short and stared.

"What—well, I'll—— And she's sitting here playing the piano!"

"Yes. Aren't you fond of music, Herr Brock?"

"I'll pay you out for this," he said, shaking a finger at her. "Just you wait and see, little lady, if I don't pay you out, with interest!" And he turned and went upstairs, chuckling as he went.

Peer was sitting at the writing-table in his study when Klaus came in. "I'm just sealing up the letter with the money for Martin Bruvold," he said, setting the taper to a stick of sealing wax. "I've signed it: 'From the shark fishers.'"

"Yes, it was a capital idea of Ferdinand's.

What d'you think the poor old fellow'll say when he opens it and the big notes tumble out?"

"I'd like to see his face," said Peer, as he wrote the address on the envelope.

Klaus dropped into a leather armchair and leaned back comfortably. "I've been downstairs flirting a little with your wife," he said. "Your wife's a wonder, Peer."

Peer looked at him, and thought of the old days when the heavy-built, clumsy doctor's son had run about after the servant-girls in the town. He had still something of his old lurching walk, but intercourse with the ladies of many lands had polished him and given lightness and ease to his manner.

"What was I going to say?" Klaus went on. "Oh yes—our friend Ferdinand's a fine fellow, isn't he?"

"Yes, indeed."

"I felt yesterday exactly as I used to feel when we three were together in the old days. When I listen to his talk I can't help agreeing with him—and then you begin to speak, and what you say, too, seems to be just what I've been thinking in my inmost soul. Do you think I've become shallow, Peer?"

"Well, your steam ploughs look after themselves, I suppose, and the ladies of your harem don't trouble you overmuch. Do you read at all?"

"Best not say too much about that," said Klaus

with a sigh, and it suddenly struck Peer that his friend's face had grown older and more worn.

"No," said Klaus again. "Better not say much about that. But tell me, old fellow—you mustn't mind my asking—has Ferdinand ever spoken to you as his brother . . . or . . ."

Peer flushed hotly. "No," he said after a pause.

"No?"

"I owe more to him than to anybody in the world. But whether he regards me as a kinsman or simply as an object for his kindness to wreak itself on is a matter he's always left quite vague."

"It's just like him. He's a queer fellow. But there's another thing. . . ."

"Well?" said Peer, looking up.

"It's—er—again it's rather a delicate matter to touch on. I know, of course, that you're in the enviable position of having your fortune invested in the best joint-stock company in the world——"

"Yes; and so are you."

"Oh, mine's a trifle compared with yours. Have you still the whole of your money in Ferdinand's company?"

"Yes. I've been thinking of selling a few shares, by the way. As you may suppose, I've been spending a good deal just lately—more than my income."

"You mustn't sell just now, Peer. They're—I daresay you've seen that they're down—below par, in fact."

"What—below par! No, I had no idea of that."

"Oh, only for the time being, of course. Just a temporary drop. There's sure to be another run on them soon, and they'll go up again. But the Khedive has the controlling interest, you know, and he's rather a ticklish customer. Ferdinand is all for extension—wants to keep on buying up new land—new desert, that is. Irrigation there's just a question of power—that's how he looks at it. And of course the bigger the scale of the work the cheaper the power will work out. But the Khedive's holding back. It may be just a temporary whim—may be all right again to-morrow. But you never know. And if you think Ferdinand's the man to give in to a cranky Khedive, you're much mistaken. His idea now is to raise all the capital he can lay hands on, and buy him out! What do you say to that? Buy the Khedive clean out of the company. It's a large order. And if I were you, old man, as soon as the shares go up again a bit, I'd sell out some of my holding, and put the money into something at home here. After all, there must be plenty of quite useful things to be had here."

Peer frowned, and sat for a while looking straight before him. "No," he said at last. "As things stand between Ferdinand Holm and me—well, if either of us goes back on the other, it's not going to be me."

"Ah, in that case—I beg your pardon," said Klaus, and he rose and departed.

The christening was a great occasion, with a houseful of guests, and a great deal of speech-making. The host was the youngest and gayest of the party. The birth of his son should be celebrated in true Ethiopian fashion, he declared—with bonfires and boating parties.

The moon was hidden that evening behind thick dark clouds, but the boats full of guests glided over the black water to the accompaniment of music and laughter. The young madcap of a lawyer was there, again sitting on the lap of someone else's wife, and playing a concertina, till people in the farms on shore opened their windows and put their heads out to listen.

Later on the bonfires blazed up all along the lake shore and shone like great flaming suns in the water below. The guests lay on the grass in little groups round picnic suppers, and here and there a couple wandered by themselves, talking in whispers.

Merle and Peer stood together for a moment beside one of the bonfires. Their faces and figures were lit by the red glow; they looked at each other and exchanged a smile. He took her hand and led her outside the circle of light from the fire, and pointed over to their home, with all its windows glowing against the dark.

"Suppose this should be the last party we give, Merle."

"Peer, what makes you say that?"

"Oh, nothing—only I have a sort of feeling, as

if something had just ended and something new was to begin. I feel like it, somehow. But I wanted to thank you, too, for all the happy times we've had.''

''But Peer—what——'' She got no farther, for Peer had already left her and joined a group of guests, where he was soon as gay as the rest.

Then came the day when the two visitors were to leave. Their birthday gift to the young gentleman so lately christened Lorentz Uthoug stood in the drawing-room; it was a bust in red granite, the height of a man, of the Sun-god Re Hormachis, brought with them by the godfathers from Alexandria. And now it sat in the drawing-room between palms in pots, pressing its elbows against its sides and gazing with great dead eyes out into endless space.

Peer stood on the quay waving farewell to his old comrades as the steamer ploughed through the water, drawing after it a fan-shaped trail of little waves.

And when he came home, he walked about the place, looking at farms and woods, at Merle and the children, with eyes that seemed to her strange and new.

Next night he stayed up once more alone, pacing to and fro in the great hall, and looking out of the windows into the dark.

Was he ravelling out his life into golden threads that vanished and were forgotten?

Was he content to be fuel instead of light?

What was he seeking? Happiness? And beyond it? As a boy he had called it the anthem, the universal hymn. What was it now? God? But he would hardly find Him in idleness.

You have drawn such nourishment as you could from joy in your home, from your marriage, your fatherhood, nature, and the fellowmen around you here. There are unused faculties in you that hunger for exercise; that long to be set free to work, to strive, to act.

You should take up the barrage on the Besna, Peer. But could you get the contract? If you once buckle-to in earnest, no one is likely to beat you—you'll get it, sure enough. But do you really want it?

Are you not working away at a mowing-machine as it is? Better own up that you can't get on without your old craft, after all—that you must for ever be messing and meddling with steel and fire. You can't help yourself.

All the things your eyes have been fixed on in these last years have been only golden visions in a mist. The steel has its own will. The steel is beginning to wake in you—singing—singing—bent on pressing onward. You have no choice.

The world-will goes on its way. Go with it or be cast overboard as useless.

And still Peer walked up and down, up and down.

Next morning he set off for the capital. Merle watched the carriage as it drove away, and thought to herself: "He was right. Something new is beginning."

Chapter IX

THERE came a card from Peer, with a brief message: "Off to inspect the ground." A fortnight later he came home, loaded with maps and plans. "Of course I'm late for the fair, as usual," he said. "But wait a bit."

He locked himself into his room. At last Merle knew what it was like to have him at work. She could hear him in the mornings, walking up and down and whistling. Then silence—he would be standing over his table, busy with notes and figures. Then steps again. Now he was singing— and this was a novelty to himself. It was as if he carried in him a store of happiness, a treasure laid by of love, and the beauty of nature, and happy hours, and now it found its way out in song. Why should he not sing over the plans for a great barrage? Mathematics are dry work enough, but at times they can be as living visions, soaring up into the light. Peer sang louder. Then silence again. Merle never knew now when he stopped work and came to bed. She would fall asleep to the sound of his singing in his own room, and when she woke he would already be tramping up and down again in there; and to her his steps seemed like the imperious tread of a great commander.

He was alight with new visions, new themes, and his voice had a lordly ring. Merle looked at him through half-closed eyes with a lingering glance. Once more he was new to her: she had never seen him like this.

At last the work was finished, and he sent in his tender. And now he was more restless than ever. For a week he waited for an answer, tramping in and out of the place, going off for rides on Bijou, and coming back with his horse dripping with sweat. An impatient man cannot possibly ride at any pace but a gallop. The days passed; Peer was sleepless, and ate nothing. More days passed. At last he came bursting into the nursery one morning: "Trunk call, Merle; summons to a meeting of the Company Directors. Quick's the word. Come and help me pack—sharp." And in no time he was off again to the city.

Now it was Merle's turn to walk up and down in suspense. It mattered little to her in itself whether he got the work or not, but she was keenly anxious that he should win.

A couple of days later a telegram came: "Hurrah, wife!" And Merle danced round the room, waving the telegram above her head.

The next day he was back home again and tramping up and down the room. "What do you think your father will say to it, Merle—ha!"

"Father? Say to what?"

"When I ask him to be my surety for a couple of hundred thousand crowns?"

"Is father to be in it, too?" Merle looked at him open-eyed.

"Oh, if he doesn't want to, we'll let him off. But at any rate I'll ask him first. Goodbye." And Peer drove off into town.

In Lorentz Uthoug's big house you had to pass through the hardware shop to get to his office, which lay behind. Peer knocked at the door, with a portfolio under his arm. Herr Uthoug had just lit the gas, and was on the point of sitting down at his American roll-top desk, when Peer entered. The grey-bearded head with the close thick hair turned towards him, darkened by the shadow from the green shade of the burner.

"You, is it?" said he. "Sit down. You've been to Christiania, I hear. And what are you busy with now?"

They sat down opposite each other. Peer explained, calmly and with confidence.

"And what does the thing amount to?" asked Uthoug, his face coming out of the shadow and looking at Peer in the full light.

"Two million four hundred thousand."

The old man laid his hairy hands on the desk and rose to his feet, staring at the other and breathing deeply. The sum half-stunned him. Beside it he himself and his work seemed like dust in the balance. Where were all his plans and achievements now, his greatness, his position, his authority in the town? Compared with amounts like this, what were the paltry sums he had been used to handle?

"I—I didn't quite catch——" he stammered. "Did you say two millions?"

"Yes. I daresay it seems a trifle to you," said Peer. "Indeed, I've handled contracts myself that ran to fifty million francs."

"What? How much did you say?" Uthoug began to move restlessly about the room. He clutched his hair, and gazed at Peer as if doubting whether he was quite sober.

At the same time he felt it would never do to let himself be so easily thrown off his balance. He tried to pull himself together.

"And what do you make out of it?" he asked.

"A couple of hundred thousand, I hope."

"Oh!" A profit on this scale again rather startled the old man. No, he was nothing; he never had been anything in this world!

"How do you know that you will make so much?"

"I've calculated it all out."

"But if—but how can you be sure of it? Suppose you've got your figures wrong?" His head was thrust forward again into the full light.

"I'm in the habit of getting my figures right," said Peer.

When he broached the question of security, the old man was in the act of moving away from him across the room. But he stopped short, and looked back over his shoulder.

"What? Security? You want me to stand security for two million crowns?"

"No; the Company asks for a guarantee for four hundred thousand."

After a pause the old man said: "I see. Yes, I see. But—but I'm not worth as much as that altogether."

"I can put in three hundred thousand of the four myself, in shares. And then, of course, I have the Loreng property, and the works. But put it at a round figure—will you guarantee a hundred thousand?"

There was another pause, and then the reply came from the far end of the room to which Uthoug had drifted: "Even that's a big sum."

"Of course if you would rather not, I could make other arrangements. My two friends, who have just been here——" He rose and began to gather up his papers.

"No, no; you mustn't be in such a hurry. Why, you come down on a man like an avalanche. You must give me time to think it over—till to-morrow at least. And the papers—at any rate, I must have a look at them."

Uthoug passed a restless and troubled night. The solid ground seemed to have failed him; his mind could find no firm foothold. His son-in-law must be a great man—he should be the last to doubt it. But a hundred thousand—to be ventured, not in landed property, or a big trade deal, but on the success of a piece of construction work.

This was something new. It seemed fantastic—
suited to the great world outside perhaps, or the
future. Had he courage enough to stand in? Who
could tell what accidents, what disasters might not
happen? No! He shook his head. He could not.
He dared not. But—the thing tempted him. He
had always wanted to be something more than a
whale among the minnows. Should he risk it?
Should he not? It meant staking his whole fortune, his position, everything, upon the outcome
of a piece of engineering that he understood nothing whatever about. It was sheer speculation; it
was gambling. No, he must say: No. Then he
was only a whale among the minnows, after all.
No, he must say: Yes. Good God! He clenched
his hands together; they were clammy with sweat,
and his brain was in a whirl. It was a trial, a
temptation. He felt an impulse to pray. But
what good could that do—since he had himself
abolished God.

Next day Merle and Peer were rung up by telephone and asked to come in to dinner with the old
folks.

But when they were all sitting at table, they
found it impossible to keep the conversation going.
Everyone seemed shy of beginning on the subject
they were all thinking about. The old man's face
was grey with want of sleep; his wife looked from
one to the other through her spectacles. Peer was
calm and smiling.

At last, when the claret came round, Fru Uthoug

lifted her glass and drank to Peer. "Good fortune!" she said. "We won't be the ones to stand in your way. Since you think it is all right, of course it is. And we all hope it will turn out well for you, Peer."

Merle looked at her parents; she had sat through the meal anxious and troubled, and now the tears rose into her eyes.

"Thanks," said Peer, lifting his glass and drinking to his host and hostess. "Thanks," he repeated, bowing to old Uthoug. The matter was arranged. Evidently the two old folks had talked it over together and come to an agreement.

It was settled, but all four felt as if the solid ground were rocking a little under their feet. All their future, their fate, seemed staked upon a throw.

A couple of days later, a day of mild October sunshine, Peer happened to go into the town, and, catching sight of his mother-in-law at the window, he went off and bought some flowers, and took them up to her.

She was sitting looking out at the yellow sky in the west, and she hardly turned her head as she took the flowers. "Thanks, Peer," she said, and continued gazing out at the sky.

"What are you thinking of, dear mother?" asked Peer.

"Ah! it isn't a good thing always to tell our thoughts," she said, and she turned her spectacled eyes so as to look out over the lake.

"I hope it was something pleasant?"

"I was thinking of you, Peer. Of you and Merle."

"It is good of you to think of us."

"You see, Peer, there is trouble coming for you. A great deal of trouble." She nodded her head towards the yellow sky in the west.

"Trouble? Why? Why should trouble come to us?"

"Because you are happy, Peer."

"What? Because I am——?"

"Because all things blossom and flourish about you. Be sure that there are unseen powers enough that grudge you your happiness."

Peer smiled. "You think so?" he asked.

"I know it," she answered with a sigh, gazing out into the distance. "You have made enemies of late amongst all those envious shadows that none can see. But they are all around us. I see them every day; I have learned to know them, in all these years. I have fought with them. And it is well for Merle that she has learned to sing in a house so full of shadows. God grant she may be able to sing them away from you too."

When Peer left the house he felt as if little shudders of cold were passing down his back. "Pooh!" he exclaimed as he reached the street. "She is not right in her head." And he hurried to his carriole and drove off home.

"Old Rode will be pleased, anyhow," he thought. "He'll be his own master in the workshop now——

the dream of his life. Well, everyone for himself. And the bailiff will have things all his own way at Loreng for a year or two. Well, well! Come up, Brownie!"

Chapter X

"PEER, you're surely not going away just now? Oh, Peer, you mustn't. You won't leave me alone, Peer!"

"Merle, dear, now do be sensible. No, no—do let go, dear." He tried to disengage her hands that were clasped behind his neck.

"Peer, you have never been like this before. Don't you care for me any more—or the children?"

"Merle, dearest, you don't imagine that I like going. But you surely don't want me to have another big breach this year. It would be sheer ruin, I do assure you. Come, come now; let me go."

But she held him fast. "And what happens to those dams up there is more to you now than what becomes of me!"

"You will be all right, dear. The doctor and the nurse have promised to be on the spot the moment you send word. And you managed so well before. . . . I simply cannot stay now, Merle. There's too much at stake. There, there, goodbye! Be sure you telegraph——" He kissed her over the eyes, put her gently down into a chair, and hurried out of the room, feeling her terrified glance follow him as he went.

The April sun had cleared away the snow from the lowlands, but when Peer stepped out of the train up in Espedal he found himself back in winter—farms and fields still covered, and ridges and peaks deep in white dazzling snow. And soon he was sitting wrapped in his furs, driving a miserable dun pony up a side-valley that led out on to the uplands.

The road was a narrow track through the snow, yellow with horse-dung, and a mass of holes and ruts, worn by his own teams that had hauled their heavy loads of cement this way all through that winter and the last, up to the plateau and across the frozen lakes to Besna.

The steel will on. The steel cares nothing for human beings. Merle must come through it alone.

When a healthy, happy man is hampered and thwarted in a great work by annoyances and disasters, he behaves like an Arab horse on a heavy march. At first it moves at a brisk trot, uphill and downhill, and it goes faster and faster as its strength begins to flag. And when at last it is thoroughly out of breath and ready to drop, it breaks into an easy gallop.

This was not the work he had once dreamed of finding. Now, as before, his hunger for eternal things seemed ever at the side of his accomplishment, asking continually: Whither? Why? and What then?

But by degrees the difficulties had multiplied and mounted, till at last his whole mind was taken up by the one thought—to put it through. Good or bad in itself—he must make a success of it. He had undertaken it, and he must see it through. He must not be beaten.

And so he fought on. It was merely a trial of strength; a fight with material difficulties. Aye, but was that all it was? Were there not times when he felt himself struggling with something greater, something worse? A new motive force seemed to have come into his life—misfortune. A power outside his own will had begun to play tricks with him.

Your calculations may be sound, correct in every detail, and yet things may go altogether wrong.

Who could include in his calculations the chance that a perfectly sober engineer will get drunk one day and give orders so crazy that it costs tens of thousands to repair the damage? Who could foresee that against all probability a big vein of water would be tapped in tunnelling, and would burst out, flooding the workings and overwhelming the workmen—so that the next day a train of unpainted deal coffins goes winding out over the frozen lakes?

More than once there had been remarks and questions in the newspapers: "Another disaster at the Besna Falls. Who is to blame?"

It was because he himself was away on a business journey and Falkman had neglected to take

elementary precautions that the big rock-fall oc-
curred in the tunnel, killing four men, and destroy-
ing the new Belgian rock-drill, that had cost a good
hundred thousand, before it had begun to work.
This sort of thing was not faulty calculation—it
was malicious fate.

"Come up, boy! We must get there to-night.
The flood mustn't have a chance this year to lay
the blame on me because I wasn't on the spot."

And then, to cap the other misfortunes, his chief
contractor for material had gone bankrupt, and
now prices had risen far above the rates he had
allowed for—adding fresh thousands to the extra
expenditure.

But he would put the thing through, even if he
lost money by it. His envious rivals who had
lately begun to run down his projects in the technical papers—he would make them look foolish
yet.

And then?

Well, it may be that the Promethean spirit is
preparing a settling day for the universe somewhere out in infinity. But what concern is that of
mine? What about my own immortal soul?

Silence—push on, push on. There may be a
snowstorm any minute. Come up—get along, you
scarecrow.

The dun struggles on to the end of a twelve-
mile stage, and then the valley ends and the full
blast from the plateau meets them. Here lies the
posting station, the last farm in the valley. He

swings into the yard and is soon sitting in the
room over a cup of coffee and a pipe.

Merle? How are things with Merle now?

Ah! here comes his own horse, the big black
stallion from Gudbrandsdal. This beast's trot is
a different thing from the poor dun's—the sleigh
flies up to the door. And in a moment Peer is sitting in it again in his furs.

Ah! what a relief to have a fresh horse, and one
that makes light of the load behind him. Away
he goes at a brisk trot, with lifted head and bells
jingling, over the frozen lakes. Here and there
on the hillslopes a grey hut or two show out—
sæters, which have lain there unchanged for perhaps a couple of thousand years. But a new time
is coming. The sæter-horns will be heard no
longer, and the song of the turbines will rise in
their place.

An icy wind is blowing; the horse throws up its
head and snorts. Big snowflakes come driving on
the wind, and soon a regular snowstorm is raging,
lashing the traveller's face till he gasps. First the
horse's mane and tail grow white with snow, then
its whole body. The drifts grow bigger, the black
has to make great bounds to clear them. Bravo,
old boy! we must get there before dark. There
are brushwood brooms set out across the ice to
mark the way, but who could keep them in sight
in a driving smother like this? Peer's own face
is plastered white now, and he feels stunned and
dazed under the lash of the snow.

He has worked under the burning suns of Egypt —and now here. But the steel will on. The wave rolls on its way over all the world.

If this snow should turn to rain now, it will mean a flood. And then the men will have to turn out to-night and work to save the dams.

One more disaster, and he would hardly be able to finish within the contract time. And that once exceeded, each day's delay means a penalty of a thousand crowns.

It is getting darker.

At last there is nothing to be seen on the way but a shapeless mass of snow struggling with bowed head against the storm, wading deep in the loose drifts, wading seemingly at haphazard—and trailing after it an indefinable bundle of white—dead white. Behind, a human being drags along, holding on for dear life to the rings on the sleigh. It is the post-boy from the last stage.

At last they were groping their way in the darkness towards the shore, where the electric lights of the station showed faintly through the snow-fog. And hardly had Peer got out of the sleigh before the snow stopped suddenly, and the dazzling electric suns shone over the place, with the workmen's barracks, the assistants' quarters, the offices, and his own little plank-built house. Two of the engineers came out to meet him, and saluted respectfully.

"Well, how is everything getting on?"

The greybeard answered: "The men have struck work to-day."

"Struck? What for?"

"They want us to take back the machinist that was dismissed the other day for drunkenness."

Peer shook the snow from his fur coat, took his bag, and walked over to the building, the others following. "Then we'll have to take him back," he said. "We can't afford a strike now."

A couple of days later Peer was lying in bed, when the post-bag was brought in. He shook the letters out over the coverlet, and caught sight of one from Klaus Brock.

What was this? Why did his hand tremble as he took it up? Of course it was only one of Klaus's ordinary friendly letters.

DEAR FRIEND,—This is a hard letter to write. But I do hope you have taken my advice and got some of your money at any rate over to Norway. Well, to be as brief as possible! Ferdinand Holm has decamped, or is in prison, or possibly worse— you know well enough it's no good asking questions in a country like this when a big man suddenly disappears. He had made enemies in the highest places; he was playing a dangerous game —and this is the end of it.

You know what it means when a business goes into liquidation out here, and no strong man on the spot to look after things. We Europeans can whistle for our share.

You'll take it coolly, I know. I've lost every penny I had—but you've still got your place over there and the workshops. And you're the sort of fellow to make twice as much next time, or I don't know you. I hope the Besna barrage is to be a success.

Yours ever,

KLAUS BROCK.

P.S.—Of course you'll understand that now my friend has been thrown overboard it will very likely be my turn next. But I can't leave now—to try would rouse suspicion at once. We foreigners have some difficult balancing to do, to escape a fall. Well, if by chance you don't hear from me again, you'll know something has happened!

Outside, the water was streaming down the channels into the fall. Peer lay still for a while, only one knee moving up and down beneath the clothes. He thought of his two friends. And he thought that he was now a poor man—and that the greater part of the burden of the security would fall now on old Lorentz D. Uthoug.

Clearly, Fate has other business on hand than making things easy for you, Peer. You must fight your fight out single-handed.

Chapter XI

One evening in the late autumn Merle was sitting at home waiting for her husband. He had been away for several weeks, so it was only natural that she should make a little festivity of his return. The lamps were lit in all the rooms, wood fires were crackling in all the stoves, the cook was busy with his favourite dishes, and little Louise, now five years old, had on her blue velvet frock. She was sitting on the floor, nursing two dolls, and chattering to them. "Mind you're a good girl now, Josephine. Your grandpa will be here directly." Merle looked in through the kitchen door: "Have you brought up the claret, Bertha? That's right. You'd better put it near the stove to warm." Then she went round all the rooms again. The two youngest children were in bed—was there anything more to be done?

It would be an hour at least before he could be here, yet she could not help listening all the time for the sound of wheels. But she had not finished yet. She hurried up to the bathroom, turned on the hot water, undressed, and put on an oilskin cap to keep her hair dry, and soon she was splashing about with soap and sponge. Why not make

herself as attractive as she could, even if things
did look dark for them just now?

A little stream of talk went on in her brain.
Strange that one's body could be so great a pleasure to another. Here he kissed you—and here—
and here—and often he seemed beside himself with
joy. And do you remember—that time? You held
back and were cold often—perhaps too often—is
it too late now? Ah! he has other things to think
of now. The time is gone by when you could be
comfort enough to him in all troubles. But is it
quite gone by? Oh yes; last time he came home,
he hardly seemed to notice that we had a new little girl, that he had never seen before. Well, no
doubt it must be so. He did not complain, and
he was calm and quiet, but his mind was full of
a whole world of serious things, a world where
there was no room for wife and children. Will
it be the same this evening again? Will he notice
that you have dressed so carefully to please him?
Will it be a joy to him any more to feel his arms
around you?

She stood in front of the big, white-framed mirror, and looked critically at herself. No, she was
no longer young as she had been. The red in her
cheeks had faded a little these last few years,
and there were one or two wrinkles that could not
be hidden. But her eyebrows—he had loved to
kiss them once—they were surely much as before. And involuntarily she bent towards the

glass, and stroked the dark growth above her eyes as if it were his hand caressing her.

She came down at last, dressed in a loose blue dress with a broad lace collar and blond lace in the wide sleeves. And not to seem too much dressed, she had put on a red-flowered apron to give herself a housewifely look.

It was past seven now. Louise came whimpering to her, and Merle sank down in a chair by the window, and took the child on her lap, and waited.

The sound of wheels in the night may mean the approach of fate itself. Some decision, some final word that casts us down in a moment from wealth to ruin—who knows? Peer had been to England now, trying to come to some arrangement with the Company. Sh!—was that not wheels? She rose, trembling, and listened.

No, it had passed on.

It was eight o'clock now, time for Louise to go to bed; and Merle began undressing her. Soon the child was lying in her little white bed, with a doll on either side. "Give Papa a tiss," she babbled, "and give him my love. And Mama, do you think he'll let me come into his bed for a bit to-morrow morning?"

"Oh yes, I'm sure he will. And now lie down and go to sleep, there's a good girl."

Merle sat down again in the room and waited. But at last she rose, put on a cloak and went out. The town lay down there in the autumn dark-

ness under a milk-white mist of light. And over
the black hills all around rose a world of stars.
Somewhere out there was Peer, far out maybe
upon some country road, the horse plodding on
through the dark at its own will, its master sitting
with bowed head, brooding.

"Help us, Thou above—and help him most, he
has had so much adversity in these last days."

But the starry vault seems icy cold—it has heard
the prayers of millions and millions before—the
hearts of men are nothing to the universe.

Merle drooped her head and went in again to
the house.

It was midnight when Peer drove up the hill
towards his home. The sight of the great house
with its brilliantly lighted windows jarred so
cruelly on his wearied mind that he involuntarily
gave the horse a cut with his whip.

He flung the reins to the stable-boy who had
come out with a lantern, and walked up the steps,
moving almost with a feeling of awe in this great
house, as if it already belonged to someone else.

He opened the door of the drawing-room—no
one there, but light, light and comfort. He passed
through into the next room, and there sat Merle,
alone, in an armchair, with her head resting on
the arm, asleep.

Had she been waiting so long?

A wave of warmth passed through him; he stood
still, looking at her; and presently her bowed figure slowly straightened; her pale face relaxed into

a smile. Without waking her, he went on into the nursery, where the lights were still burning. But here the lights shone only on three little ones, lying in their clean night-clothes, asleep.

He went back to the dining-room; more lights, and a table laid for two, a snowy cloth and flowers, and a single carnation stuck into his napkin—that must be from Louise—little Louise.

At last Merle was awakened by the touch of his hand on her shoulder.

"Oh, are you there?"

"Good-evening, Merle!" They embraced, and he kissed her forehead. But she could see that his mind was busy with other things.

They sat down to table, and began their meal. She could read the expression of his face, his voice, his calm air—she knew they meant bad news.

But she would not question him. She would only try to show him that all things else could be endured, if only they two loved each other.

But the time had passed when an unexpected caress from her was enough to send him wild with joy. She sat there now trembling inwardly with suspense, wondering if he would notice her—if he could find any comfort in having her with him, still young and with something of her beauty left.

He looked over to her with a far-away smile. "Merle," he asked, "what do you think your father is worth altogether?" The words came like a quiet order from a captain standing on the bridge, while his ship goes down.

"Oh, Peer, don't think about all that to-night. Welcome home!" And she smiled and took his hand.

"Thanks," he said, and pressed her fingers; but his thoughts were still far off. And he went on eating without knowing what he ate.

"And what do you think? Louise has begun the violin. You've no idea how the little thing takes to it."

"Oh?"

"And Asta's got another tooth—she had a wretched time, poor thing, while it was coming through."

It was as if she were drawing the children up to him, to show him that at least he still had them.

He looked at her for a moment. "Merle, you ought never to have married me. It would have been better for you and for your people too."

"Oh, nonsense, Peer—you know you'll be able to make it all right again."

They went up to bed, and undressed slowly. "He hasn't noticed me yet," thought Merle.

And she laughed a little, and said, "I was sitting thinking this evening of the first day we met. I suppose you never think of it now?"

He turned round, half undressed, and looked at her. Her lively tone fell strangely on his ears. "She does not ask how I have got on, or how things are going," he thought. But as he went on looking at her he began at last to see through her smile to the anxious heart beneath.

Ah, yes; he remembered well that far-off summer when life had been a holiday in the hills, and a girl making coffee over a fire had smiled at him for the first time. And he remembered the first sun-red night of his love on the shining lake-mirror, when his heart was filled with the rush of a great anthem to heaven and earth.

She stood there still. He had her yet. But for the first time in their lives she came to him now humbly, begging him to make the best of her as she was.

An unspeakable warmth began to flow through his heavy heart. But he did not rush to embrace her and whirl her off in a storm of passionate delight. He stood still, staring before him, and, drawing himself up, swore to himself with fast-closed lips that he would, he *would* trample a way through, and save things for them both, even yet.

The lights were put out, and soon they lay in their separate beds, breathing heavily in the dark. Peer stretched himself out, with his face up, thinking, with closed eyes. He was hunting in the dark for some way to save his dear ones. And Merle lay so long waiting for one caress from him that at last she had to draw out her handkerchief and press it over her eyes, while her body shook with a noiseless sobbing.

OLD Lorentz D. Uthoug rarely visited his rich sister at Bruseth, but to-day he had taken his weary way up there, and the two masterful old folks sat now facing each other.

"So you've managed to find your way up here?" said Aunt Marit, throwing out her ample bosom and rubbing her knees like a man.

"Why, yes—I thought I'd like to see how you were getting on," said Uthoug, squaring his broad shoulders.

"Quite well, thanks. Having no son-in-law, I'm not likely to go bankrupt, I daresay."

"I'm not bankrupt, either," said old Uthoug, fixing his red eyes on her face.

"Perhaps not. But what about him?"

"Neither is he. He'll be a rich man before very long."

"He!—rich! Did you say rich?"

"Before a year's out," answered the old man calmly. "But you'll have to help."

"I!" Aunt Marit shifted her chair backwards, gaping. "I, did you say? Ha-ha-ha! Just tell me, how many hundreds of thousands did he lose over that ditch or drain or whatever it was?"

"He was six months behind time in finishing it,

I know. But the Company agreed to halve the forfeit for delay when they'd seen what a masterpiece the work was."

"Ah, yes—and what about the contractors, whom he couldn't pay, I hear?"

"He's paid them all in full now. The Bank arranged things."

"I see. After you and he had mortaged every stick and rag you had in the world. Yes, indeed— you deserve a good whipping, the pair of you!"

Uthoug stroked his beard. "From a financial point of view the thing wasn't a success for him, I'll admit. But I can show you here what the engineering people say about it in the technical papers. Here's an article with pictures of him and of the barrage."

"Well! he'd better keep his family on pictures in the papers then," said the widow, paying no attention to the paper he offered.

"He'll soon be on top again," said her brother, putting the papers back in his pocket. He sat there in front of her quite unruffled. He would let people see that he was not the man to be crushed by a reverse; that there were other things he valued more than money.

"Soon be on top?" repeated Aunt Marit. "Has he got round you again with some nonsense?"

"He's invented a new mowing machine. It's nearly finished. And the experts say it will be worth a million."

"Ho! and you want to come over me with a tale

like that?" The widow shifted her chair a little farther back.

"You must help us to carry on through this year—both of us. If you will stand security for thirty thousand, the bank . . ."

Aunt Marit of Bruseth slapped her knees emphatically. "I'll do nothing of the sort!"

"For twenty thousand, then?"

"Not for twenty pence!"

Lorentz Uthoug fixed his gaze on his sister's face; his red eyes began to glow.

"You'll have to do it, Marit," he said calmly. He took a pipe from his pocket and set to work to fill and light it.

The two sat for a while looking at each other, each on the alert for fear the other's will should prove the stronger. They looked at each other so long that at last both smiled involuntarily.

"I suppose you've taken to going to church with your wife now?" asked the widow at last, her eyes blinking derision.

"If I put my trust in the Lord," he said, "I might just sit down and pray and let things go to ruin. As it is, I've more faith in human works, and that's why I'm here now."

The answer pleased her. The widow at Bruseth was no churchgoer herself. She thought the Lord had made a bad mistake in not giving her any children.

"Will you have some coffee?" she asked, rising from her seat.

"Now you're talking sense," said her brother, and his eyes twinkled. He knew his sister and her ways. And now he lit his pipe and leaned back comfortably in his chair.

Chapter XIII

ONCE more Peer stood in his workroom down at the foundry, wrestling with fire and steel.

A working drawing is a useful thing; an idea in one's head is all very well. But the men he employed to turn his plans into tangible models worked slowly; why not use his own hands for what had to be done?

When the workmen arrived at the foundry in the morning there was hammering going on already in the little room. And when they left in the evening, the master had not stopped working yet. When the good citizens of Ringeby went to bed, they would look out of their windows and see his light still burning.

Peer had had plenty to tire him out even before he began work here. But in the old days no one had ever asked if he felt strong enough to do this or that. And he never asked himself. Now, as before, it was a question of getting something done, at any cost. And never before had there been so much at stake.

The wooden model of the new machine is finished already, and the castings put together. The whole thing looks simple enough, and yet—what a distance from the first rough implement to this thing, which seems almost to live—a thing with a brain of metal at least. Have not these wheels and axles had their parents and ancestors—their pedigree stretching back into the past? The steel has brought forth, and its descendants again in turn, advancing always toward something finer, stronger, more efficient. And here is the last stage reached by human invention in this particular work up to now—yet, after all, is it good enough? An invention successful enough to bring money in to the inventor—that is not all. It must be more; it must be a world-success, a thing to make its way across the prairies, across the enormous plains of India and Egypt—that is what is needed. Sleep? rest? food? What are such things when so much is at stake!

There was no longer that questioning in his ear: Why? Whither? What then? Useless to ponder on these things. His horizon was narrowed down to include nothing beyond this one problem. Once he had dreamed of a work allied to his dreams of eternity. This, certainly, was not it. What does the gain amount to, after all, when humanity has one more machine added to it? Does it kindle a single ray of dawn the more in a human soul?

Yet this work, such as it was, had now become his all. It must and should be all. He was fast bound to it.

When he looked up at the window, there seemed to be faces at each pane staring in. "What? Not finished yet?" they seemed to say. "Think what it means if you fail!" Merle's face, and the children's: "Must we be driven from Loreng, out into the cold?" The faces of old Uthoug and his wife: "Was it for this you came into an honourable family? To bring it to ruin?" And behind them, swarming, all the town. All knew what was at stake, and why he was toiling so. All stared at him, waiting. The Bank Manager was there too—waiting, like the rest.

One can seize one's neck in iron pincers, and say: You shall! Tired? difficulties? time too short?—all that doesn't exist. You shall! Is this thing or that impossible? Well, make it possible. It is your business to make it possible.

He spent but little time at home now; a sofa in the workshop was his bed. Often Merle would come in with food for him, and seeing how pale and grey and worn out he was, she did not dare to question him. She tried to jest instead. She had trained herself long ago to be gay in a house where shadows had to be driven off with laughter.

But one day, as she was leaving, he held her back, and looked at her with a strange smile.

"Well, dear?" she said, with a questioning look.

He stood looking at her as before, with the same far-off smile. He was looking through her into the little world she stood for. This home, this family that he, a homeless man, had won through her, was it all to go down in shipwreck?

Then he kissed her eyes and let her go.

And as her footsteps died away, he stood a moment, moved by a sudden desire to turn to some Power above him with a prayer that he might succeed in this work. But there was no such Power. And in the end his eyes turned once more to the iron, the fire, his tools, and his own hands, and it was as though he sighed out a prayer to these: "Help me—help me, that I may save my wife and children's happiness."

Sleep? rest? weariness? He had only a year's grace. The bank would only wait a year.

Winter and spring passed, and one day in July he came home and rushed in upon Merle crying, "To-morrow, Merle! They will be here to-morrow!"

"Who?"

"The people to look at the machine. We're going to try it to-morrow."

"Oh, Peer!" she said breathlessly, gazing at him.

"It's a good thing that I had connections abroad," he went on. "There's one man coming from an English firm, and another from America. It ought to be a big business."

The morrow came. Merle stood looking after her husband as he drove off, his hat on the back of his head, through the haze that followed the night's rain. But there was no time to stand trembling; they were to have the strangers to dinner, and she must see to it.

Out in the field the machine stood ready, a slender, newly painted thing. A boy was harnessing the horses.

Two men in soft hats and light overcoats came up; it was old Uthoug, and the Bank Manager. They stopped and looked round, leaning on their sticks; the results of the day were not a matter of entire indifference to these two gentlemen. Ah! here was the big carriage from Loreng, with the two strangers and Peer himself, who had been down to fetch them from the hotel.

He was a little pale as he took the reins and climbed to his seat on the machine, to drive it himself through the meadow of high, thick timothy-grass.

The horses pricked up their ears and tried to break into a gallop, the noise of the machine behind them startling them as usual at first, but they soon settled down to a steady pace, and the steel arm bearing the shears swept a broad swath through the meadow, where the grass stood shining after the rain.

The two strangers walked slowly in the rear, bending down now and again to look at the stubble, and see if the shears cut clean. The tall man with the heavy beard and pince-nez was the agent for John Fowler of Leeds; the little clean-shaven one with the Jewish nose represented Harrow & Co. of Philadelphia.

Now and again they called to Peer to stop, while they investigated some part of the machine.

They asked him then to try it on different

ground; on an uneven slope, over little tussocks; and at last the agent for Fowler's would have it that it should be tried on a patch of stony ground. But that would spoil the shears? Very likely, but Fowler's would like to know exactly how the shears were affected by stones on the ground.

At last the trials were over, and the visitors nodded thoughtfully to each other. Evidently they had come on something new here. There were possibilities in the thing that might drive most other types out of the field, even in the intense competition that rages all round the world in agricultural machinery.

Peer read the expression in their eyes—these cold-blooded specialists had seen the vision; they had seen gold.

But all the same there was a hitch—a little hitch.

Dinner was over, the visitors had left, and Merle and Peer were alone. She lifted her eyes to his inquiringly.

"It went off well then?" she asked.

"Yes. But there is just one little thing to put right."

"Still something to put right—after you have worked so hard all these months?" She sat down, and her hands dropped into her lap.

"It's only a small detail," he said eagerly, pacing up and down. "When the grass is wet, it sticks between the steel fingers above the shears and accumulates there and gets in the way. It's the devil and all that I never thought of testing it myself in wet weather. But once I've got that right, my girl, the thing will be a world-success.''

Once more the machine was set up in his workshop, and he walked around it, watching, spying, thinking, racking his brain to find the little device that should make all well. All else was finished, all was right, but he still lacked the single happy thought, the flash of inspiration—that given, a moment's work would be enough to give this thing of steel life, and wings with which to fly out over the wide world.

It might come at any moment, that happy thought. And he tramped round and round his machine, clenching his fists in desperation because it was so slow in coming.

The last touch only, the dot upon an i, was wanting. A slight change in the shape or position of the fingers, or the length of the shears—what was it he wanted? How could he sleep that night?

He felt that he stood face to face with a difficulty that could have been easily solved had he come fresh to the work, but that his tortured brain was too worn out to overcome.

But when an Arab horse is ready to drop with fatigue, then is the time when it breaks into a gallop.

He could not wait. There were the faces at the window again, staring and asking: ''Not finished yet?'' Merle, the children, Uthoug and his wife, the Bank Manager. And there were his com-

petitors the world over. To-day he was a length
ahead of them, but by to-morrow he might be left
behind. Wait? Rest? No!

It was autumn now, and sleepless nights drove
him to a doctor, who prescribed cold baths, per-
fect quiet, sleeping draughts, iron and arsenic. Ah,
yes. Peer could swallow all the prescriptions—
the one thing he could not do was rest or sleep.

He would sit late into the night, prostrate with
exhaustion, watching the dying embers of the
forge, the steel, the tools. And innumerable sparks
would begin to fly before his eyes, and masses of
molten iron to creep about like living things over
walls and floor.—And over by the forge was something more defined, a misty shape, that grew in
size and clearness and stood at last a bearded,
naked demigod, with fire in one hand and sledge-
hammer in the other.

"What? Who is that?"

"Man, do you not know me?"

"Who are you, I ask?"

"I have a thing to tell you: it is vain for you to
seek for any other faith than faith in the evolution
of the universe. It will do no good to pray. You
may dream yourself away from the steel and the
fire, but you must offer yourself up to them at
last. You are bound fast to these things. Outside them your soul is nothing. God? happiness?
yourself? eternal life for you? All these are nothing. The will of the world rolls on towards its

eternal goal, and the individual is but fuel for the fire.''

Peer would spring up, believing for a moment that someone was really there. But there was nothing, only the empty air.

Now and again he would go home to Loreng, but everything there seemed to pass in a mist. He could see that Merle's eyes were red, though she sang cheerily as she went about the house. It seemed to him that she had begged him to go to bed and rest, and he had gone to bed. It would be delicious to sleep. But in the middle of the night it was borne in upon him that the fault lay in the shape of the shears after all, and then there was no stopping him from getting up and hurrying in to the workshop. Winter has come round again, and he fights his way in through a snow-storm. And in the quiet night he lights his lamp, kindles the forge fire, screws off the blades of the shears once more. But when he has altered them and fixed them in place again, he knows at once that the defect was not in them after all.

Coffee is a good thing for keeping the brain clear. He took to making it in the workshop for himself—and at night especially a few cups did him good. They were so satisfying too, that he felt no desire for food. And when he came to the conclusion that the best thing would be to make each separate part of the machine over again anew, coffee was a great help, keeping him awake through many a long night.

It began to dawn upon him that Merle and his father-in-law and the Bank Manager had taken to lurking about the place night and day, watching and spying to see if the work were not nearly done. Why in the devil's name could they not leave him in peace—just one week more? In any case, the machine could not be tried before next summer. At times the workers at the foundry would be startled by their master suddenly rushing out from his inner room and crying fiercely: "No one is to come in here. I *will* be left in peace!"

And when he had gone in again, they would look at each other and shake their heads.

One morning Merle came down and walked through the outer shops, and knocked at the door of her husband's room. There was no answer; and she opened the door and went in.

A moment after, the workmen heard a woman's shriek, and when they ran in she was bending over her husband, who was seated on the floor, staring up at her with blank, uncomprehending eyes.

"Peer," she cried, shaking his shoulder—"Peer, do you hear? Oh, for God's sake—what is it, my darling——"

· · · · ·

One April day there was a stir in the little town of Ringeby, and a stream of people, all in their best clothes (though it was only Wednesday), was moving out along the fjord road to Loreng. There were the two editors, who had just settled one of their everlasting disputes, and the two lawyers, each still intent on snatching any scraps of business that offered; there were tradesmen and artisans; and nearly everyone was wearing a long overcoat and a grey felt hat. But the tanner had put on a high silk hat, so as to look a little taller.

Where the road left the wood most of them stopped for a moment to look up at Loreng. The great white house seemed to have set itself high on its hill to look out far and wide over the lake and the country round. And men talked of the great doings, the feasting and magnificence, the great house had seen in days gone by, from the time when the place had been a Governor's residence until a few years back, when Engineer Holm was in his glory.

But to-day the place was up to auction, with stock and furniture, and people had walked or driven over from far around. For the bank management felt they would not be justified in giving any longer grace, now that Peer Holm was lying sick in hospital, and no doctor would undertake to say whether he would ever be fit to work again.

The courtyard was soon crowded. Inside, in the great hall, the auctioneer was beginning to put up the lots already, but most people hung back a little, as if they felt a reluctance to go in. For the air in there seemed charged with lingering memories of splendour and hospitality, from the days when cavaliers with ruffles and golden spurs had done homage there to ladies in sweeping silk robes

—down to the last gay banquets to which the famous engineer from Egypt had loved to gather all the gentry round in the days of his prosperity.

Most of the people stood on the steps and in the entrance-hall. And now and again they would catch a glimpse of a pale woman, dressed in black, with thick dark eyebrows, crossing the courtyard to a servant's house or a storehouse to give some order for moving the things. It was Merle, now mistress here no longer.

Old Lorentz D. Uthoug met his sister, the mighty lady of Bruseth, on the steps. She looked at him, and there was a gleam of derision in her narrowed eyes. But he drew himself up, and said as he passed her, "You've nothing to be afraid of. I've settled things so that I'm not bankrupt yet. And you shall have your share—in full."

And he strode in, a broad-shouldered, upright figure, looking calmly at all men, that all might see he was not the man to be crushed by a reverse.

Late in the day the chestnut, Bijou, was put up for sale. He was led across the courtyard in a halter, and as he came he stopped for a moment, and threw up his head, and neighed, and from the stables the other horses neighed in answer. Was it a farewell? Did he remember the day, years ago, when he had come there first, dancing on his white-stockinged feet, full of youth and strength?

But by the woodshed there stood as usual a little grey old man, busy sawing and chopping, as if nothing at all was the matter. One master left, another took his place; one needed firewood, it seemed to him, as much as the other. And if they came and gave him notice—why, thank the Lord, he was stone deaf. Thud, thud, the sound of the axe went on.

A young man came driving up the hill, a florid-faced young man, with very blue eyes. He took off his overcoat in the passage, revealing a long black frock coat beneath and a large-patterned waist-coat. It was Uthoug junior, general agent for English tweeds. He had taken no part in his brother-in-law's business affairs, and so he was able to help his father in this crisis.

But the auction at Loreng went on for several days.

BOOK III

Chapter I

ONCE more a deep valley, with sun-steeped farms
on the hillsides between the river and the moun-
tain-range behind.

One day about midsummer it was old Raastad
himself that came down to meet the train, driving
a spring-cart, with a waggon following behind.
Was he expecting visitors? the people at the station asked him. "Maybe I am," said old Raastad,
stroking his heavy beard, and he limped about
looking to his horses. Was it the folk who had
taken the Court-house? "Ay, it's likely them,"
said the old man.

The train came in, and a pale man, with grey
hair and beard, and blue spectacles, stepped out,
and he had a wife and three children with him.
"Paul Raastad?" inquired the stranger. "Ay,
that's me," said the old man. The stranger looked
up at the great mountains to the north, rising diz-
zily into the sky. "The air ought to be good here,"
said he. "Ay, the air's good enough, by all accounts," said Raastad, and began loading up the
carts.

They drove off up the hill road. The man and
his wife sat in the spring-cart, the woman with a
child in her lap, but a boy and a girl were seated

on the load in the baggage-waggon behind Raastad. "Can we see the farm from here?" asked the woman, turning her head. "There," said the old man, pointing. And looking, they saw a big farmstead high up on a sunny hill-slope, close under the crest, and near by a long low house with a steep slate roof, the sort of place where the district officers used to live in old days. "Is that the house we are to live in?" she asked again. "Ay, that's it, right enough," said old Raastad, and chirruped to his horses.

The woman looked long at the farm and sighed. So this was to be their new home. They were to live here, far from all their friends. And would it give him back his health, after all the doctors' medicines had failed?

A Lapland dog met them at the gate and barked at them; a couple of pigs came down the road, stopped and studied the new arrivals with profound attention, then wheeled suddenly and galloped off among the houses.

The farmer's wife herself was waiting outside the Court-house, a tall wrinkled woman with a black cap on her head. "Welcome," she said, offering a rough and bony hand.

The house was one of large low-ceiled rooms, with big stoves that would need a deal of firewood in winter. The furniture was a mixture of every possible sort and style: a mahogany sofa, cupboards with painted roses on the panels, chairs covered with "Old Norse" carving, and on the

walls appalling pictures of foreign royal families
and of the Crucifixion. "Good Heavens!" said
Merle, as they went round the rooms alone: "how
shall we ever get used to all this?"

But just then Louise came rushing in, breathless with news. "Mother—father—there are goats
here!" And little Lorentz came toddling in after
her: "Goats, mother," he cried, stumbling over
the doorstep.

The old house had stood empty and dead for
years. Now it seemed to have wakened up again.
Footsteps went in and out, and the stairs creaked
once more under the tread of feet, small, patter-
ing, exploring feet, and big feet going about on
grown-up errands. There was movement in every
corner: a rattle of pots and pans in the kitchen;
fires blazed up, and smoke began to rise from the
chimney; people passing by outside looked up at
it and saw that the dead old house had come to
life again.

Peer was weak still after his illness, but he could
help a little with the unpacking. It took very little, though, to make him out of breath and giddy,
and there was a sledge-hammer continually
thumping somewhere in the back of his head. Suppose—suppose, after all, the change here does you
no good? You are at the last stage. You've managed to borrow the money to keep you all here
for a year. And then? Your wife and children?
Hush!—better not think of that. Not that; think
of anything else, only not that.

Clothes to be carried upstairs. Yes, yes—and to think it was all to end in your living on other people's charity. Even that can't go on long. If you should be no better next summer—or two years hence?—what then? For yourself—yes, there's always one way out for you. But Merle and the children? Hush, don't think of it! Once it was your whole duty to finish a certain piece of work in a certain time. Now it is your duty to get well again, to be as strong as a horse by next year. It is your duty. If only the sledge-hammer would stop, that cursed sledge-hammer in the back of your head.

Merle, as she went out and in, was thinking perhaps of the same thing, but her head was full of so much else—getting things in order and the household set going. Food had to be bought from the local shop; and how many litres of milk would she require in the morning? Where could she get eggs? She must go across at once to the Raastads' and ask. So the pale woman in the dark dress walked slowly with bowed head across the courtyard. But when she stopped to speak to people about the place, they would forget their manners and stare at her, she smiled so strangely.

"Father, there's a box of starlings on the wall here," said Louise as she lay in bed with her arms round Peer's neck saying good-night. "And there's a swallow's nest under the eaves too."

"Oh, yes, we'll have great fun at Raastad—just you wait and see."

Soon Merle and Peer too lay in their strange beds, looking out at the luminous summer night.

They were shipwrecked people washed ashore here. But it was not so clear that they were saved.

Peer turned restlessly from side to side. He was so worn to skin and bone that his nerves seemed laid bare, and he could not rest in any position. Also there were three hundred wheels whirring in his head, and striking out sparks that flew up and turned to visions.

Rest? why had he never been content to rest in the days when all went well?

He had made his mark at the First Cataract, yes, and had made big sums of money out of his new pump; but all the time there were the gnawing questions: Why? and whither? and what then? He had been Chief Engineer and had built a railway, and could have had commissions to build more railways—but again the questions: Why? and what then? Home, then, home and strike root in his native land—well, and had that brought him rest? What was it that drove him away again? The steel, the steel and the fire.

Ah! that day when he had stepped down from the mowing machine and had been ensnared by the idea of improving it. Why had he ever taken it up? Did he need money? No. Or was the work at a standstill? No. But the steel would on; it had need of a man; it had taken him by the throat and said, "You shall!"

Happiness? Rest? Ah no! For, you see, a stored-up mass of knowledge and experience turns one fine day into an army of evil powers, that lash you on and on, unceasingly. You may stumble, you may fall—what does it matter? The steel squeezes one man dry, and then grips the next. The flame of the world has need of fuel—bow thy head, Man, and leap into the fire.

To-day you prosper—to-morrow you are cast down into a hell on earth. What matter? You are fuel for the fire.

But I will not, I will not be swallowed up in the flame of the world, even though it be the only god-head in the universe. I will tear myself loose, be something in and for myself. I will have an immortal soul. The world-transformation that progress may have wrought a thousand years hence—what is it to me?

Your soul? Just think of all your noble feelings towards that true-born half-brother of yours—ha-ha-ha! Shakespeare was wrong. It's the bastard that gets cheated.

"Dearest Peer, do, for God's sake, try to get to sleep."

"Oh yes. I'll get to sleep all right. But it's so hot." He threw off the clothes and lay breathing heavily.

"I'm sure you're lying thinking and brooding over things. Can't you do what the Swedish doctor told you—just try to think that everything is dark all round you."

Peer turns round, and everything around him is dark. But in the heart of that darkness waves arise, waves of melody, rolling nearer, nearer. It is the sound of a hymn—it is Louise standing playing, his sister Louise. And what peace—O God, what peace and rest!

But soon Louise fades away, she fades away, and vanishes like a flame blown out. And there comes a roaring noise, nearer and nearer, grinding, crashing, rattling—and he knows now what it is only too well: it is the song of the steel.

The roar of steel from ships and from railway-trains, with their pairs of yellow evil eyes, rushing on, full of human captives, whither? Faster, faster—driven by competition, by the steel demon that hunts men on without rest or respite—that hurries on the pulse of the world to fever, to hallucination, to madness.

Crashing of steel girders falling, the hum of wheels, the clash of cranes and winches and chains, the clang of steam-hammers at work—all are in that roar. The fire flares up with hellish eyes in every dark corner, and men swarm around in the red glow like evil angels. They are the slaves of steel and fire, lashed onwards, never resting.

Is this the spirit of Prometheus? Look, the will of steel is flinging men up into the air now. It is conquering the heavens. Why? That it may rush the faster. It craves for yet more speed, quicker, quicker, dizzier yet, hurrying—wherefore?— whither? Alas! it knows not itself.

Are the children of the earth grown so home-less? Do they fear to take a moment's rest? Do they dread to look inward and see their own empti-ness? Are they longing for something they have lost—some hymn, some harmony, some God?

God? They find a bloodthirsty Jehovah, and an ascetic on the cross. What gods are these for mod-ern men? Religious history, not religion.

"Peer," says Merle again, "for God's sake try to sleep."

"Merle, do you think I shall get well here?"

"Why, don't you feel already how splendid the air is? Of course you'll get well."

He twined his fingers into hers, and at last the sound of Louise's hymn came to him once more, lifting and rocking him gently till his eyes closed.

A LITTLE road winds in among the woods, two wheel-tracks only, with a carpet of brown pine-needles between; but there are trees and the sky, quiet and peace, so that it's a real blessing to walk there. It rises and falls so gently, that no one need get out of breath; indeed, it seems to go along with one all the time, in mere friendliness, whispering: "Take it easy. Take your time. Have a good rest here." And so on it goes, winding in among the tree-trunks, slender and supple as a young girl.

Peer walked here every day. He would stop and look up into the tops of the fir trees, and walk on again; then sit down for a moment on a mossy stone; but only for a moment—always he was up again soon and moving on, though he had nowhere to go. But at least there was peace here. He would linger watching an insect as it crept along a fir branch, or listening to the murmur of the river in the valley far below, or breathing in the health-giving scent of the resin, thick in the warm air.

This present life of his was one way of living. As he lay, after a sleepless night, watching the window grow lighter with the dawn, he would think: Yet another new day—and nothing that I can do in it.

And yet he had to get up, and dress, and go down and eat. His bread had a slightly bitter taste to him—it tasted of charity and dependence, of the rich widow at Bruseth and the agent for English tweeds. And he must remember to eat slowly, to masticate each mouthful carefully, to rest after meals, and above all not to think—not to think of anything in the wide world. Afterwards, he could go out and in like other people, only that all his movements and actions were useless and meaningless in themselves; they were done only for the sake of health, or to keep thoughts away, or to make the time go by.

How had this come to pass? He found it still impossible to grasp how such senseless things can happen and no Providence interfere to set them right. Why should he have been so suddenly doomed to destruction? Days, weeks and months of his best manhood oozing away into empty nothingness—why? Sleeplessness and tortured nerves drove him to do things that his will disowned; he would storm at his wife and children if a heel so much as scraped on the floor, and the remorse that followed, sometimes ending in childish tears, did no good, for the next time the same thing, or worse, would happen again. This was the burden of his days. This was the life he was doomed to live.

But up here on the little forest track he harms no one; and no racking noises come thrusting sharp knives into his spine. Here is a great peace; a peace that does a man good. Down on the grassy slope below stands a tumble-down grey barn; it reminds him of an old worn-out horse, lifting its head from grazing to gaze at you—a lonely forsaken creature it seems—to-morrow it will sink to the ground and rise no more—yet *it* takes its lot calmly and patiently.

Ugh! how far he has got from Raastad. A cold sweat breaks out over his body for fear he may not have strength to walk back again uphill. Well, pull yourself together. Rest a little. And he lies down on his back in a field of clover, and stares up at the sky.

A stream of clean air, fresh from the snow, flows all day long down the valley; as if Jotunheim itself, where it lies in there beneath the sky, were breathing in easy well-being. Peer fills his lungs again and again with long deep draughts, drinking in the air like a saving potion. "Help me then, oh air, light, solitude! help me that I may be whole once more and fit to work, for this is the one and only religion left me to cling to."

High above, over the two mountain ranges, a blue flood stands immovable, and in its depths eternal rest is brooding. But is there a will there too, that is concerned with men on earth? You do not believe in it, and yet a little prayer mounts up to it as well! Help me—thou too. Who? Thou that hearest. If Thou care at all for the miserable things called men that crawl upon the earth—

help me! If I once prayed for a great work that could stay my hunger for things eternal, I repent me now and confess that it was pride and vanity. Make me a slave, toiling at servile tasks for food, so that Merle and the children be not taken from me. Hearest Thou?

Does anyone in heaven find comfort in seeing men tortured by blind fortune? Are my wife and my children slaves of an unmeaning chance—and yet can smile and laugh? Answer me, if Thou hearest—Thou of the many names.

A grasshopper is shrilling in the grass about him. Suddenly he starts up sitting. A railway-train goes screaming past below.

And so the days go on.

Each morning Merle would steal a glance at her husband's face, to see if he had slept; if his eyes were dull, or inflamed, or calm. Surely he must be better soon! Surely their stay here must do him good. She too had lost faith in medicines, but this air, the country life, the solitude—rest, rest—surely there must soon be some sign that these were helping him.

Many a time she rose in the morning without having closed her eyes all night. But there were the children to look after, the house to see to, and she had made up her mind to get on without a maid if she possibly could.

"What has taken you over to the farm so much lately?" she asked one day. "You have been sit-

ting over there with old Raastad for hours together.''

"I—I go over to amuse myself and pass the
time," he said.

"Do you talk politics?"

"No—we play cards. Why do you look at me
like that?"

"You never cared for cards before."

"No; but what the devil am I to do? I can't
read, because of these cursed eyes of mine—and
the hammering in my head. . . . And I've counted
all the farms up and down the valley now. There
are fifty in all. And on the farm here there are
just twenty-one houses, big and little. What the
devil am I to take to next?"

Merle sighed. "It is hard," she said. "But
couldn't you wait till the evening to play cards—
till the children are in bed—then I could play with
you. That would be better."

"Thank you very much. But what about the
rest of the day? Do you know what it's like to go
about from dawn to dark feeling that every minute
is wasted, and wasted for nothing? No, you can't
know it. What am I to do with myself all through
one of these endless, deadly days? Drink myself
drunk?"

"Couldn't you try cutting firewood for a little?"

"Firewood?" He whistled softly. "Well,
that's an idea. Ye—yes. Let's try chopping firewood for a change."

Thud, thud, thud!

But as he straightened his back for a breathing-space, the whirr, whirr of Raastad's mowing machine came to him from the hill-slope near by where it was working, and he clenched his teeth as if they ached. He was driving a mowing machine of his own invention, and it was raining continually, and the grass kept sticking, sticking—and how to put it right—put it right? It was as if blows were falling on festering wounds in his head, making him dance with pain. Thud, thud, thud! —anything to drown the whirr of that machine.

But a man may use an axe with his hands, and yet have idiotic fancies all the time bubbling and seething in his head. The power to hold in check the vagaries of imagination may be gone. From all sides they come creeping out in swarms, they swoop down on him like birds of prey—as if in revenge for having been driven away so often before—they cry: here we are! He stood once more as an apprentice in the mechanical works, riveting the plates of a gigantic boiler with a compressed-air tube—cling, clang! The wailing clang of the boiler went out over the whole town. And now that same boiler is set up inside his head—cling-clang—ugh! A cold sweat breaks out upon his body; he throws down the axe; he must go—must fly, escape somewhere—where, he cannot tell. Faces that he hates to think of peer out at him from every corner, yapping out: "Heh!—what did we say? To-day a beggar—to-morrow a madman in a cell."

But it may happen, too, that help comes in the night. Things come back to a man that it is good to remember. That time—and that other. . . . A woman there—and the one you met in such a place. There is a picture in the Louvre, by Veronese: a young Venetian woman steps out upon the marble stairway of a palace holding a golden-haired boy by the hand; she is dressed in black velvet, she glows with youth and happiness. A lovers' meeting in her garden? The first kiss! Moonlight and mandolins!

A shudder of pleasure passes through his weary body. Bright recollections and impressions flock towards him like spirits of light—he can hear the rushing sound of their wings—he calls to them for aid, and they encircle him round; they struggle with the spirits of darkness for his soul. He has known much brightness, much beauty in his life— surely the bright angels are the stronger and must conquer. Ah! why had he not lived royally, amidst women and flowers and wine?

One morning as he was getting up, he said: "Merle, I must and will hit upon something that'll send me to bed thoroughly tired out."

"Yes dear," she answered. "Do try."

"I'll try wheeling stones to begin with," he said. "The devil's in it if a day at that doesn't make a man sleep."

So that day and for many days he wheeled stones from some newly broken land on the hillside down to a dyke that ran along the road.

Calm, golden autumn days; one farm above another rising up towards the crest of the range, all set in ripe yellow fields. One little cottage stands right on the crest against the sky itself, and it, too, has its tiny patch of yellow corn. And an eagle sails slowly across the deep valley from peak to peak.

People passing by stared at Peer as he went about bare-headed, in his shirt-sleeves, wheeling stones. "Aye, gentlefolks have queer notions," they would say, shaking their heads.

"That's it—keep at it," a dry, hacking voice kept going in Peer's head. "It is idiocy, but you are doomed to it. Shove hard with those skinny legs of yours; many a jade before you has had to do the same. You've got to get some sleep to-night. Only ten months left now; and then we shall have Lucifer turning up at the cross-roads once more. Poor Merle—she's beginning to grow grey. And the poor little children—dreaming of father beating them, maybe, they cry out so often in their sleep. Off now, trundle away. Now over with that load; and back for another."

"You, that once looked down on the soulless toil for bread, you have sunk now to something far more miserable. You are dragging at a load of sheer stupidity. You are a galley-slave, with calamity for your task-master. As you move the chains rattle. And that is your day."

He straightens himself up, wipes the sweat from

his forehead, and begins heaving up stones into
his barrow again.

How long must it last, this life in manacles?
Do you remember Job? Job? Aye, doubtless
Jehovah was sitting at some jovial feast when he
conceived that fantasy of a drunken brain, to let
Satan loose upon a happy man. Job? His seven
sons and daughters, and his cattle, and his calves
were restored unto him, but we read nothing of
any compensation made him for the jest itself.
He was made to play court fool, with his boils
and his tortures and his misery, and the gods
had their bit of sport gratis. Job had his actual
outlay in cattle and offspring refunded, and that
was all. Ha-ha!

Prometheus! Is it you after all that are the
friend of man among the gods? Have you indeed
the power to free us all some day? When will you
come, then, to raise the great revolt?

Come, come—up with the barrow again—you
see it is full.

"Father, it's dinner-time. Come along home,"
cries little Louise, racing down the hill with her
yellow plaits flying about her ears. But she stops
cautiously a little distance off—there is no knowing what sort of temper father may be in.

"Thanks, little monkey. Got anything good for
dinner to-day?"

"Aha! that's a secret," said the girl in a teasing
voice; she was beaming now, with delight at find-

ing him approachable. "Catch me, father! I can run quicker than you can!"

"I'm afraid I'm too tired just now, my little girl."

"Oh, poor papa! are you tired?" And she came up and took him by the hand. Then she slipped her arm into his—it was just as good fun to walk up the hill on her father's arm like a grown-up young lady.

Then came the frosts. And one morning the hilltops were turned into leaden grey clouds from which the snow came sweeping down. Merle stood at the window, her face grey in the clammy light. She looked down the valley to where the mountains closed it in; it seemed still narrower than before; one's breath came heavily, and one's mind seemed stifled under cold damp wrappings.

Ugh! Better go out into the kitchen and set to work again—work—work and forget.

Then one day there came a letter telling her that her mother was dead.

Chapter III

Dear Klaus Brock,—

Legendary being! Cast down from Khedivial heights one day and up again on high with Kitchener the next. But, in Heaven's name, what has taken you to the Soudan? What made you go and risk your life at Omdurman? The same old desperation, I suppose, that you're always complaining about. And why, of all things, plant yourself away in an outpost on the edge of the wilderness, to lie awake at nights nursing suicidal thoughts over Schopenhauer? You have lived without principles, you say. And wasted your youth. And are homeless now all round, with no morals, no country, no religion. But will you make all this better by making things much worse?

You've no reason to envy me my country life, by the way, and there's no sense in your going about longing for the little church of your childhood, with its Moses and hymns and God. Well, longing does no harm, perhaps, but don't ever try to find it. The fact is, old fellow, that such things are not to be found any more.

I take it that religion had the same power on you in your childhood as it had with me. We were wild young scamps, both of us, but we liked going

283

to church, not for the sake of the sermons, but to
bow our heads when the hymn arose and join in
singing it. When the waves of the organ-music
rolled through the church, it seemed—to me at
least—as if something were set swelling in my own
soul, bearing me away to lands and kingdoms
where all at last was as it should be. And when
we went out into the world we went with some echo
of the hymn in our hearts, and we might curse
Jehovah, but in a corner of our minds the hymn
lived on as a craving, a hunger for some world-
harmony. All through the busy day we might
bear our part in the roaring song of the steel, but
in the evenings, on our lonely couch, another power
would come forth in our minds, the hunger for the
infinite, the longing to be cradled and borne up
on the waves of eternity, whose way is past all
finding out.

Never believe, though, that you'll find the church
of your childhood now in any of our country
places. We have electric light now everywhere,
telephones, separators, labour unions and political
meetings, but the church stands empty. I have
been there. The organ wails as if it had the tooth-
ache, the precentor sneezes out a hymn, the congregation does not lift the roof off with its voice,
for the very good reason that there is no congregation there. And the priest, poor devil, stands
up in his pulpit with his black moustache and
pince-nez; he is an officer in the army reserve, and
he reads out his highly rational remarks from a

manuscript. But his face says all the time—"You two paupers down there that make up my congregation, you don't believe a word I am saying; but never mind, I don't believe it either." It's a tragic business when people have outgrown their own conception of the divine. And we—we are certainly better than Jehovah. The dogma of the atonement, based on original sin and the bloodthirstiness of God, is revolting to us; we shrug our shoulders, and turn away with a smile, or in disgust. We are not angels yet, but we are too good to worship such a God as that.

There is some excuse for the priest, of course. He must preach of some God. And he has no other.

Altogether, it's hardly surprising that even ignorant peasants shake their heads and give the church a wide berth. What do they do on Sundays, then? My dear fellow, they have no Sunday. They sit nodding their heads over a long table, waiting for the day to pass. They remind one of plough horses, that have filled their bellies, and stand snoring softly, because there's no work today.

The great evolutionary scheme, with its wonders of steel and miracles of science, goes marching on victoriously, I grant you, changing the face of the world, hurrying its pulse to a more and more feverish beat. But what good will it do the peasant to be able to fly through the air on his wheelbarrow, while no temple, no holy day, is left him any more on earth? What errand can he have up among the clouds, while yet no heaven arches above his soul?

This is the burning question with all of us, with you in the desert as with us up here under the Pole. To me it seems that we need One who will make our religion new—not merely a new prophet, but a new God.

You ask about my health—well, I fancy it's too early yet to speak about it. But so much I will say: If you should ever be in pain and suffering, take it out on yourself—not on others.

Greetings from us all.

Yours,
PEER DALESMAN.

Chapter IV

CHRISTMAS was near, the days were all grey twilight, and there was a frost that set the wall-timbers cracking. The children went about blue with cold. When Merle scrubbed the floors, they turned into small skating-rinks, though there might be a big fire in the stove. Peer waded and waded through deep snow to the well for water, and his beard hung like a wreath of icicles about his face.

Aye, this was a winter.

Old Raastad's two daughters were in the dairy making whey-cheese. The door was flung open, there was a rush of frosty air, and Peer stood there blinking his eyes.

"Huh! what smokers you two are!"

"Are we now?" And the red-haired one and the fair-haired one both giggled, and they looked at each other and nodded. This queer townsman-lodger of theirs never came near them that he didn't crack jokes.

"By the way, Else, I dreamed last night that we were going to be married."

Both the girls shrieked with delight at this.

"And Mari, you were married to the bailiff."

"Oh my! That old creature down at Moen?"

"He was much older. Ninety years old he was."

"Uf!—you're always at your nonsense," said the red-haired girl, stirring away at her huge, steaming cauldron.

Peer went out again. The girls were hardly out of their teens, and yet their faces seemed set already and stiff with earnestness. And whenever Peer had managed to set them laughing unawares, they seemed frightened the next minute at having been betrayed into doing something there was no profit in.

Peer strode about in the crackling snow with his fur cap drawn down over his ears. Jotunheim itself lay there up north, breathing an icy-blue cold out over the world.

And he? Was he to go on like this, growing hunchbacked under a burden that weighed and bowed him down continually? Why the devil could he not shake it off, break away from it, and kick out bravely at his evil fate?

"Peer," asked Merle, standing in the kitchen, "what did you think of giving the children for a Christmas present?"

"Oh, a palace each, and a horse to ride, of course. When you've more money than you know what to do with, the devil take economy. And what about you, my girl? Any objection to a couple of thousand crowns' worth of furs?"

"No, but seriously. The children haven't any ski—nor a hand-sleigh."

"Well, have you the money to buy them? I haven't."

"Suppose you tried making them yourself?"

"Ski?" Peer turned over the notion, whistling. "Well, why not? And a sleigh? We might manage that. But what about little Asta?—she's too little for that sort of thing."

"She hasn't any bed for her doll."

Peer whistled again. "There's something in that. That's an idea. I'm not so handless yet that I couldn't——"

He was soon hard at it. There were tools and a joiner's bench in an outhouse, and there he worked. He grew easily tired; his feet tried constantly to take him to the door, but he forced himself to go on. Is there anything in the notion that a man can get well by simply willing it? I will, will, will. The thought of others besides himself began to get the upper hand of those birds of prey ravening in his head. Presents for the children, presents that father had made himself—the picture made light and warmth in his mind. Drive ahead then.

When it came to making the iron ribbons for the sleigh runners he had to go across to the smithy; and there stood a cottar at work roughing horseshoes. Red glowing iron once more, and steel. The clang of hammer on anvil seemed to tear his ears; yet it drew him on too. It was long since last he heard that sound. And there were memories.

"Want this welded, Jens? Where's the borax? Look here, this is the way of it."

"Might ha' been born and bred a smith," said

Jens, as he watched the deft and easy hammer-strokes.

Christmas Eve came, and the grey farm-pony dragged up a big wooden case to the door. Peer opened it and carried in the things—a whole heap of good things for Christmas from the Ringeby relations.

He bit his lips when he saw all the bags piled up on the kitchen table. There had been a time not long ago when Merle and he had loaded up a sledge at the Loreng storehouse and driven off with Christmas gifts to all the poor folk round. It was part of the season's fun for them. And now—now they must even be glad to receive presents themselves.

"Merle—have *we* nothing we can give away this year?"

"I don't know. What do you think?"

"A poor man's Christmas it'll be with a vengeance—if we're only to take presents, and haven't the least little thing to give away."

Merle sighed. "We must hope it won't happen to us again," she said.

"I won't have it happen to us now," he said, pacing up and down. "There's that poor devil of a joiner down at Moen, with consumption. I'm going down there with a bit of a parcel to chuck in at his door, if I have to take your shift and the shirt off my back. You know yourself it won't be any Christmas at all, if we don't do something."

"Well—if you like. I'll see if we can't find

something among the children's clothes that they can do without."

The end of it was that Merle levied toll on all the parcels from home, both rice and raisins and cakes, and made up little packets of them to send round by him. That was Merle's way; let her alone and she would hit upon something.

The snow creaked and crackled underfoot as Peer went off on his errand. A starry sky and a biting wind, and light upon light from the windows of the farms scattered over the dark hillsides. High above all, against the sky, there was one little gleam that might be a cottage window, or might be a star.

Peer was flushed and freshened up when he came back into the warmth of the room. And a chorus of joyful shouts was raised when Merle announced to the children: "Father's going to bath you all to-night."

The sawed-off end of a barrel was the bathing-tub, and Peer stood in the kitchen with his sleeves rolled up, holding the naked little bodies as they sprawled about in the steaming water.

Mother was busy with something or other in the sitting-room. But it was a great secret, and the children were very mysterious about it. "No, no, you mustn't go in," they said to little Asta, who went whimpering for her mother to the door.

And later in the evening, when the Christmas-tree was lit up, and the windows shone white with frost, there were great doings all about the sitting

room floor. Louise got her ski on and immediately
fell on her face; Lorentz, astride of the new sleigh,
was shouting "Hi, hi!—clear the course there!",
and over in a corner sat little Asta, busy putting
her baby to bed and singing it to sleep.

Husband and wife looked at each other and
smiled.

"What did I tell you?" said Merle.

Slowly, with torturing slowness, the leaden-grey
winter days creep by. For two hours in the middle of the day there is pale twilight—for two hours
—then darkness again. Through the long nights
the north wind howls funeral dirges—hu-u-u-u—
and piles up the snow into great drifts across the
road, deep enough, almost, to smother a sleigh and
its driver. The days and nights come and go, mo-
notonous, unchanged; the same icy grey daylight,
and never a human soul to speak to. Across the
valley a great solid mountain wall hems you in,
and you gaze at it till it nearly drives you mad.
If only one could bore a hole through it, and steal
a glimpse of the world beyond, or could climb up
to the topmost ridge and for a moment look far
round to a wide horizon, and breathe freely once
more.

At last one day the grey veil lifts a little. A
strip of blue sky appears—and hearts grow lighter
at the sight. The snow peaks to the south turn
golden. What? Is it actually the sun? And day
by day now a belt of gold grows broader, comes

lower and lower on the hillside, till the highest-lying farms are steeped in it and glow red. And at last one day the red flame reaches the Court-house, and shines in across the floor of the room where Merle is sitting by the window patching the seat of a tiny pair of trousers.

What life and cheer it brings with it!

"Mother—here's the sun," cries Louise joyfully from the doorway.

"Yes, child, I see it."

But Louise has only looked in for a moment to beg some cake for Lorentz and herself, and be off again on her ski to the hill-slopes. "Thank you, mother—you're a darling!" And with a slice in each hand she dashes out, glowing with health and the cold air.

If only Peer could glow with health again! But though one day they might persuade themselves that now—now at last he had turned the corner—the next he would be lying tossing about in misery, and it all seemed more hopeless than ever. He had taken to the doctors' medicines again—arsenic and iron and so forth—and the quiet and fresh air they had prescribed were here in plenty; would nothing do him any good? There were not so many months of their year left now.

And then? Another winter here? And living on charity—ah me! Merle shook her head and sighed.

The time had come, too, when Louise should go to school.

"Send the children over to me—all three of them, if you like," wrote Aunt Marit from Bruseth. No, thanks; Merle knew what that meant. Aunt Marit wanted to keep them for good.

Lose her children—give away her children to others? Was the day to come when that burden, too, would be laid upon them?

But schooling they must have; they must learn enough at least to fit them to make a living when they grew up. And if their own parents could not afford them schooling, why—why then perhaps they had no right to keep them?

Merle sewed and sewed on, lifting her head now and again, so that the sunlight fell on her face.

How the snow shone—like purple under the red flood of sunlight. After all, their troubles seemed a little easier to bear to-day. It was as if something frozen in her heart were beginning to thaw.

Louise was getting on well with her violin. Perhaps one day the child might go out into the world, and win the triumphs that her mother had dreamed of in vain.

There was a sound of hurried steps in the passage, and she started and sat in suspense. Would he come in raging, or in despair, or had the pains in his head come back? The door opened.

"Merle! I have it now. By all the gods, little woman, something's happened at last!"

Merle half rose from her seat, but sank back again, gazing at his face.

"I've got it this time, Merle," he said again.

"And how on earth I never hit on it before—when it's as simple as shelling peas!"

He was stalking about the room now, with his hands in his pockets, whistling.

"But what is it, Peer?"

"Why, you see, I was standing there chopping wood. And all the time swarms of mowing machines—nine million of them—were going in my head, all with the grass sticking fast to the shears and clogging them up. I was in a cold sweat—I felt myself going straight to hell—and then, in a flash—a flash of steel—it came to me. It means salvation for us, Merle, salvation."

"Oh, do talk so that I can understand a little of what you're saying."

"Why, don't you see—all that's wanted is a small movable steel brush above the shears, to flick away the grass and keep them clear. Hang it all, a child could see it. By Jove, little woman, it'll soon be changed times with us now."

Merle laid her work down in her lap and let her hands fall. If this were true!

"I'll have the machine up here, Merle. Making the brushes and fixing them on will be no trouble at all—I can do it in a day in the smithy here."

"What—you had better try! You're just beginning to get a little better, and you want to spoil it all again!"

"I shall never get well, Merle, as long as I have that infernal machine in my head balancing between world-success and fiasco. It presses on my brain like a leaden weight, I shall never have a decent night's sleep till I get rid of it. Oh, my great God—if times were to change some day— even for us! Well! Do you think I wouldn't get well when that day came!"

This time she let him take her in his arms. But when he had gone, she sat still, watching the sun sink behind the snow-ranges, till her eyes grew dim and her breath came heavily.

A week later, when the sun was flaming on the white roofs, the grey pony dragged a huge packing-case up to Raastad. And the same day a noise of hammer and file at work was heard in the smithy.

What do a few sleepless nights matter now? And they are sleepless not so much from anxiety —for this time things go well—as because of dreams. And both of them dream. They have bought back Loreng, and they wander about through the great light rooms once more, and all is peace and happiness. All the evil days before are as a nightmare that is past. Once more they will be young, go out on ski together, and dine together after, and drink champagne, and look at each other with love in their eyes. Once more— and many times again.

"Good-night, Merle."

"Good-night, Peer, and sleep well."

Day after day the hammering went on in the smithy.

A few years back he could have finished the

whole business in a couple of days. But now, half
an hour's work was enough to tire him out. It is
exhausting work to concentrate your thoughts
upon a single point, when your brain has long been
used to play idly with stray fancies as they came.
He found, too, that there were defects to be put
right in the parts he thought were complete before, and he had no assistants now, no foundry to
get castings from, he must forge out each piece
with his own hands, and with sorry tools.

What did it matter?

He began to discipline his brain, denying himself every superfluous thought. He drew dark cur-
tains across every window in his consciousness,
save one—the machine. After half an hour's work
he would go back to bed and rest—just close his
eyes, and rest. This too was discipline. Again
he flooded all his mind with darkness, darkness,
to save his strength for the half-hour of work next
day.

Was Merle fearful and anxious? At all events
she said no word about the work that so absorbed
him. He was excited enough as it was. And now
when he was irritable and angry with the children,
she did not even look at him reproachfully. They
must bear it, both she and the children—it would
soon be all over now.

In the clear moonlight nights, when the children
were in bed, the two would sometimes be seen wandering about together. They went with their arms
about each other's waists, talking loudly, laughing

a great deal, and sometimes singing. People going by on the road would hear the laughter and singing, and think to themselves: It's either someone that's been drinking, or else that couple from the Court-house.

The spring drew on and the days grew lighter.

But at the Hamar Agricultural Exhibition, where the machine was tried, an American competitor was found to be just a little better. Everyone thought it a queer business; for even if the idea hadn't been directly stolen from Peer, there could be no doubt that his machine had suggested it. The principles adopted were the same in both cases, but in the American machine there was just enough improvement in carrying them out to make it doubtful whether it would be any use going to law over the patent rights. And besides—it's no light matter for a man with no money at his back to go to law with a rich American firm.

In the mighty race, with competitors the wide world over, to produce the best machine, Peer had been on the very point of winning. Another man had climbed upon his chariot, and then, at the last moment, jumped a few feet ahead, and had thereby won the prize.

So that the achievement in itself be good, the world does not inquire too curiously whether it was honestly achieved.

And there is no use starting a joint-stock company to exploit a new machine when there is a better machine in the field.

The steel had seized on Peer, and used him as a springboard. But the reward was destined for another.

Chapter V

HERR UTHOUG JUNIOR, Agent for English tweeds, stepped out of the train one warm day in July, and stood for a moment on the station platform looking about him. Magnificent scenery, certainly. And this beautiful valley was where his sister had been living for more than a year. Splendid air—and yet somehow it didn't seem to have done his brother-in-law much good. Well, well! And the neatly dressed young gentleman set off on foot towards Raastad, asking his way from time to time. He wanted to take them by surprise. There had been a family council at Ringeby, and they had agreed that some definite arrangement must be made for the future of the sister and her husband, with whom things had gone so hopelessly wrong.

As he turned up the by-road that led to the farm, he was aware of a man in his shirt-sleeves, wheeling a barrow full of stones. What? He thought—could he be mistaken? No—sure enough it was Peer Holm—Peer Holm, loading up stones and wheeling them down the hill as zealously as if he were paid for every step.

The Agent was not the man for lamentations or condolences. "Hullo!" he cried. "Hard at it, aren't you? You've taken to farming, I see."

Peer stood up straight, wiped his hands on his trousers, and came towards him. "Good heavens! how old he has grown!" thought Uthoug to himself. But aloud he said, "Well, you do look fit. I'd hardly have known you again."

Merle caught sight of the pair from the kitchen window. "Why, I do believe——" she exclaimed, and came running out. It was so long since she had seen any of her people, that she forgot her dignity and in a moment had her arms round her brother's neck, hugging him.

No, certainly Uthoug junior had not come with lamentations and condolences. He had a bottle of good wine in his bag, and at supper he filled the glasses and drank with them both, and talked about theatres and variety shows, and gave imitations of well-known actors, till he had set the two poor harassed creatures laughing. They must need a little joy and laughter—ah! well he knew how they must need it.

But he knew, too, that Merle and Peer were on tenterhooks waiting to know what the family had decided about their future. The days of their life here had been evil and sad, but they only hoped now that they might be able to stay on. If the help they had received up to now were taken from them, they could neither afford to stay here nor to go elsewhere. What then could they do? No wonder they were anxious as they sat there.

After supper he went out for a stroll with Peer, while Merle waited at home in suspense. She

understood that their fate was being settled as she waited.

At last they returned—and to her astonishment they came in laughing.

Her brother said good-night, and kissed her on the forehead, and patted her arm and was kindness itself. She took him up to his room, and would have liked to sit there a while and talk to him; but she knew Peer had waited till they were alone to tell her the news that concerned them so nearly. "Good-night, then, Carsten," she said to her brother, and went downstairs.

And then at last she and Peer were sitting alone together, at her work-table by the window.

"Well?" said Merle.

"The thing is this, Merle. If we have courage to live at all, we must look facts in the face as they are."

"Yes, dear, but tell me . . ."

"And the facts are that with my health as it now is I cannot possibly get any employment. It is certain that I cannot. And as that is the case, we may as well be here as anywhere else."

"But can we stay on here, Peer?"

"If you can bear to stay with a miserable bungler like me—that, of course, is a question."

"Answer me—can we stay here?"

"Yes. But it may be years, Merle, before I'm fit to work again—we've got to reckon with that. And to live on charity year after year is what I cannot and will not endure."

"But what are we to do, then, Peer? There seems to be no possible way for me to earn any money."

"I can try, at any rate," he answered, looking out of the window.

"You? Oh no, Peer. Even if you could get work as a draughtsman, you know quite well that your eyes would never stand . . ."

"I can do blacksmith's work," he said.

There was a pause. Merle glanced at him involuntarily, as if she could hardly believe her ears. Could he be in earnest? Was the engineer of the Nile Barrage to sink into a country blacksmith?

She sighed. But she felt she must not dishearten him. And at last she said with an effort: "It would help to pass the time, I daresay. And perhaps you would get into the way of sleeping better." She looked out of the window with tightly compressed lips.

"And if I do that, Merle, we can't stay on in this house. In fact a great box of a place like this is too big for us in any case—when you haven't even a maid to help you."

"But do you know of any smaller house we could take?"

"Yes, there's a little place for sale, with a rood or two of ground. If we had a cow and a pig, Merle—and a few fowls—and could raise a bushel or two of corn—and if I could earn a few shillings a week in the smithy—we wouldn't come on the parish, at any rate. I could manage the little jobs that I'd get—in fact, pottering about at them would do me good. What do you say?"

Merle did not answer; her eyes were turned away, gazing fixedly out of the window.

"But there's another question—about you, Merle. Are you willing to sink along with me into a life like that? I shall be all right. I lived in just such a place when I was a boy. But you! Honestly, Merle, I don't think I should ask it of you." His voice began to tremble; he pressed his lips together and his eyes avoided her face.

There was a pause. "How about the money?" she said, at last. "How will you buy the place?"

"Your brother has promised to arrange about a loan. But I say again, Merle—I shall not blame you in the least if you would rather go and live with your aunt at Bruseth. I fancy she'd be glad to have you, and the children too."

Again there was silence for a while. Then she said: "If there are two decent rooms in the cottage, we could be comfortable enough. And as you say, it would be easier to look after."

Peer waited a little. There was something in his throat that prevented speech. He understood now that it was to be taken for granted, without words, that they should not part company. And it took him a little time to get over the discovery.

Merle sat facing him, but her eyes were turned to the window as before. She had still the same beautiful dark eyebrows, but her face was faded and worn, and there were streaks of grey in her hair.

At last he spoke again. "And about the children, Merle."

She started. "The children—what about them?" Had it come at last, the thing she had gone in fear of so long?

"Aunt Marit has sent word to ask if we will let your brother take Louise over to stay with her."

"No!" Merle flung out. "No, Peer. Surely you said no at once. Surely you wouldn't let her go. You know what it means, their wanting to have her over there."

"I know," he nodded. "But there's another question: in Louise's own interest, have we any right to say no?"

"Peer," she cried, springing up and wringing her hands, "you mustn't ask it of me. You don't want to do it yourself. Surely we have not come to that—to begin sending—giving away—no, no, no!" she moaned. "Do you hear me, Peer? I cannot do it."

"As you please, Merle," he said, rising, and forcing himself to speak calmly. "We can think it over, at any rate, till your brother leaves to-morrow. There are two sides to the thing: one way of it may hurt us now; the other way may be a very serious matter for Louise, poor thing."

Next morning, when it was time to wake the children, Peer and Merle went into the nursery together. They stopped by Louise's bed, and stood looking down at her. The child had grown a great deal since they came to Raastad; she lay now with her nose buried in the pillow and the fair hair hiding her cheek. She slept so soundly and securely. This was home to her still; she was safer with father and mother than anywhere else in the world.

"Louise," said Merle, shaking her. "Time to get up, dear."

The child sat up, still half asleep, and looked wonderingly at the two faces. What was it?

"Make haste and get dressed," said Peer. "Fancy! You're going off with Uncle Carsten to-day, to see Aunt Marit at Bruseth. What do you say to that?"

The little girl was wide awake in a moment, and hopped out of bed at once to begin dressing. But there was something in her parents' faces which a little subdued her joy.

That morning there was much whispering among the children. The two youngest looked with wondering eyes at their elder sister, who was going away. Little Lorentz gave her his horse as a keepsake, and Asta gave her youngest doll. And Merle went about trying to make believe that Louise was only going on a short visit, and would soon be coming back.

By dinner-time they had packed a little trunk, and Louise, in her best dress, was rushing about saying goodbye all round the farm, the harvesters, whom she had helped to drive in the hay, coming in for a specially affectionate farewell. Her last visit was to Musin, the grey horse, that was grazing tethered behind the smithy. Musin was busy cropping the turf, but he just lifted his head and looked at her—she plucked a handful of grass, and offered it, and when he had disposed of that, she patted his muzzle, and he let her cling round his neck for a moment.

"I'll be sure to write," she cried out to no one in particular, as she went back over the courtyard again.

The train moved out of the station, taking with it Uthoug junior and Louise, each waving from one of the windows of the compartment.

And Peer and Merle were left on the platform, holding their two youngest children by the hand. They could still see a small hand with a white handkerchief waving from the carriage window. Then the last carriage disappeared into the cutting, and the smoke and the rumble of the train were all that was left.

The four that were left behind stood still for a little while, but they seemed to have moved unconsciously closer together than before.

SOME way up from the high-road there stands a little one-storeyed house with three small windows in a row, a cowshed on one side of it and a smithy on the other. When smoke rises from the smithy, the neighbours say: "The engineer must be a bit better to-day, since he's at it in the smithy again. If there's anything you want done, you'd better take it to him. He doesn't charge any more than Jens up at Lia."

Merle and Peer had been living here a couple of years. Their lives had gone on together, but there had come to be this difference between them: Merle still looked constantly at her husband's face, always hoping that he would get better, while he himself had no longer any hope. Even when the thump, thumping in his head was quiet for a time, there was generally some trouble somewhere to keep him on the rack, only he did not talk about it any more. He looked at his wife's face, and thought to himself: "She is changing more and more; and it is you that are to blame. You have poured out your own misery on her day and night. It is time now you tried to make some amends." So had begun a struggle to keep silence, to endure, if possible to laugh, even when he could have found it in his heart to weep. It was difficult enough, especially at first, but each victory gained brought with it a certain satisfaction which strengthened him to take up the struggle again.

In this way, too, he learned to look on his fate more calmly. His humour grew lighter; it was as if he drew himself up and looked misfortune in the eyes, saying: "Yes, I know I am defenceless, and you can plunge me deeper and deeper yet; but for all that, if I choose to laugh you cannot hinder me."

How much easier all things seemed, now that he looked no longer for any good to come to him, and urged no claims against anyone either in heaven or on earth. But when he was tired out with his work at the forge, there was a satisfaction in saying to his wife: "No, Merle, didn't I tell you I wouldn't have you carrying the water up? Give me the bucket." "You?—you look fit for it, don't you?" "Hang it all, am I a man, or am I not? Get back to your kitchen—that's the place for a woman." So he carried water, and his mood was the brighter for it, though he might feel at times as if his back were breaking. And sometimes, "I'm feeling lazy, to-day, Merle," he would say. "If you don't mind I'll stay in bed a bit longer." And she understood. She knew from experience that these were the days when his nightmare headache was upon him, and that it was to spare her he called it laziness.

They had a cow now, and a pig and some fowls.

It was not exactly on the same scale as at Loreng, but it had the advantage that he could manage it all himself. Last year they had raised so many potatoes that they had been able to sell a few bushels. They did not buy eggs any more—they sold them. Peer carried them down himself to the local dealer, sold them at market price, and bought things they might need with the money. Why not? Merle did not think it beneath her to wash and scrub and do the cooking. True enough, things had been different with them once, but it was only Merle now who ever had moments of dreaming that the old days might come back. Otherwise, for both him and her it was as if they had been washed ashore on a barren coast, and must try to live through the grey days as best they could.

It would happen once in a while that a mowing machine of the new American type would be sent in by some farmer to the smithy for repairs. When this happened, Peer would shut his lips close, with a queer expression, look at the machine for a moment, and swallow something in his throat. The man who had stolen this thing from him and bettered it by a hairsbreadth was doubtless a millionaire by now on the strength of it.

It cost him something of an effort to take these repairs in hand, but he bowed his head and set to. Merle, poor girl, needed a pair of shoes.

At times, too, he would turn from the anvil and the darkness within and come out into the doorway for a breath of air; and here he would look out upon the day—the great broad empty day.

A man with a sledge-hammer in his hands instinctively looks up at the heavens. He has inherited that instinct from his great ancestor, who brought down fire and thought to men, and taught them to rebel against God.

Peer looked at the sky, and at the clouds, sweeping across it in a meaningless turmoil. Rebellion against someone up there? But heaven is empty. There is no one to rebel against.

But then all the injustice, the manifold iniquity! Who is to sit in judgment on it at the great day?

Who? No one.

What? Think of the millions of all kinds of martyrs, who died under the bloodiest torments, yet innocent as babes at the breast—is there to be no day of reparation for them?

None.

But there must be a whole world-full of victims of injustice, whose souls flit restlessly around, because they died under a weight of undeserved shame—because they lost a battle in which the right was theirs—because they suffered and strove for truth, but went down because falsehood was the stronger. Truth? Right? Is there no one, then, who will one day give peace to the dead in their graves and set things in their right places? Is there no one?

No one.

The world rolls on its way. Fate is blind, and God smiles while Satan works his will upon Job.

Hold your peace and grip your sledge-hammer, idiot. If ever your conscience should embrace the universe, that day the horror of it would strike you dead. Remember that you are a vertebrate animal, and it is by mistake that you have developed a soul.

Cling, clang. The red sparks fly from the anvil. Live out your life as it is.

But there began to dawn in him a strange longing to be united to all those unfortunates whom fate had blindly crushed; to gather them together, not to a common lamentation, but to a common victory. Not for vengeance, but for a song of praise. Behold, Thou eternal Omnipotence, how we requite Thy cruelty—we praise life: see how much more godlike we are than Thou.

A temple, a temple for the modern spirit of man, hungry for eternity—not for the babbling of prayers, but for a hymn from man's munificent heart sent pealing up to heaven. Will it come—will it one day be built?

One evening Peer came home from the post-office apparently in high spirits. "Hi, Merle, I've got a letter from the Bruseth lady."

Merle glanced at Lorentz, who had instinctively come close to her, and was looking at his father.

"From Bruseth? How is Louise getting on?" she asked.

"You can see for yourself. Here's the letter," said he.

Merle read it through hurriedly, and glanced at Lorentz once more.

That evening, after the children had gone to bed, the father and mother sat up talking together in a low voice.

And Merle had to admit that her husband was right. It would be selfish of them to keep the boy here, when he might be heir to Bruseth some day if they let him go.

Suppose he stayed and worked here under his father and learned to be a smith? The blacksmith's day is over—factories do all the work now.

And what schooling could he get away here in the country? Aunt Marit offered to send him to a good school.—And so the die was cast for him too.

But when they went with the boy to see him off at the station, the mother's handkerchief was at her eyes all the time, do what she would.

And when they came home she had to lie down in bed, while Peer went about the place, humming to himself, while he got ready a little supper and brought it to her bedside.

"I can't understand how you can take it so easily," she burst out.

"No—no," he laughed a little oddly. "The less said about that the better, perhaps."

But the next day it was Peer who said he felt

lazy again and would lie still a bit. Merle looked at him and stroked his forehead.

And the time went on. They worked hard and constantly to make both ends meet without help, and they were content to take things as they came. When the big dairy was started close by, he made a good deal of money setting up the plant, but he was not above sharpening a drill for the road-gangs either. He was often to be seen going down to the country store in a sleeved waistcoat with a knapsack on his back. He carried his head high, the close-trimmed beard was shading over into white, his face often had the strained look that comes from sleeplessness, but his step was light, and he still had a joke for the girls whom he met.

In summer, the neighbours would often see them shutting up the house and starting off up the hill with knapsack and coffee-kettle and with little Asta trotting between them. They were gone, it might be, to try and recapture some memory of old days, with coffee in the open air by a picnic fire.

In the autumn, when the great fields yellowed all the hillsides, Peer and Merle had a little plot of their own that showed golden too. The dimensions of things had shrunk not a little for these two. A bushel of corn was much to them now. It hit them hard if their potato-patch yielded a couple of measures less than they had reckoned on. But the housewives from the farms near by would often look in on Merle to see how bright and clean she

kept her little house; and now that she had no one
to help her, she found time herself to teach the
peasant girls something of cooking and sewing.

But one habit had grown upon her. She would
stand long and long by the window looking down
the valley to where the hills closed it in. It was
as if she were looking constantly for something
to come in sight, something that should bring them
better days. It was a kind of Sunday for her to
stand there and look and wait.

And the time went on.

Chapter VII

Dear Klaus Brock,

I write to tell you of what has lately happened to us here, chiefly in the hope that it may be some comfort to yourself. For I have discovered, dear friend, that this world-sorrow of ours is something a man can get over, if only he will learn to see with his own eyes and not with those of others.

Most men would say things have steadily gone from bad to worse with me, and certainly I shall not pretend to feel any love for suffering in itself. On the contrary, it hurts. It does not ennoble. It rather brutalises, unless it becomes so great that it embraces all things. I was once Engineer in charge at the First Cataract—now I am a blacksmith in a country parish. And that hurts. I am cut off from reading because of my eyes, and from intercourse with people whose society would be a pleasure because there are no such people here. All this hurts, even when you've grown used to it —a good thing in itself it is not. Many times I have thought that we must have reached the very bottom of the inclined plane of adversity, but always it proved to be only a break. The deepest deep was still to come. You work on even when your head feels like to split; you save up every pin, every match; and yet the bread you eat often tastes of charity. That hurts. You give up hoping that things may be better some day; you give up all hope, all dreams, all faith, all illusions— surely you have come to the end of all things. But no; the very roots of one's being are still left; the most precious thing of all is still left. What can that be, you ask?

That is what I was going to tell you.

The thing that happened came just when things were beginning to look a little brighter for us. For some time past my head had been less troublesome, and I had got to work on a new harrow— steel again; it never lets one rest—and you know what endless possibilities a man sees in a thing like that. Merle was working with fresh courage. What do you think of a wife like that? taking up the cross of her own free will, to go on sharing the life of a ruined man? I hope you may meet a woman of her sort one day. True, her hair is growing grey, and her face lined. Her figure is not so straight as once it was; her hands are red and broken. And yet all this has a soul of its own, a beauty of its own, in my eyes, because I know that each wrinkle is a mark left by the time when some new trouble came upon us, and found us together. Then one day she smiles, and her smile has grown strained and full of sadness, but again it brings back to me times when both heaven and earth breathed cold upon us and we drew closer to each other for warmth. Our happiness and our sufferings have moulded her into what she now is. The world may think perhaps that she is growing old; to me she is only more beautiful than before.

And now I am coming to what I was going to tell you. You will understand that it was not easy to send away the two children, and it doesn't make things better to get letters from them constantly begging us to let them come home again. But we had still one little girl left, little Asta, who was just five. I wish you could have seen her. If you were a father and your tortured nerves had often made you harsh and unreasonable with the two elder ones, you would try—would you not?—to make it up in loving-kindness to the one that was left. Asta—isn't it pretty? Imagine a sunburnt little being with black hair, and her mother's beautiful eyebrows, always busy with her dolls, or fetching in wood, or baking little cakes of her own for father when mother's baking bread for us all, chattering to the birds on the roof, or singing now and then, just because some stray note of music has come into her head. When mother is busy scrubbing the floor, little Asta must needs get hold of a wet rag behind her back and slop away at a chair, until she has got herself in a terrible mess, and then she gets smacked, and screams for a moment, but soon runs out and sings herself happy again. When you're at work in the smithy, there comes a sound of little feet, and "Father, come to dinner"; and a little hand takes hold of you and leads you to the door. "Are you

going to bath me to-night, father?" Or "Here's
your napkin, father." And though there might
be only potatoes and milk for dinner, she would
eat as if she were seated at the grandest banquet.
"Aren't potatoes and milk your favourite dish,
father?" And she makes faces at you in the eager-
ness of her questionings. At night she slept in a
box at the foot of our bed, and when I was lying
sleepless, it would often happen that her light,
peaceful breathing filled me too with peace; and
it was as if her little hand took mine and led me
on to sleep itself, to beautiful, divine sleep.

And now, as I come to the thing that happened,
I find it a little hard to write—my hand begins to
tremble. But my hope is that there may be some
comfort in it for you too, as there has proved to
be for Merle and me in the end.

Our next neighbours here were a brazier and
his wife—poor folks, like ourselves. Soon after
we first came I went over to have a talk with him.
I found him a poor wizened little creature, pottering about with his acids, and making a living as
best as he could, soldering and tinning kettles and
pans. "What do you want?" he asked, looking
askance at me; and as I went out, I heard him bolt
the door behind me. Alas! he was afraid—afraid
that I was come to snatch his daily bread from
him. His wife was a big-boned fleshy lump of a
woman, insolent enough in her ways, though she
had just been in prison for criminal abetment in
the case of a girl that had **got** into trouble.

One Sunday morning I was standing looking at some apple trees in bloom in his garden. One of them grew so close to the fence that the branches hung over on my side, and I bent one down to smell the blossom. Then suddenly I heard a cry: "Hi, Tiger! catch him!" and the brazier's great wolf-dog came bounding down, ready to fly at my throat. I was lucky enough to get hold of its collar before it could do me any harm, and I dragged it up to its owner, and told him that if anything of the sort happened again I'd have the sheriff's officer after him. Then the music began. He fairly let himself go and told me what he thought of me. "You hold your jaw, you cursed pauper, coming here taking the bread out of honest working people's mouths," and so on. He hissed it out, flourishing his arms about, and at last it seemed to me he was fumbling about for a knife or something to throw at my head. I couldn't help laughing. It was a scene in the grand style between two Great Powers in the world-competition.

A couple of days later I was standing at the forge, when I heard a shriek from my wife. I rushed out—what could be the matter? Merle was down by the fence already, and all at once I saw what it was—there was Asta, lying on the ground under the body of a great beast.

And then—— Well, Merle tells me it was I that tore the thing away from the little bundle of clothes beneath it, and carried our little girl home.

A doctor is often a good refuge in trouble, but

though he may sew up a ragged tear in a child's throat ever so neatly, it doesn't necessarily follow that it will help much.

There was a mother, though, that would not let him go—that cried and prayed and clung about him, begging him to try once more if nothing could be done. And when at last he was gone, she was always for going after him again, and grovelled on the floor and tore her hair—could not, would not, believe what she knew was true.

And that night a father and mother sat up together, staring strangely in front of them. The mother was quiet now. The child was laid out, decked and ready. The father sat by the window, looking out. It was in May, and the night was grey.

Now it was that I began to realise how every great sorrow leads us farther and farther out on the promontory of existence. I had come to the outermost point now—there was no more.

And I discovered too, dear friend, that these many years of adversity had shaped me not in one but in various moulds, for I had in me the stuff for several quite distinct persons, and now the work was done, and they could break free from my being and go their several ways.

I saw a man rush out into the night, shaking his fist at heaven and earth; a madman who refused to play his part in the farce any more, and so rushed down towards the river.

But I myself sat there still.

And I saw another, a puny creature, let loose; a humble, ashen-grey ascetic, that bent his head and bowed under the lash, and said: "Thy will be done. The Lord gave, the Lord hath taken away——" A pitiful being this, that stole out into the night and disappeared.

But I myself sat there still.

I sat alone on the promontory of existence, with the sun and the stars gone out, and ice-cold emptiness above me, about me, and in me, on every side.

But then, my friend, by degrees it dawned on me that there was still something left. There was one little indomitable spark in me, that began to glow all by itself—it was as if I were lifted back to the first day of existence, and an eternal will rose up in me, and said: Let there be light!

This will it was that by and by grew and grew in me, and made me strong.

I began to feel an unspeakable compassion for all men upon earth, and yet in the last resort I was proud that I was one of them.

I understood how blind fate can strip and plunder us of all, and yet something will remain in us at the last, that nothing in heaven or earth can vanquish. Our bodies are doomed to die, and our spirit to be extinguished, yet still we bear within us the spark, the germ of an eternity of harmony and light both for the world and for God.

And I knew now that what I had hungered after in my best years was neither knowledge, nor honour, nor riches; nor to be a priest or a great

creator in steel; no, friend, but to build temples;
not chapels for prayers or churches for wailing
penitent sinners, but a temple for the human spirit
in its grandeur, where we could lift up our souls
in an anthem as a gift to heaven.

I could never do this now. Perhaps there was
nothing that I could do any more. And yet it
seemed to me as I sat there that I had conquered.

What happened then? Well, there had been a
terrible drought all that spring—it is often so in
this valley. The eternal north wind sent the dry
mould sweeping in clouds over the whole countryside, and we were threatened with one of our worst
years of scarcity if the rain didn't come.

At last people ventured to sow their corn, but
then the frosts set in, and snow and sleet, and the
seed froze in the earth. My neighbour the brazier
had his patch of ground sown with barley—but
now he would have to sow it again, and where was
he to get the seed? He went from farm to farm
begging for some, but people hated the sight of
him after what had happened about Asta—no one
would lend him any, and he had no money to buy.
The boys on the roads hooted after him, and some
of the neighbours talked of driving him out of the
parish.

I wasn't able to sleep much the next night either,
and when the clock struck two I got up. "Where
are you going?" asked Merle. "I want to see if
we haven't a half-bushel of barley left," I said.
"Barley—what do you want with barley in the

middle of the night?" "I want to sow the brazier's plot with it," I said, "and it's best to do it now, so that nobody will know it was me."

She sat up and stared at me. "What? His—the—the brazier's?"

"Yes," said I. "It won't do us any good, you know, to see his bit of field lying bare all summer."

"Peer—where are you going?"

"I've told you," said I, and went out. But I knew that she was dressing and meant to come too.

It had rained during the night, and as I came out the air was soft and easy to breathe. The morning still lay in a grey half-light with yellow gleams from the wind-clouds to the north. The scent of the budding birches was in the air, the magpies and starlings were up and about, but not a human soul was to be seen; the farms were asleep, the whole countryside was asleep.

I took the grain in a basket, climbed over the neighbour's fence and began to sow. No sign of life in the house; the sheriff's officer had come over and shot the dog the day before; no doubt the brazier and his wife were lying sleeping, dreaming maybe of enemies all around, trying their best to do them harm.

Dear friend, is there any need to tell the rest? Just think, though, how one man may give away a kingdom, and it costs him nothing, and another may give up a few handfuls of corn, and it means to him not only all that he has, but a world of struggle and passion before he can bring his soul to make that gift. Do you think that is nothing? As for me—I did not do this for Christ's sake, or because I loved my enemy; but because, standing upon the ruins of my life, I felt a vast responsibility. Mankind must arise, and be better than the blind powers that order its ways; in the midst of its sorrows it must take heed that the god-like does not die. The spark of eternity was once more aglow in me, and said: Let there be light.

And more and more it came home to me that it is man himself that must create the divine in heaven and on earth—that that is his triumph over the dead omnipotence of the universe. Therefore I went out and sowed the corn in my enemy's field, that God might exist.

Ah, if you had known that moment! It was as if the air about me grew alive with voices. It was as though all the unfortunates I had seen and known were bearing me company; more and more they came; the dead too were joined to us, an army from times past and long ago. Sister Louise was there, she played her hymn, and drew the voices all together into a choir, the choir of the living and the dead, the choir of all mankind. See, here are we all, your sisters and brothers. Your fate is ours. We are flung by the indifferent law of the universe into a life that we cannot order as we would; we are ravaged by injustice, by sickness and sorrow, by fire and blood. Even the happiest must die. In his own home he is but on a visit. He never knows but that he may be gone to-morrow. And yet man smiles and laughs in the face of his tragic fate. In the midst of his thraldom he has created the beautiful on earth; in the midst of his torments he has had so much surplus energy of soul that he has sent it radiating forth into the cold deeps of space and warmed them with God.

So marvellous art thou, O spirit of man! So godlike in thy very nature! Thou dost reap death, and in return thou sowest the dream of everlasting life. In revenge for thine evil fate thou dost fill the universe with an all-loving God.

We bore our part in his creation, all we who now are dust; we who sank down into the dark like flames gone out;—we wept, we exulted, we felt the ecstasy and the agony, but each of us brought our ray to the mighty sea of light, each of us, from the negro setting up the first mark above the grave of his dead to the genius raising the pillars of a temple towards heaven. We bore our part, from the poor mother praying beside a cradle, to the hosts that lifted their songs of praise high up into boundless space.

Honour to thee, O spirit of man. Thou givest a soul to the world, thou settest it a goal, thou art the hymn that lifts it into harmony; therefore turn back into thyself, lift high thy head and meet proudly the evil that comes to thee. Adversity can crush thee, death can blot thee out, yet art thou still unconquerable and eternal.

Dear friend, it was thus I felt. And when the corn was sown, and I went back, the sun was glancing over the shoulder of the hill. There by the fence stood Merle, looking at me. She had drawn a kerchief forward over her brow, after the fashion of the peasant women, so that her face was in shadow; but she smiled to me—as if she, too, the stricken mother, had risen up from the ocean of her suffering that here, in the daybreak, she might take her share in the creating of God. . . .

THE END

TRANSLATOR'S NOTE

Pronunciation of Proper Names

For the convenience of readers a few points in which Norwegian pronunciation differs from English are noted below:

The vowels *a, e,* and *i* in the middle of words are pronounced much as in Italian.

aa = long *o,* as in "post" or "pole."

e final is sounded, as in German; thus Louisë, Merlë, etc.

d final is nearly always elided; thus Raastad = Rōsta'.

g before *e* or *i* is hard; thus Ringëby, not Rinjeby.

j = the English *y;* thus Bojer = Boyer, Jens = Yens.

l before another consonant is sounded; thus Hŏlm, not Home.

Currency

The unit of currency in Norway is the crown (kronë), which in normal conditions is worth something over thirteen pence, so that about eighteen crowns go to the pound sterling. Thus Peer Holm's fortune in the Savings Bank represented about £100 in English money, and a million crowns is equivalent to about $260,000 in American money.

To avoid encumbering the reader unnecessarily with the details of Norwegian currency, small amounts have been represented in this translation by their equivalents in English money.